# STILL WA

Rebecca Pert was born in 1990. She grew up in a small town in Devon before attending Cardiff University, where she received an MA in Creative Writing. She now lives in Gloucestershire with her husband, son and dog. *Still Water* is her first novel.

Praise for *Still Water:*

'Beautiful and brutal . . . a breathtaking debut'
Joanna Cannon

'An atmospheric slow burn . . . with a sense of foreboding
that grows with each page'
*Good Housekeeping*

'Atmospheric and compelling'
Kate Sawyer, author of the Costa-shortlisted *The Stranding*

'A hauntingly beautiful, shattering book'
Dinah Jefferies

'A stunning, explosive novel, shot through with vicious
beauty. An eerie hypnotic book'
Hayley Scrivenor

'A haunting story . . . told with compassion and
even tenderness'
Katie Munnik

'Intense, unflinching, honest . . . beautifully told'
Lucie McKnight Hardy, author of *Dead Relatives*

# STILL WATER
## REBECCA PERT

THE BOROUGH PRESS

The Borough Press
An imprint of HarperCollins*Publishers* Ltd
1 London Bridge Street
London SE1 9GF

www.harpercollins.co.uk

HarperCollins Publishers
Macken House,
39/40 Mayor Street Upper,
Dublin 1
D01 C9W8
Ireland

This paperback edition 2023

1

First published by HarperCollins*Publishers* 2022

A catalogue record for this book is available from the British Library

ISBN: 978-0-00-831170-4

This novel is entirely a work of fiction.
The names, characters and incidents portrayed in it are
the work of the author's imagination. Any resemblance to
actual persons, living or dead, events or localities is
entirely coincidental.

Set in Bell MT by Palimpsest Book Production Ltd,
Falkirk, Stirlingshire

Printed and bound in the UK using 100% Renewable Electricity by CPI Group (UK) Ltd

MIX
Paper | Supporting
responsible forestry
FSC™ C007454

This book is produced from independently certified FSC™ paper to ensure
responsible forest management.

For more information visit: www.harpercollins.co.uk/green

For my husband, Lewis; my son, Arthur; and my parents, Lynda and Bill, with love.

# Prologue

There is something floating in Crowholt quarry.

It is late autumn. A chill mist sits on the water. The limestone cliffs rise from the edge, the rock rim fringed with hawthorn, ash, sycamore, birch, their leaves yellowing, curling, drifting to the pool below. A flock of swallows wheel in the air, preparing for their winter migration.

A week passes. Two. A skein of geese glide overhead, their straggling V reflected in the water. Still the thing floats in the centre of the lake, moving gently with unseen currents. The temperature inches downwards. One night, the quarry freezes, a sheet of ice as thin as the skin on a healing scar.

In the morning two girls come, in their school uniforms. They stand on the shore and smoke thin cigarettes and hurl stones at the ice, relishing the glacial crack and splinter. They toe the edge of the lake, pressing on the surface, shrieking as their boots flood. One of them registers something caught fast in the frozen water. A dead fish? A pale branch, stripped of its bark? But then snow begins to fall, and the girls open their mouths to it, and the thing in the ice is forgotten.

Weak sunlight breaks through the cloud. The lake thaws. Rain comes. The bare black trees drip. A man arrives with a spaniel. He picks up sticks, throws them at the lake, and the dog leaps in after

1

them. The man used to swim in the quarry too, when he was young, in the long hot summers, soon after the drilling and blasting had stopped and the pit had been abandoned and left to fill with ground-water. Memories surface – stepping into the pool, the soft slime of rotting leaves between his toes, the tang of cannabis hanging in the air. The summers at the swimming hole; the heat shimmering off the pale cliffs. The best days of his life.

But then two boys from his school had drowned. Twelve years old, their boyish faces just beginning to harden. The swimming hole was fenced off, signs installed at the shoreline:

NO SWIMMING

DEEP WATER

DANGER OF DEATH

The man has a teenage son of his own, now. He imagines him, floating face down in that cold water, and feels a lurch of fear in his gut.

The dog swims across the lake, cleaving the water. There is something floating nearby, something ripe with strange scents: cloth, mud, fat, rot, bone. It turns, swims towards it.

The man is looking at the sky, lost in thought, and doesn't notice what the dog has brought him until he bends to pick it up. His fingers are an inch from it before he notices.

The man stares at it, the pale thing glistening wetly on the shore, remembering, with a slow, low creep of terror, the woman who went missing all those years ago; the black and white face that stared out from every lamp post, every shop window. He remembers the lines of yellow-jacketed officers spreading over the fields, the frogmen slipping silently into the water, the headlines in the papers.

The man stares at the thing at his feet. Then he pulls his mobile phone from his pocket and, with shaking fingers, calls the police.

# Chapter One

Jane is lying with her head on Mike's chest, blinking at the morning light filtering through the curtains. The shapes of the room are drained of colour. Her clothes, heaped on a chair, his orange oilskins hanging from the back of his door, his boots, two empty glasses. A condom wrapper gleams dully on the bedside table.

She listens to Mike's heartbeat: lub-dup, lub-dup, lub-dup; the low thrum and rumble of it.

The air in the room is cold. Under Mike's duvet their bodies are warm. She breathes his smell, the faint salt of his skin, the slight tang of his armpits. It is intoxicating, this being close to another person. Six months ago she hadn't touched, really touched, another human being in ten years. The skin she was used to was that of dead fish; the ice-cold slither of salmon under her hand. And yet now here she is, naked under a duvet with a man, up close, his chest hair tickling her nose, the rushing of his blood in her ears.

She is very happy. She doesn't think she's ever been this happy. She wants to stay here forever. But the clock on the bedside table reads 07:32, and she's going to be late for work.

Jane sits up; yawns in the frail blueish light. Looks at Mike. He is a big man. She is tall, but he is taller than her, and broad, his dome of a head like a mountain top, crowned with rust-coloured hair, fringed with a thick beard.

Mike stirs, grunts. Rolls onto his side, blinks up at her. Jane's self-conscious, suddenly. She wonders what she must look like from that angle; if she has a double chin, if her armpits stink. She squeezes her elbows to her sides.

'I've got to get up,' she says.

'Mm.' Mike rubs his eyes.

'Do you want a coffee?'

'Mm,' says Mike, reaching for her. 'No. Stay a minute.'

He kisses the side of her, just below the ribcage. His beard tickles her skin and she shivers.

'I can't,' she says. 'I'll be late.'

But within ten seconds she's back down under the duvet, tasting his sleep-ripe mouth.

The factory hoves into view, the huge white box of it gleaming in the winter sunshine. Jane's car judders over the cattle grid, and she pulls up in the car park with a squeal of brakes. She checks her watch. The time is eight fifteen.

'Shit,' she says.

She steps out of the car, slams the door shut. The trawlers are unloading in the dock, bright crates being winched onto the shore by men in orange overalls. It was where she first met Mike, on a fag break; he was a trawlerman back then. He asked her for a light and as she handed him her Zippo their fingers touched, and something happened to her – a chain reaction of explosions travelling down her body, klaxons sounding, red lights flashing, an announcement on a tannoy: human touch, we have human touch. She hadn't realised how touch-starved she was. And the brush of warmth, the feeling of a man's hand, wakened something, some deep primal urge, a fire lit in her loins. She'd felt dried up down below, no sexual urges for years and years, but she swore she felt her ovaries release an egg then and there, like a rusty old gumball machine given a kick. Rolling it down the fallopian tubes.

She hadn't planned to be in a relationship. It was the last thing she'd wanted. She'd been living like a nun, a neat, small, serious life. But her body had overruled her brain, drunk on pheromones. They'd had sex that evening, after a few pints in the bar of the Baltasound Hotel, stumbling back to her caravan, buttons pinging off, their mouths hungry, skin fizzing with electricity.

As she hurries across the car park towards the factory, she thinks back to this morning, straddling Mike, her hands gripping the headboard. The orgasm she'd had, slow-spreading and radiant. She feels heat rise in her cheeks as she pushes in through the metal doors, into the women's changing room. It is empty. She unhooks her pair of yellow vinyl dungarees from a peg, pulls them on over her jeans, jams her rubber boots on her feet, tucks her hair up into the hairnet.

A middle-aged woman with a buzzcut slams the door open.

'There you fuckin' are.'

'Sorry, Pat,' says Jane.

'You're late.'

'I know.'

'Well?'

'I'm sorry.'

'Am I not going to get an explanation?'

Jane thinks back to pulling her underwear on hurriedly, back to front, Mike laughing in bed, and tries not to grin.

'Car wouldn't start,' she says, shoving her bag in the locker.

Pat shakes her head. 'I've no idea how that rattle o' shite is still on the road,' she says. 'It's more rust than car.'

'The sea air,' says Jane, slamming her locker shut, pocketing the key. 'Not good for it.'

Pat looks at her clipboard. Narrows her eyes.

'Heading,' she says. 'Get a move on. And don't be late again.'

'Yes Pat,' says Jane.

The factory stinks of fish and ice and blood and metal. The machinery roars and hums and hisses. Salmon come tumbling down a chute to Jane's right, and the man next to her – Anthony, his name is written in marker pen on the back of his overalls – jostles them free from the packing ice, spreads them out, passes them to Jane one by one.

In front of Jane is a guillotine, a blade that she controls with a foot pedal. She slides the fish beneath it, presses the pedal, and the blade comes down, cutting the head from the body, the skin splitting cleanly like rubber, blood spitting out. The heads tumble onto a little conveyor belt running along the floor, rumbling off to be made into cat food. Then Jane slides the headless body to her left, where another pair of gloved hands slices the fishes' bellies from neck to tail. Then a string in their necks is cut, their insides hoovered out, the roe stripped, sun-bright gelatinous eggs, scooped into buckets. Round they go, a never-ending stream of fish, slid from hand to hand across the stainless steel, until they end up in their tin cans, clean and neat and bloodless.

The job is monotonous but Jane doesn't mind it too much. When she first got here, she treated it as a punishment. Like a self-flagellating monk, she let the noise, the smell, the cold, the sheer backbreaking tedium of it batter her, exhaust her, obliterate everything else. At the end of each day she was so aching and drained that sleep came mercifully quickly. But now she's used to it. She's stronger, and faster, and she doesn't mind the monotony. It's almost meditative. As she heads the salmon, she daydreams. About Mike, mainly. About Mike, and her, and what they are to each other. About their future.

He quit the trawlers a couple of months after they met. Took over his uncle's mussel farm. 'Aquaculture,' he told her. 'That's where the future is.' He'd taken her out on his boat one morning, as dawn broke across the ocean; showed her how they hauled up the ropes, encrusted with oil-black shellfish, how they chipped away at the months-old seaweed, green and purple, to reveal the mussels clinging to the rope, thick as grapes on a vine.

Business is booming. He has a slick website full of artsy black and white photographs: lines of floats in the bay, the wet deck of a fishing boat, Mike's hands shucking a mussel. 'The most northerly British mussels,' it reads, 'washed by the purest North Atlantic water. Organic, sustainable, natural.' Mike had cooked some for her one evening, with white wine, garlic, and cream. They'd been full of flesh, fat and delicious, the butterfly shells vulval, aphrodisiac, tasting only faintly of the ocean. Heart-shaped, too. Was it a coincidence that was the night she told him she loved him?

At lunchtime the klaxon sounds, and Jane peels off her gloves, stretches, pulls a pack of Marlboros from her pocket and goes outside. She lights her cigarette and peels a blob of fish meat from her overalls, flicks it to the ground. A seagull swoops down and gobbles it up.

The sun has gone in. The sea is slate-grey beneath a sky the shade of mother-of-pearl, a tanker crawling across it in the distance. Jane breathes the cold air deeply, trying to clear her nose of the stench of fish guts. A truck rumbles past with the cannery's logo on the side: a blue mermaid. Jane always thought that logo was strange. Suggesting what? If they caught a mermaid they'd can her? Crack her carapace, scoop out her roe, hoover out her guts, behead her, fillet her?

She smokes her cigarette. She should quit, she knows. Mike's trying, at the moment. Chews the gum, puts the patches on his upper arm, shiny squares of film. She's smoked for eighteen years now. Since she was thirteen years old. As a child she'd been fascinated by her mum's smoking, the silver machine she used. She'd lick the paper, line the little hammock, pack the shreds of tobacco in it, then squeeze with her one hand and pop! Like a magic trick, out the cigarette rolled, perfect and smooth. Sometimes she'd get Jane to roll for her instead. Shreds of baccy would stick to Jane's fingertips, and she'd nibble at them, wrinkling her nose at the tang of it, spicy on the tip of her tongue.

She was always nibbling, chewing, as a child. Always had a strand of hair pulled into her mouth, leaching the faint shampoo taste from it. If not her hair, it was paper, torn from the back of exercise books, or plastic – the ends of biros, the lids of Smarties tubes. As they bent between her molars they'd heat up, and she'd touch the warm plastic to her tongue. 'Will you stop chewing?' her mother would say. 'You look like a bloody cow in the field. Chewing the cud. Spit it out. That hair will stay in your stomach and then the doctor will have to cut you open and scoop it out.'

What was that all about? Jane thinks, as she takes a drag on her cigarette. All that nibbling, chewing? Could be that she'd had a deficiency. Iron or something, like those pregnant women who suddenly get a taste for chalk or soil. When she was a teenager, a friend had told her about oral regression. People put things in their mouths to mimic their mother's breasts. Trying to get back to that warm soft place, that comfort. Bullshit, Jane had said. The thought had made her feel sick.

Why is she thinking about her mother? She doesn't want to think about her. She stubs out her cigarette, drops it into the metal ashtray bolted to the wall, then goes into the canteen. Grabs a tray, slides it along the rack. Looks at the vats of food beneath the heat lamps.

'Tuna pasta bake,' says a woman next to her, wrinkling her nose. 'You'd think they'd ken by now that we're all sick of fish.'

Jane shrugs. 'Doesn't bother me,' she says, and scoops some pasta onto her plate.

The woman grunts. 'I canna stomach it any more. None of it.

Anything fishy makes me heave.' She shovels chips onto her plate instead.

'How's things?' says Jane.

'Awful night. Millie's got da nirls. Chickenpox,' she says, seeing Jane's blank expression. 'Absolute nightmare, she wouldna sleep at all. She's covered. Calamine lotion won't touch it.'

They sit down at a table. Two other women are there, one with curls dyed the colour of new pennies, the other with grey hair scraped back in a bun.

'Hiya Dawn. Hiya Jude.'

'Terri. Jane. Y'all right?'

'No. I'm exhausted,' says Terri. 'Was just saying to Jane, Millie's got chickenpox. Awful. She was in tears last night with it, wouldna stop scratching.'

'Aloe vera,' says Judy. 'That's what you need.'

'No,' says Dawn. 'Oats. Fill a sock with them, tie it up, drop it in the bath – that's what my granny used to do.'

There was a moment, halfway through that sentence. A split second, a heartbeat – just after Dawn said the word 'bath' – where something shifted slightly. Nobody watching the conversation would have noticed it. But everyone at the table felt it. A change in atmosphere. A slight drop in temperature.

Jane continues eating, methodically, avoiding the women's eyes, as they move swiftly on, swapping chickenpox stories. Dawn shows a scar on her neck, Terri tells them about an attack of shingles she had ten years ago, and Jane is quiet, the gluey pasta sticking in her throat.

This is her dynamic with the group. She listens to them, their small gripes and grievances, their family quarrels, their gossip and jokes, and feels a longing; looking in at their lives like standing out in a cold dark street, peering at lit windows. What must it be like to live a life like that? No shadows. No feeling of the past lying in wait for you, a black hole ready to trip you up, suck you down, make your lunch stick in your craw.

'Oh, Jane,' says Judy, turning towards her. 'Don't forget – it's Pat's birthday next week. Her fiftieth. We're going to the hotel bar after work next Friday. Stuart's doing the card and collection. Will you come? Bring your fella. I'm dying to meet him.'

'Oh,' says Jane. 'Maybe. Not sure I'm free.'

Dawn rolls her eyes. 'What else are you gonna be doing?' she says. 'Sitting in your caravan, staring out the window?'

'Dawn,' says Terri.

Jane shrugs. 'Maggie might need me, is all.'

Dawn raises her eyebrows. 'Suit yourself,' she says.


Jane looks at the back of the cubicle door as she pisses. There's a poster Blu-Tacked there, curling at the corners. 'KNOW YOUR BREASTS,' it says. 'It may save your life!' She looks at the diagrams: hard lump, sunken nipple, orange-peel texture, discharge. Pat put it up there, years ago now, after her double mastectomy. Her hair had fallen out from the chemo, and for a while she'd worn a wig, a stiff black bob, shiny as an oil slick, stark against her eyebrowless face, until one hot day she'd got so sick of its itching that she'd ripped it off and thrown it in the bin in the ladies' loo. Terri had found it and shrieked, thinking there was a dead rat in amongst the paper towels. Pat's hair never grew back properly. She keeps it buzzed short now.

As Jane's wiping, she hears the door open, close. Two women, talking.

'Why d'you even bother asking her?' Jane recognises Dawn's voice. 'We ask her to everything. The Chinese nights. The Sunday Teas. She never turns up.'

'Well. It's polite to ask,' says Judy.

The cubicle doors open, shut. The sound of zips, the clank of toilet seats. Jane listens.

'It's pointless. I'm not being nasty, I'm just saying. She's so –

aloof, you know? Thinks she's better than the rest of us. Stuck up soothmoother.'

'Oh, I wouldna say that. She's friendly enough. Some folk just like their own company.'

The flush of two toilets. The opening of cubicle doors. Water running.

'God I need my roots doing,' says Judy. 'Look at those. Shocking.'

'It just doesn't make sense,' says Dawn, 'her living like some tramp in a caravan when she owns that croft. You ken my brother wanted to buy it off her? Still would. He offered a good price – too good a price, I thought. He wants to knock it down, build a holiday let there. It's such a bonnie spot, you know? Looking out over the sound, Keen of Hamar right on the doorstep. Would be an absolute money-spinner in the summer. But she wouldna entertain the idea. Flat out refused.'

Jane hears the roll of paper towels rumbling in the dispenser.

'It's just such a waste, the place sitting empty like that. All boarded up with the roof falling in. It's an eyesore. Gives me the creeps. *She* gives me the creeps.'

'Oh, Dawn.'

'It's true though, isn't it? She's a bit oorie. All pale and quiet. I know what happened to her was sad and that, but . . .'

The door shuts. The only sound is the dripping tap.

Jane sits there for a moment. Then flushes. Opens the toilet, washes her hands, looks at herself in the mirror as she shakes the drops into the sink. Her cheeks are burning.

Then she tucks her hair back up into the net, walks back through the canteen, to the factory floor, takes up her place at the conveyor belt. Grabs a fish. Slices its head off.

A wooden ladder is propped against the front wall of Mike's cottage. At the top is Mike, in his oilskins, a knitted cap on his head, a bucket in one hand. Jane feels a sudden fear, seeing him up high like that.

'Mike.'

He looks down, raises a hand, hooks the bucket over one arm, descends. Jane doesn't realise she's been holding her breath until he has both feet on the ground.

'Just clearing out the gutters,' he says. He flicks a handful of moss and sludge into the bucket.

'Oh.'

'You all right? Come straight from work?'

'Yeah.'

He kisses her.

'How was your day?'

She shrugs. 'Same old. Grab the fish, head the fish, pass it on. You know how it goes.'

Mike looks at her. 'You sure you're okay?'

'Yeah,' she says. 'Just tired.'

'Ah well. Weekend now.'

'Want a cuppa?'

'Sure,' he says. 'I'll be in in a sec.'

She watches him climb the ladder again.

'Be careful up there,' she says, wrapping her arms about herself. Then she turns and heads indoors.

She makes tea in the kitchen, two sugars for him. Leaves his mug steaming on the counter, goes into the living room, flops onto the sofa, switches the telly on. Some programme about buying a house in Spain. Sun-warmed brown hills and olive groves. She watches a middle-aged couple poke around a derelict barn and imagines what it would be like to live somewhere hot and bright instead of damp and windy. If the scorching sun would burn the past away, chase away the shadows. She blows on her tea, sips it. Maybe one day she and Mike could move to Spain. She imagines it. Sipping *cervezas* under a parasol, getting brown and old, tanning and shrivelling like a pair of raisins.

Maybe that's what she should have done in the first place, instead of coming back here. Back to Shetland. Made a clean break, a fresh start, somewhere new. But she was sixteen when she ran away, alone, without a passport, and it was the only place she could think of to go. And besides, she'd been homesick. For Unst, for the sea air, the clear skies. For the people. People who knew her before it all happened. When she'd stepped off the ferry and Maggie had rushed forward to hold her, she'd felt something ease deep in her chest, some tight knot loosen.

But maybe, Jane thinks, draining her mug of tea, it's time to move on. She's got enough money, that's for sure. Has saved nearly every penny she's earnt, squirrelling it away in the savings account her nan set up for her as a child. More than enough to buy a little *casa de pueblo*.

Jane rubs her eyes. Lies down, watches the presenter on the telly talk about the heat-retaining properties of adobe walls. She yawns. Before she knows it, she's fallen asleep.

Mike's coat is spread over her, the room lamplit. She can hear him in the kitchen, the rattle of the cutlery drawer, the chink of plates, the opening and shutting of the oven. She blinks at the TV. A comedy programme, a panel show.

Mike comes in with two plates. 'I was just gonna wake you,' he says. He hands her a plate, a burger in a bun. 'You must have been shattered. You were out like a light.'

They eat with the plates on their laps. Mike squirts brown sauce on his burger. Jane watches him.

'Give us some of that,' she says.

'I thought you hated brown sauce?'

'Yeah. I do. I just fancy some. Dunno why.'

She takes the bottle, squirts a bit on the side of her plate, dips her finger in it, licks. The tartness zings across her tongue. She scoops some more up with her finger, sucks at it, then squeezes a glob into her burger.

They eat. Watch the telly. Jane thinks of Dawn. Of what she said in the toilets. She chews, swallows, glances at Mike.

'Am I creepy?' she says.

Mike looks at her. 'Creepy?'

She pauses, then says: 'Dawn said I was creepy. Oorie.'

'Dawn. Which one's Dawn?'

'Dawn Henderson. Curly hair. Pete's sister.'

'Oh, her. She called you creepy?'

'She was talking about her brother buying the croft again.' She dabs at some loose sesame seeds on her plate, pops them in her mouth. 'Her brother wants the land. Wants to build a holiday let. Maybe I should just sell it. Be done with it.'

'But I thought you didn't want to? That you wanted to do it up – that's the plan, right?'

'I know. I just – it's been thirteen years, now, Mike. Thirteen. And I still can't face the thought of it. I keep thinking, next year I'll do it, next year, when the spring comes, when the weather's good, when I've saved a bit more money, and the next year comes, and . . . I can't even stand to step inside the place. But I can't bear to sell it either, you know? It's still – it's still got everything in it. My dad's stuff. Charlie's.'

They are quiet for a moment. Then she says: 'Maybe I should just go. Just leave. Sell the croft and fuck off to – to Spain.'

'Spain?'

'Somewhere bright and hot. And dry. Where nobody knows me.'

'You serious? You want to emigrate?'

'No,' she says. 'I don't really mean it. Sometimes I feel like I want to go somewhere totally new. Leave everything behind. Not you,' she says. 'But everything else. Just . . . go. That's

14

why I like living in the caravan, you know? If I wanted to, I could just hitch it to the back of the car and drive off.'

Mike puts his plate down. 'Come here,' he says, and Jane leans against him, breathing in his smell, of saltwater, damp wool, engine oil. He holds her, and says, 'Why don't you take a holiday? You haven't had a break in years, Jane. You work like a dog. Go somewhere for a fortnight. A month, even. Go and sit on a beach somewhere warm and drink cocktails.'

Jane grimaces. 'No. I couldn't.'

'Why not?'

'It just seems – I dunno. Self-indulgent.'

'You can treat yourself now and again, you know. Live a little. Sometimes it feels like you're . . .'

'What?'

'Well – punishing yourself for something.'

Jane looks at the television. '*Judge John Deed*'s on in a mo,' she says. 'Can you turn it up?'


In the morning Jane wakes to an empty bed and a note on the bedside table: 'Didn't want to wake you. Phil called – starter motor's blown on the voe boat. Gone to sort it. Might be out all day. Love you. M.'

She eats toast and watches TV. A breakfast programme. The presenters have tanned skin and straight teeth and sunny faces. Then she goes into the bathroom, tugs on the light switch, looks at herself in the mirror. Pale. Dark shadows under her eyes. Her father's colouring; he had an Italian grandmother. The darkness around his blue eyes had made them gleam. On her they just look muddy, like old bruises.

Her hair hangs around her face, limp and dark and fine, the same as her mother's. She remembers her trying to fluff it up, spraying her updo with a cloud of Elnett. 'It's like a bloody oil slick,' she'd say. 'Can't do anything with it.'

15

Jane pushes her hair behind her ears, scrapes it back from her forehead, then lets it flop again.

*Creepy*, she thinks.

She brushes her teeth, steps into the shower, lathering herself with Mike's soap, something green that smells of pine trees. As she soaps her chest, she winces a little. Her breasts feel tender, tight. She looks down at them. Thinks for a moment of Pat's poster on the back of the cubicle door. Runs her hands over the skin. No lumps. Some hormonal thing, probably. She makes a mental note to buy tampons later.

She gets dressed – thermal top under her jumper, knitted snood, parka, fingerless gloves – and steps out of the front door. The cold wind buffets her, whips her hair about her face. She heaves the car door open against the wind, slides herself in, shuts it.

It is a ten-minute run from Mike's cottage to her caravan, from Haroldswick to Baltasound, just time enough for a cigarette. The smoke spools up to the open window as she drives; the tarmac sizzles beneath the wheels. The road winds like a ribbon through the landscape, swooping through the open vista of sky and moor and sea, past the steely glint of lochs, the tumbledown ruins of crofts and kirks. She's heard people say Shetland is bleak, desolate, and she supposes in the winter it can be, the grey cliffs plunging into the grey ocean, the barren, wind-scoured hills. But she loves it. The hills and moorland remind her of the pelt of an animal, a great sleeping beast, something furred and scabbed and scarred. And even on the greyest of days there's still a beauty to the place, a subtle beauty – you just have to know how to look. Like the salmon at the factory – just silver fish, until you look up close, and you see they're magnificent: leopard-spotted, iridescent, the colour of clouds.

She turns off, down a single-track road, past the ancient ruin of a cottage, a few sheep sheltering beside it, their fleeces ruffling in the wind. She still has some cigarette left by the time she parks up. She switches the engine off and sits for a moment, taking a last few drags.

She looks at the house in front of her, the big white building with attached barn. Maggie's house. In the front garden is a jumble of detritus from when it was a working farm – an ancient tractor tyre, rolls of chicken wire, the bucket of a digger, two old pink bathtubs which served as troughs for the animals. A wind turbine whirls in the field behind it, and next to the green front door is a huge orange buoy, HAMARSGARTH painted on it in large letters.

Jane looks down, past the house, along the rutted track which cuts through the fields, through a gate in a low stone wall, to the croft. Her croft. Peerie Hamarsgarth. A small building overlooking the sound. She looks at its dirty whitewash, its slipped roof tiles, its boarded-up windows.

Just across from the croft is her caravan. A 1979 Bailey Mikado. Made the same year she was born. She'd bought it from a man on the mainland five years ago, a replacement for her first caravan, after the summer gales in 2005 had ripped its roof clean off. This one had been kept in a garage for nearly its whole life, a seventies time capsule, with an avocado green tip-up sink, floral orange curtains, a brown and beige carpet with a pattern like a Magic Eye picture. She loves it. Her tin can, Maggie calls it. As if she herself is salmon, processed and packed.

Jane stubs out her cigarette in the Micra's ashtray, gets out of the car into the buffeting wind, and trudges up to Maggie's front door. A woman opens it, a small woman with a face like a dried-out apple, her wild hair a white corona around her head.

'Oh!' she says, drawing her shawl more tightly round her shoulders and gesturing for Jane to come in. 'That wind! It's blowin' a hooley!'

Jane steps into the porch, the friendly porch full of wellie boots, coats, potted plants, and shuts the door against the weather. A collie dog appears, whimpering with joy, tail wagging.

17

'Hey, Nell,' Jane says, letting the dog lick her hand. Nell rolls over and Jane rubs her white belly.

'Daft old thing,' says Maggie. 'That was good timing. I've just got off the phone. Been talking to Dave.'

'Oh? How is he?'

'Same as ever,' says Maggie, pinching a couple of dead leaves from a potted plant. 'Busy at work, always busy. But okay. Wants me to talk to him and the bairns on the computer. On the video, you know. I said, I've tried that before, with Steven. Hated it. Was like shouting down a well to them, the connection was that bad, there was an awful delay . . . he said oh but the kids would love to see you. Kids, I said? Baby goats? *Kids*. Dreadful American slang. I said you've been living out there too long, you've started talking like a Yank. And Steven's just as bad, sounds like Crocodile Dundee. I just despair. Why they had to move so far away . . .' She drops the shrivelled leaves into a bin. 'Anyway. I've just made a coffee, d'you want one?'

'No, you're all right,' says Jane, giving the dog's belly one last pat before standing up. 'Got to get on. Got your list?'

Maggie rummages in her pocket, draws out a folded piece of paper.

'I'm hoping the shelves won't be bare,' she says. 'Gales forecast tomorrow, ferry won't be coming. Will you be all right out there?' Maggie looks out of the porch window, in the direction of the caravan.

'Aye. I've got the ground anchors on, I'll be safe as houses.'

Maggie makes a sceptical noise. 'Wish you'd spend the night here,' she says.

'I'll be fine, Mags.'

Maggie looks at Jane. Her eyes are a piercing blue. 'How many years has it been now?'

'Thirteen,' says Jane.

'Thirteen,' says Maggie. 'Jane – if it's money you need . . .'

'Mags. You know it's not that. I've got my savings.'

Maggie shrugs. 'Well. You know the offer's here if you ever need it. Now have you got any laundry? I'm putting a whites wash on this afternoon.'

'I'm okay thanks. I did mine at Mike's the other day.'

Maggie's eyes gleam. 'When am I going to meet this fella? Bring him round for Sunday lunch tomorrow. I'm doing roast beef.'

'Soon,' she says. 'Not yet. But soon. Now do you need anything doing about the house? That lightbulb in the bathroom?'

'Oh, I did that myself.'

'How did you reach?'

'Stood on a chair.'

'Maggie. I don't want you climbing on chairs.'

Maggie waves a hand dismissively.

'All right. Back in a bit,' says Jane, and steps out of the house. She looks at the list. Milk, two tins of baked beans, bread (white), two tins of soup, margarine, toilet roll, and three packets of Aberdeen butteries. Jane sets off up the road, head lowered and hood up against the wind.

The shop is busy when she arrives, people stocking up. She fills her basket, looks around her as she waits in the queue at the till. There are sometimes a few tourists, livening up the place with their strange accents and impractical clothes, paying a visit to the most northerly shop in Britain to stock up on postcards of Shetland ponies or tins of fudge for relatives back down south. But not today – just windswept islanders, in their wellies and parkas and Fair Isle knits.

As she waits, as she pays, as she walks home, Jane thinks again of Spain. Of selling up, of moving away. But she can't. Unst is home. She belongs here. She loves the rhythms of the place, the colours of it, the textures of it, even in the winter. No, she won't leave, she thinks, as she turns up the road to

Maggie's house, eyes screwed up against the wind. She won't be made to feel like an outsider, won't be forced off the island, not again—

But when she reaches the gate, she sees something that stops her in her tracks.

Pulled up next to the building, its yellow and blue livery shocking against the muted greens and greys of the grass and sky, is a police cruiser.

Maggie is standing in her doorway, shawl drawn tightly around her, talking to the police officer. PC Barry French, the only policeman on the island. He looks nervous, clutching his cap in his hands, his receding hair ruffling in the wind. They both look at Jane as she walks towards them.

Jane's heart is thudding in her chest. Her mouth is dry. She grips the plastic bag of groceries tightly.

'Jane,' says Barry. 'I have some news. Shall we go inside? Sit down?' He gestures to the house.

'Is this about the planning permission for the caravan?' says Jane. 'Because I sorted that all out with the council, I've got all the documents – it's for ancillary use while I renovate the croft – so if someone's been complaining—'

'No, it's not about the caravan.'

She stares at him.

'Am I in trouble?' she says. 'Have I done something?'

'Maggie – would you mind giving us a bit of privacy, please?'

'Oh,' says Maggie, who had been straining to hear. 'Sure.' She takes the shopping bags from Jane, gives her a look, then shuts the door behind her.

Jane turns to the policeman. 'Well?' she says.

'I have some news, Jane. About your mother.'

Jane feels suddenly bloodless, hollow.

'They've found her?' she says. Her voice comes out small and hoarse.

PC French opens his mouth, closes it. His Adam's apple bobs as he swallows.

'No,' he says. 'No. Not exactly. I – I had a call from the Devon and Cornwall Police,' he says. 'They've found – what they think . . .' He hesitates. 'They've found a prosthetic forearm. Floating in a lake – a flooded quarry, in Devon. Crowholt.'

Jane feels as if the ground has dropped from beneath her. The world spins. Black spots swarm at the edge of her vision. She puts a hand on the wall of the house to steady herself.

'Jane, are you sure you don't want to go inside? It must be a shock, I understand.'

Jane shakes her head. Tries to breathe.

'They don't know for certain it's your mother's,' says PC French. 'They're pretty sure, but they still need to run some forensic tests, which—'

'Tests?' says Jane.

'Well, DNA matching, to confirm it's hers, and—'

'Of course it's hers,' says Jane. 'Of course it is. It's an arm, a prosthetic arm. How many people with prosthetic arms have gone missing in Crowholt, for fuck's sake?'

Her breaths come fast and shallow.

'Jane, are you sure you don't want to sit down? Have a cup of tea?'

But Jane is already pushing past him, down the track, past her croft, across the field, barging into the little white caravan sheltering behind the low stone wall. She slams the door behind her and stands for a few moments in the small space, breathing hard.

Then she turns, slides open the worktop, and throws up in the sink.

Night falls quickly, like a trap snapping shut. The wind tears over the island. The caravan creaks, groans, strains against the land anchors, the steel spikes that tether it to the ground. Inside, Jane lies on the bed, staring up at the roof, at a watermark left behind from an ancient leak. She is thinking of her mother's arm. She remembers it – its cool smooth beigeness, its oval fingernails, the way the fingers and thumb were positioned, the palm cupped slightly, like the Queen's when she waves to a crowd. The gash near the wrist from when her dad hit a tin can with a weed strimmer while her mother was sunbathing. The yellow stain between the first two fingers from the cigarettes.

She remembers asking her mother what would happen to the arm when she died. Her mother was smoking and watching *Coronation Street*.

'Mum.'

'What?' Sylvia had said, her eyes fixed to the screen.

'What'll happen to your arm when you die?'

Jane remembers the slow turn of her mother's face. The cigarette smoke curling from her mouth. The expression of disgust.

'That's morbid,' she'd said. 'That's a horrible thing to say.'

Jane had felt her face burning as her mother tapped her cigarette on the ashtray and turned back to the TV.

Jane hadn't asked her again. But it had bothered her; she'd lain awake that night, thinking about it. She knew about cremations, about bodies all burned up and turned to ash, but she knew that plastic didn't burn, because once her mother had left a plastic bowl on top of the stove, and it had melted, great long gloopy strands of it stretching like cheese on a pizza when she picked it up. The kitchen had smelt acrid for days.

What if she was buried instead of cremated? But she knew that plastic didn't rot, either, because once Maggie's old collie dog had buried her Sindy doll, and it had turned up a year later when Maggie was digging the flowerbeds, and the doll had still been exactly the same, except with dirt matted in her hair. Jane had thrown her away after that; there was something frightening about the fact she'd been underground for so long. So if plastic didn't rot, her mother would decompose to a skeleton in her coffin; all bones, apart from one peach-coloured arm. That didn't seem right.

Plastic may not burn, or rot, Jane thinks, staring at the water-mark on the caravan ceiling, goosebumps prickling her skin. But it does float.

The police had searched the flooded quarry, all those years ago. But it was deep and murky, and the bottom was littered with dumped machinery, and the divers had abandoned the search. Was her mother down there? Buried beneath one hundred feet of stagnant water, in that great pit which plunged into the earth like a cavity in a rotten tooth?

If so, why now? Why, after all these years, would the arm appear?

Maybe she's not at the bottom of the lake, Jane thinks, a cold finger of fear tracing up her spine. Maybe she's still alive.

Jane imagines her mother standing on the shore, flinging the arm out over the water, laughing to herself, then turning, running into the trees.

When she was younger, Jane was convinced her mother was still out there somewhere. Perhaps she'd run off – to Russia maybe, or South America, or Africa. Somewhere she could disappear. Caught a plane. Donned a wig. Forged some papers. Changed her name. For years Jane kept thinking she saw her – in crowds, on a passing bus, turning down a side street – the back of a head, dark hair in a ponytail. A whiff of Anaïs Anaïs perfume. Once, as a teenager, she'd had a phone call from an unknown number. Someone breathing down the line. 'Mum?' she'd whispered, her blood icy with fear. The other person had put the phone down.

She could be on her way to me now, thinks Jane. On the over-night ferry. Standing on the deck, the wind whipping her hair. Maybe she's already on the island, trudging across the windswept grass, past the croft, down towards the caravan. Creeping up to the window. Her pale face there, just there, behind those curtains

– Jane turns her head to look at them, the orange fabric with yellow chrysanthemums, her heart thudding in her chest.

Get a grip, she thinks. Your mother is dead. Long dead.

But still, she can't bring herself to switch off the light.

Night. Jane is at the quarry. Standing on the shoreline, looking out over the still water. Everything is silver-black, the pale cliffs lunar in the moonlight. An owl hoots.

And she is afraid. God, she's afraid.

She hears a noise behind her. A word. Her name. Her old name, spoken in a voice like dry leaves. And she doesn't want to turn. Doesn't want to turn around. Because Jane knows it's her. She knows it's her mother calling. Jane can feel her at her back.

But her mother calls. Again and again.

Hannah, she says.

Hannah.

And Jane has to turn.

Out from the trees she comes. Stepping forward into the moonlight. Her mother. She is naked. She is dead. Her eyes milk white, her hair matted, her skin veined like marble. Jane cannot move.

Hannah, her mother says, her jaw flopping open. She reaches out with her hand. Her rotting mouth turns down at the corners. A tragic mask.

Hannah.

Jane sucks air into her lungs and screams and screams until she surfaces in a mess of tangled sheets, wailing.

Jane pushes the roast beef around her plate. Maggie watches her, a line between her brows.

'Come on, Jane,' she says softly. 'Tell me what's wrong.'

Jane presses her lips together. Looks at Nell, stretched in front of the fire. Then looks at Maggie.

'They found her arm,' Jane says.

There is a silence. The carriage clock on the mantelpiece ticks. Nell makes a noise in her sleep, a low yip, deep in the throat.

Maggie stares. 'What?'

'Her prosthesis,' says Jane. 'In a flooded quarry. In Crowholt. They searched it when . . . at the time. But didn't find anything. Someone's dog found it, floating in the water.' She grimaces.

'Christ, Jane.'

Jane pokes at the beef.

'I just wanted her gone, Maggie,' she says, her voice trembling. 'I just wanted her to disappear forever. If they could have found her – found all of her – then good. I could get rid of her, move on. But this – it feels deliberate, somehow.'

'What do you mean?'

Jane sits back in her chair, sighs. 'Like – I've just started to feel safe. You know? I've built a little life of my own here. It's not much, but it's mine. And I was just starting to relax. To *breathe* a little. To plan a wee bit of a future, and it's like she's – she's left this morbid little reminder. Ah, no no no, Jane, don't forget about your past, remember me – remember . . .' she trails off, swallows hard. Stares at the fireplace. A log settles, sending a shower of sparks up the chimney.

'I just wish that it would end,' she says. 'I wish they'd find her. *All* of her,' she says. 'So I know she's gone for good.'

Maggie reaches across, takes Jane's hand.

'They'll find her, Jane,' she says, softly. 'And even if they don't – she's long gone. *Long* gone.'

'It doesn't feel like she's gone,' says Jane. 'It feels like I'm – like I'm fucking cursed. Haunted by her. Christ. I'll never escape her, will I? No matter what I do, where I go. She's always there . . .' Jane makes a gesture, motioning behind her. 'I hate her, Maggie,' says Jane. 'I can't tell you how much I hate her.'

Maggie holds Jane's hand, squeezes it tight.

'Jane,' she says. 'After Laura died, I was . . . I was so bitter with rage. Sick with it. God, I wanted to murder that man. And I'm saying that in all seriousness, I could have torn him limb from limb, I wanted to torture him, I wanted to fill his days with endless agony, to make him feel even an ounce of the pain I was in. And you know I'm not a religious woman, but the vicar came to see me, and I told him that, I ranted and raved, I said some awful things, I swore, I screamed, I cursed God, I cursed the universe, I cursed the vicar himself. And he said, Maggie, you're going to hate me for saying this, but you have to try to forgive him. Because the only person you're hurting, by holding on to all that rage, all that hatred, is yourself.'

Jane sniffs. Looks at the urn on the mantelpiece, the framed photograph of the young woman with green eyes and feathered hair.

'I can't forgive her, Maggie,' says Jane. 'I can't. Laura's death was an accident; this was different, this was . . .'

'She was unwell, Jane,' says Maggie. 'You have to try and understand. There's that saying, isn't there. To understand all is to forgive all.'

'How? How could I ever begin to understand what she did?' says Jane. 'It was evil. Pure evil. A drunk driver' – she glances at the photograph again – 'that's different. What my mother did . . .' She can feel her chest tightening, her breaths coming faster, shallower.

Jane pushes her plate away. Gets up. 'I'm sorry, Maggie. I have to go. I just want to be alone for a bit.'

The wind tears in from the ocean, snatching the breath from her lungs, funnelling into her mouth, her nostrils, her ears. She battles against it, leaning herself into it, trudging up the boardwalk, stomping across the planks which cut a snaking path through the peatland. She reaches the grassy clifftop and turns right. North. To her left the sea crashes, gulls rise and fall.

She watches her boots thud across the ground – rock, grass, sheep shit, marshy patches of brown water, the skeletons of sea pink, pushing forward, forward, forward. She ignores the few other walkers she passes, with their waterproofs and binoculars, she ignores the sheep that bleat and stumble away as she disturbs their grazing. She trudges across the marshy land until she reaches the edge. The furthest north she can go.

She stops, sweating beneath her coat, and squints into the roaring wind, staring out over the restless water to the rocky islands of Muckle Flugga, the white lighthouse clinging improbably to the stone. And beyond, a small blip in the sea: Out Stack, the most northerly point of the UK.

She stands. Breathes deep. Lets the ferocious wind pummel her. A walk along the cliffs on a windy day normally makes her feel like she's been scrubbed clean with a stiff flannel. It seems to flush her head out, purify her. And being up here, at Hermaness, nearly seven hundred miles away from Crowholt, never fails to quiet her mind. But today, Jane realises, it's not working. She still feels sick, sick to her bones.

Maybe she needs to go even further north. The Faroe Islands, Greenland. The Arctic. Right to the top, to the North Pole. A vast sheet of white snow, hard and glittering. Antiseptic, blank, free from the mess and dirt of history. To fall off the edge of the map. It is appealing.

But Jane knows it wouldn't help. Like running to the highest room in the burning building, the flames will reach her eventually.

Jane, sitting on her bed, pours a couple of fingers of gin into the glass, knocks it back. It burns her throat. She screws up her eyes, her mouth, at the taste. Still, she drinks it. Another shot, and another, feeling it warm her stomach, her bones, her blood. She hasn't drunk spirits since her teenage years, but it's so familiar still, that feeling of untethering, loosening; each swallow putting distance between herself and herself.

She massages her blistered feet, winces. Looks around the caravan. Her tin can. *That's why I like living in the caravan, you know?* she'd told Mike. *If I wanted to, I could just hitch it to the back of the car and drive off.* And it's true. The idea of settling into a house – walls of stone, concrete foundations – makes her feel trapped, panicky. But now, tonight, in her flimsy metal shell, she feels exposed. She is tinned meat. She imagines a long claw piercing through the metal wall, ripping it open like a can opener.

She looks at her belongings. The little pile of books from the mobile library. Her binoculars. Her sketchpad and pencils. Her radio. One framed photograph – her and Mike. He'd taken it, using the self-timer. They are sitting on a beach, the spit of sand which connects St Ninian's Isle to the mainland, on a sunny day, in shorts and T-shirts. He is beaming widely, his arm around her. She's smiling, looking slightly dazed, as if she can't believe her luck.

These fragile things. These scraps of comfort. She's gathered them, over the years, begun to shore up a life, build a breakwater against the tide of the past. And now, in the distance, she feels a tidal wave coming. A wall of black water, ready to destroy everything.

She feels a sudden, wild rage. Wants to smash something. She kicks, blindly, slamming her foot against the drawer beneath the sink. The pain in her foot cripples her, makes her bend double. She squeezes her eyes shut, biting her lip, waiting for the burst of agony to subside.

When she opens her eyes she sees the drawer she kicked has come loose from its tracks, hanging at an angle like a busted jaw. She leans forward. Looks at it. Pulls it free. It's broken, the track buckled.

'Idiot,' she mutters.

Then she notices something, at the back of the drawer. Something she put there ten years ago, that she's ignored for an entire decade.

A biscuit tin, sealed shut with masking tape.

'Polly's Pride Crackers', reads the gilt writing on the lid. 'With Soup They're Souper!'

She knows what's inside.

She remembers finding them, under the mattress in her mother's old bedroom, the night she ran away to Crowholt. She'd been looking for hidden cash. Instead, she'd found two slim books. Her blood ran cold when she realised what they were.

She thought about handing them in to the police station as evidence, but something stopped her. She didn't want them read. Not by anyone. Had a feeling that if they were opened they'd release some curse, like Tutankhamun's tomb. So she'd put them in the tin, put the tin into her duffel bag, and they'd ridden with her on the overnight coach from Exeter to Aberdeen, then the ferry to Shetland. Since then, she'd tried to forget they existed.

*You have to try and understand,* Maggie had said. *There's that saying, isn't there. To understand all is to forgive all.*

Jane takes a swig of gin, looks at the tin. Then she puts the bottle down, digs at the tape with her thumbnail, peels it away, pops the lid off. Inside are the two slim books, one dove-grey leather with a rusting gilt lock, one black. Both embossed with the word DIARY.

Jane stares at them, her heart thumping. Then she grabs the grey one, prises the rusted lock from the catch. Opens the front cover, the spine cracking. She expects the pages to be crinkled, stuck together with damp, but they aren't. They are crisp, the edges sharp enough to cut, and covered in spidery blue writing.

Jane swallows hard.

Almost against her will, she starts to read.

*   *   *

*13 August 1978*

I don't know what to write in here.

My name's Sylvia. Sylvia Anne Legg.

Today is my sixteenth birthday. Mum got me this diary as a present. And this fountain pen, too.

This is stupid. What's the point of writing this stuff? Nobody is going to read it except me. I've never written a diary. Or anything really. Only stuff for school.

Well, not any more. I've left school now. My last day was a few weeks ago.

I don't know if I'm happy or sad about leaving school. There were bits of school I liked and bits I didn't.

Bits I liked:

French, because of Monsieur Leclerc. He had wavy dark hair and the most amazing green eyes. I loved the way he pronounced my name. Seel-vya.

Sitting on the playing field in summer with Sally and Judith. English, because I was good at it. Miss Dawes said I have a poetic streak. I liked Miss Dawes, she had loads of plants in her classroom, geraniums mainly, and I liked the way they made the room smell, like soil and leaves and sort of peppery.

Bits I hated:

Cross-country running, especially in the autumn when craneflies would come flapping up from the wet grass.

PE in general, actually. For obvious reasons.

Maths.

I don't know what else to write. Maybe I should introduce myself properly. My name is Sylvia Anne Legg – oh, I've already said that. I live in Crowholt, in Devon. Crowholt is a small town. It's the most boring small town on the planet. Nothing ever happens here. Three years ago a cow escaped from the field up the road and came into our front garden and ate our hedge.

And we still talk about it now. That's how boring life is here.

There's nothing to do here. There's a primary school and a secondary school and some shops and a few pubs and a bookies and a hairdresser and a church. And that's pretty much it. Nothing decent like a cinema or swimming pool or anything. There was a swimming pool fundraising campaign for a while, until the guy running it pocketed all the money and fled the country.

I live on the council estate at the edge of the town. Number 41. Mum says it's the best house on the whole estate. We're set back from the road behind a grass verge with two conifers on it, which means we aren't overlooked, and we've got the biggest back garden of the lot, a double plot, because we're on a corner. It's a massive garden actually. Mum told me they built them big after the war so that people could grow their own vegetables. Dad used to grow loads of veg until he put his back out – cabbages and runner beans and potatoes, and he had some fruit bushes too. Once me and George ate so many gooseberries I had the shits for days. My bum's clenching just thinking about it. Anyway, all the veg is gone now, and Dad doesn't garden any more. It's just Mum's flowers. My bedroom looks out over the garden. There's a jasmine bush right under my window, I can smell it now. I've got my window open because it's such a hot evening.

Behind the garden is fields, then the paper mill, then the train track, then the motorway. Mum always says the bloody motorway's ruined Crowholt; it was a nice little village before they built that, and now it's turning into a soulless commuter town. They're throwing up all these new housing estates, little boxes made of ticky-tacky, she says. Moans about the noise, too, says it keeps her up at night when the wind's blowing the wrong way and the sound travels. But I don't mind it. It's sort of comforting, the whooshing of it. I like to imagine where those people are going in their cars. What their lives are like. One day, I think, I'll be one of those people. Speeding off into the night. Away from this boring little town.

What else can I tell you? I live with my mum and my dad and my little brother, George. My mum is called Doreen. She's a dinner lady at St Theresa's, the primary school. My dad is called Alan. He was a carpenter but he doesn't work any more because of his back. My brother George is two years younger than me and is stupid and ugly and very, very annoying.

I should tell you more about me, I suppose.

My favourite band is the Bee Gees.

My favourite colour is turquoise.

My favourite film is *Saturday Night Fever*. I've seen it five times in the cinema, even though I'm not old enough. My friend Judith knows one of the ushers at the Odeon in Exeter and she persuaded him to let us in. I love John Travolta with my whole heart. He is the handsomest man on the planet, even handsomer than Monsieur Leclerc.

My favourite food is my mum's fish pie except for the prawns which I pick out and feed to Rex. Rex is our Alsatian, he's fat and lazy and farts a lot. Mum got him for protection from burglars after Nora up the road had her Toby jugs stolen. I don't know what a burglar would steal from our house, we don't have anything worth stealing. All they'd find was tins of beans and corned beef and tomatoes. Mum saves up coupons and buys in bulk from Barry's Bargains, and we don't have enough room in the cupboards, so there are piles of tins everywhere. I've got a mountain of tinned tuna in my bedroom. It's embarrassing.

What I look like:

Some people say I look like Olivia Hussey, you know that actress who played Juliet. I don't think I'm as pretty as her though. My teeth are sort of wonky.

I have long straight brown hair.

I have brown eyes.

I am 5 foot 9 inches tall.

Oh, and my right arm is missing below the elbow.

(Yeah. I'm missing an arm and my name is Legg. You can imagine the jokes. An arm and a Legg, ha fucking ha.)

I wish I had an exciting story about my arm. Sometimes if a stranger is being really nosy about it I make up a story. I was swimming in the sea and a Great White came up and snatched it off, or we were visiting the zoo and I stuck my hand in the tiger cage, or, my favourite, I have a hideous flesh-eating disease. You'd better stay back, I tell people. It's contagious.

It's not nearly as exciting as that, though. It was the tablets, the ones Mum took when she was pregnant to stop her morning sickness. Thalidomide. We've still got half a tube of them in the back of the medicine cabinet. I was one of the last ones born. They withdrew the tablets soon after Mum got pregnant – she only took a couple – but the damage was already done.

I got off lightly, really. Some of the babies were born without any arms or legs, just little flippers poking out from their torsos. Some were blind or deaf. Some were stillborn. Count your blessings, says Mum, whenever I moan about my arm. You're healthy, and you're clever, and you're pretty. But that makes it worse, in a way. Being pretty. My Auntie Wendy said once: you're so beautiful and slim, Sylvia. If it wasn't for your arm you could be a model.

I hate Auntie Wendy.

When my mum was pregnant, and the news about Thalidomide came out, Auntie Wendy went to Lourdes to pray for a miracle. She brought back this brass crucifix which Mum's nailed up in the downstairs loo. I look at that crucifix when I go to the toilet. Jesus with his arms stretched out, both of them sculpted and sinewy. Almost like he's showing off.

That's an evil wicked thought, I know. Blasphemous. I sometimes think I am evil and wicked.

I don't know how I got onto this topic. My hand's cramping now from writing so much. I have to go, anyway. I'm going to the beach with Sally and Judith. We're having a picnic for my birthday.

Who knows if I'll write in here again. Probably not.

Jane stares at the page. As she listens to the wind howling around the caravan, she imagines her mother. Lying on her bed in the inky dusk, the scent of the jasmine bush drifting through the window, the low whooshing of the motorway in the background. The nib of her fountain pen scratching on the page. Sixteen years old. About half the age Jane is now.

Jane feels ill, giddy, with a sense that time has dissolved, folded in on itself.

Before she knows what she's doing, she turns the page.

*14 August 1978*

Yesterday was so, so awful. The worst birthday ever. I just wanted to crawl into a hole and die.

We went to the beach. Down to Exmouth. Judith's new boyfriend drove us in his car, a yellow Ford Cortina. He's nineteen and has a moustache and chest hair and was wearing so much Brut that I thought I was going to puke. I had to wind down the window to breathe. He drove the whole time with one hand on the wheel and the other on Judith's leg. Sally whispered in my ear that he had a stiffy, and that set me off, we were in absolute hysterics in the back seat and he got really annoyed with us. Judith sighed and flicked her hair and said ignore them Rodney, they're so immature, and that just set us off laughing again.

We got to Exmouth and it was so hot. The beach was packed. Judith and her boyfriend went off into the dunes together, and

Sally and I decided to sunbathe. Sally had gone the whole nine yards. She had tinfoil to put under her chin and tanning oil which smelt of coconuts, and a brand-new red bikini with white hibiscus flowers on it. Sally's figure is amazing, she is short but curvy and boys go mad for her. I'm like an ironing board. In my navy blue swimming costume I looked practically prepubescent.

We lay there for a bit. Sally loves sunbathing but I think it's boring. The sun makes me scrunch my eyes up and I get a headache. I was just about to say we should go for a paddle instead when this group of boys came over, carrying surfboards. Four of them. One of them was quite cute. He had feathered hair and looked a bit like Andy Gibb. I sat up on my elbows. Tried to keep my arm out of sight. They got chatting to Sally. She likes talking to boys – she knows what to say, how to flirt without being slutty.

So they were getting along okay, and I thought I'd got away without them seeing my arm. But then I saw one of them notice.

You can tell when it happens. The exact second. Especially with men. Their faces change. It's like a cloud passing over the sun. Like shutters coming down.

One of the boys – this little runty one at the back – I saw him staring. And he nudged his friend, nodded at me. I saw the other one look, too. I heard him mutter the word. The F word.

Flid.

One by one, they all stared. Last to look was Andy Gibb. I looked away. Focused on the bright water, wishing an enormous wave would rise up, wipe me clean off the beach. Off the entire bloody planet.

Sally cottoned on to what was happening pretty quick. She grabbed our towels and said come on, Sylvia. Let's go for a swim. She took my hand and pulled me up and we walked away. And then one of them started saying stuff. Loud enough for us to hear. Spaz. Freak. Flid. Sally wheeled round and yelled at them. Think you're so big, do you? Picking on girls? You're just a bunch of knuckle-dragging Neanderthals.

I was tugging at her hand. Willing her to just walk away. More people were staring. I thought I might just spontaneously combust with embarrassment.

Come on, said Sally. Just ignore those creeps. We won't let them ruin our day.

But I didn't want to swim any more and the day was already ruined and I just wanted to go home. Sally and I went up into the dunes to find Judith and her boyfriend. They were snogging behind a patch of pampas grass and Sally kicked sand at them.

We want to go home, she said.

Well we don't, said Judith.

Well, give us the keys and we'll wait in the car.

Judith's boyfriend complained a bit but eventually gave in. Don't touch anything, he said. And don't smoke in it, I don't want it to stink.

Already stinks of your fucking aftershave, said Sally, but quietly so he didn't hear.

We sat inside the Cortina and Sally smoked a cigarette. Flicked the ash in the footwell and rubbed it in with her toe. She was raging about the boys. Calling them all sorts of names. Idiots. Ignoramuses. Dickheads. Trying to cheer me up, I think. But I was so depressed. I just wanted to go home.

When I got in the door Mum asked me if I'd had a good birthday and I burst into tears. She sat me down and made me tell her what had happened. And she started up with her usual advice. Don't pay any attention, they're just ignorant, sticks and stones may break my bones but words can never hurt me.

I know she means well but all that stuff makes me feel worse. I'm sick of hearing it. And I stared at my stupid little withered stump and blurted out what I've been wanting to say for ages:

I want a prosthesis.

Mum looked surprised.

You're fine as you are, aren't you? she said. You get along just fine.

I don't get along fine, I said. I need one.

But you don't, she said. You can do everything with your arm. A prosthesis would just get in the way. It would make you all clumsy. You hated them when you were a baby.

Well, I'm not a baby now, I said. And I don't want one for doing things with, I want one so that I look normal.

You are normal, she said. You're beautiful, you're perfect.

I'm a freak, I said. I'm a monstrous freak, and I'm never going to get a boyfriend, nobody's ever going to love me, I'm going to die alone, a dried-up lonely old spinster because I'm a mutant, I'm a cripple, I'm a flid!

And then I ran upstairs in tears and slammed my bedroom door behind me. Mum came up and knocked but I told her to leave me alone and she's gone.

And this is where I've been ever since.

She's never wanted me to have a prosthesis. I can understand why. I've seen pictures of some of the ones they gave the other kids. Scary-looking things made of leather with hinges and hooks. Gas-powered ones with steel pincers that open and close with a hiss. I would have looked even more of a freak. They tried me with things when I was a baby but apparently I just sat there and screamed until they took them off. And that was that. No more prosthetics. I learned how to do everything with my stump. Tie my shoelaces, put my hair up, use cutlery, everything. I've still got a bit of arm below my elbow that I can grip things with, so I get along okay.

When I was ten some engineering students from the local university came round and offered my mum a prototype arm they'd designed with different attachments that screwed on – a fork, a brush, a violin bow. They spread them all out on the coffee table, like salesmen with a set of steak knives. Mum got really angry with them, said that I wasn't a toy, a Barbie doll for them to play with, and they packed it all up again and went away. But I was a bit disappointed.

Mum has always wanted me to be fine without a prosthesis. You're too worried about looks, she says. Looks aren't everything, you know.

They are, though. If you're a sixteen-year-old girl trying to get a boyfriend they are.

I'm getting a prosthesis whether she likes it or not.

### 2 September 1978

The morning after I wrote that last entry, Mum came up to my room. She said she hadn't realised how sad I was. And that if that was what I really wanted, if a prosthesis would stop me thinking such awful things about myself, then we would go to the doctor's and we would get one.

So we went. And the doctor referred us to Exeter Hospital. The appointment was today. I barely slept last night; so excited I felt sick. Sweated patches under my arms in the waiting room.

The consultant was a bit of a prick. Really burst my bubble. He asked me what I wanted the prosthesis to achieve. I dunno, I said. I just want it to look good. So a cosmetic prosthesis, he said. Well, a cosmetic prosthesis is passive. A dead weight. More of a hindrance than a help in many ways. Have you considered something more functional? This, for example –

And then he showed me the prosthesis he wanted me to have. Oh my God, I nearly cried. It was horrific, this mechanical thing that looked like a silver shotgun with two orange antennae poking out of the barrel. The latest technology, apparently. He kept going on and on about it. Neoprene-lined, aluminium alloy, excellent prehension facility, blah blah blah. I told him, I said I don't want something that makes me look like a freak. I just want one that looks good. He got a bit sniffy and said: but a cosmetic prosthesis won't *do* anything.

I felt like telling him that actually, it would do a lot. It would fill out sleeves. Let me dance. Let me walk down the street without feeling that everyone is staring, whispering. Let me hold my head up high. Talk to boys. Find true love. But of course I didn't say any of that. Just kept quiet, trying not to blub. But then Mum piped up.

She's made her mind up, Doctor, she said. Give her the one she wants.

I was so grateful to her for that. And the doctor sighed and said all right. See how you get on with a passive model. Maybe once you've come to appreciate its limitations you can come back and we can fit you with something more functional.

A woman came in and did loads of measurements of my stump and then made a plaster cast of it and then it was time to go. I've got to go back in a couple of weeks to try out a dummy mould for it, and if that's fine then they'll make the real thing.

I can't believe it's finally happening.


1 October 1978

It's here!

Today was like Christmas and a birthday rolled into one.

When we got into the consultant's office the prosthesis was there, just laid out on the table next to him. I was so excited I couldn't focus on a word he said. But he waffled on for ages and ages about aftercare, fit checks, what happens if I gain weight, blah blah blah. And then finally he said, well then, let's see how it fits.

He slotted it onto my arm, and told me to take a look in the mirror. I nearly cried.

It's beautiful. It's perfect. It has slender fingers like a pianist's and long oval nails that look like they've been manicured. I turned this way and that, raised my hand, waved. Grinning from ear to ear.

Mum said oh, it looks wonderful, Sylvia, just beautiful.

Walking out of the hospital was so strange. I wondered if people were staring at it. I didn't know what to do with it, whether to tuck my hand in my pocket, cross my arms, what. It just sort of dangled there, feeling odd and heavy. And another strange thing – I was so happy as we walked through the hospital, but for a moment, as we stepped out of the doors into the bright sunshine, I suddenly wanted to cry. I was filled with this awful feeling, like – I don't know, like dread. As if the arm was something bad. It felt like a threshold had been crossed, somehow. Like by putting on the prosthesis my life had changed direction and there was no turning back. And I had this urge to rip it off, take it back, even though I'd wanted it for so long.

I think it was just nerves. By the time we got home, the feeling had gone. I ran upstairs and looked at myself in the mirror. My silhouette. It looked whole. I was so happy I even hugged George, when he came up to see. I practised waving, and tucking my hand in my pocket, and crossing my arms. I tried on my coat – I could roll my sleeve down. I raided Mum's drawers for a pair of gloves. When I put them on I couldn't believe it. I looked so normal. Nobody would ever know.

I'm even going to paint the nails. I bought polish with my birthday money, Revlon's Cherries in the Snow.

\* \* \*

*8 November 1978*

I haven't written in here for a while. I've been busy with my new hand. I've been practising with it – walking, dressing, doing my hair. Eating. Cycling, even. I'm still a bit clumsy with it. And I've worn it too much. The consultant said start with a couple of hours a day at most, but I've been wearing it all the time, and after a few days my arm ached so badly, and it rubbed a lot and gave me bruises and blisters on my elbow, so I had to stop for a bit.

But last Friday, Sally and Judith took me out to a disco in Tiverton, and I borrowed one of Sally's dresses, the green chiffon one with long sleeves, and I wore my prosthesis and I looked amazing if I say so myself. I danced all night. Two boys asked me to dance with them. I said thanks but no thanks. If they'd touched my hand accidentally I'd have been mortified. But still. I was asked to dance by a boy. That's never happened before.

It was wonderful. Do you know the relief of seeing people look you in the eye? Of not waiting for that awful moment, the moment when they notice? It felt like floating on air.

Also – I have a job. At the Pony and Trap, the roughest pub in Crowholt, but still. I'm earning money, my own money to spend exactly as I please. I thought I might struggle with my arm and would have to take it off, but actually it's okay. My plastic hand has a bit of give in it, which lets me pull a pint just fine, and I can carry empties pressed against my chest with it, and hold lemons in place as I slice them, and with my other arm I can carry trays and count change and pour from bottles and wipe down tables. I'm not the fastest barmaid in the West but I get along okay.

I am feeling good about my life now. Like stuff is happening, moving forwards. All that needs to happen now is for a John Travolta lookalike to come and sweep me off my feet.

Dream on, baby.

9 November 1978

A dramatic day.

I was sitting in my room this morning, curling my hair and listening to my new Rod Stewart LP, when George burst in. Clambered up on my bed, ripped open the curtains and pressed his face to the window. I said oi! What the hell do you think you're doing, barging into my room like that? I started giving him an earful, but he ignored me. Just stared out the window.

The paper mill's on fire, he said. Look.

I climbed up on the bed next to him. We both stared.

I couldn't believe it. The entire mill was burning. Bright orange, the exact same colour as the electric heater in the living room. I could almost feel the heat on my skin. An enormous column of black smoke rising into the air. It was apocalyptic.

George got his binoculars and we took turns pressing them to our eyes, twisting the dial. The flames were ferocious, streaming out of the windows, twisting up the sides of the mill. A proper inferno. Through the binos we could see scraps of paper fluttering out, rising into the air like birds.

And then we saw the firemen. They looked so small against the blaze, and their jets of water seemed to do nothing, thin threads swallowed up instantly by the flames. There was something awful and exciting about it, watching the mill burn, passing the binoculars between us. Our breath fogged up the window, and we wiped it away with our sleeves.

Do you think there are people in there? I said.

Probably, said George. He sounded excited. That boy's got a morbid streak a mile wide.

It's always reminded me of a dragon, the paper mill. Sitting there with its plume of steam trailing into the sky, like it's breathing smoke. Sometimes, maybe twice a year, it roars, a great boiling gush of steam pouring out of its stack. It's so loud when it happens, all the birds in the trees at the bottom of the garden fly into the air. Makes me jump out of my skin. Dad says it's called a steam blow, and it clears the pipes.

And now it's breathed fire.

We watched it for ages, until Mum shouted at us to come downstairs for our lunch and to stop gawping.

It's three o'clock now and there are still loads of fire engines there. The jets of water still falling uselessly into the flames. I wonder if anyone's dead.


*12 November 1978*

Someone's dead.

I keep thinking about how George and I watched the flames and all the while there was a man inside there, burning. George said he swore he saw someone screaming at a window and I said no he didn't, he was making it up. He's such a cretin sometimes.

It's all the village can talk about. Martin Adams was the man's name. He was the foreman at the mill. I'd served him in the pub only a week before he died. Big fat man with a sovereign ring and a moustache. Strange to think. There he was, drinking a pint of Watneys Red Barrel and smoking and playing darts, casual as anything, not knowing that seven days later he'd burn to death. Gives me the creeps thinking about it.

They reckon it was an electrical fault that did it, something overheating. Mum's been paranoid ever since, testing our smoke detector every day, getting an electrician in to check our plug sockets and fuse box. She's even banned Dad from smoking in his easy chair because he might nod off and set the house on fire.

I can't believe I was moaning at the start of this diary that nothing ever happens in Crowholt. Well, I should be careful what

I wish for, because now something HAS happened but it's horrible and frightening and I'm reminded of it every time I open my bedroom curtains and see the blackened shell of the mill. It sends a chill right through me.

20 November 1978

The most incredible thing has happened.

Today was Martin Adams' funeral, and they held his wake at the pub. I didn't know it was going to be there until Moira rang me last night and told me to wear black for my shift. Well, the only black clothes I have are a mohair jumper and a corduroy skirt from when I dressed up as a witch's cat in our school production of *Macbeth* in the fourth year. So I wore those.

Mohair was a mistake. The pub was roasting hot. Moira had both fires blazing, and there were so many people packed in, I could barely move. I was sweating absolute buckets. Anyway, the wake had been going on for a few hours, and I'd been run off my feet, and hadn't had a chance for so much as a sip of water, and hadn't eaten since breakfast either, and I was feeling really lightheaded.

There were these three men propping up the bar. As I was pulling their pints, I overheard them talking about Martin Adams. Apparently he'd got out of the mill when the fire started, but then he went back inside to check if anyone was still in there, and a huge great two-tonne roll of paper crashed right down in front of him and blocked his exit. One of the men said his body was so burnt up they could only tell it was him by his sovereign ring.

God, hearing that made me feel like I was going to pass out. I handed the men their pints, then said something to Moira about needing some fresh air, and I tried to push my way out of the bar, but everyone was packed in too close, and the heat of their bodies was too much, and the room began to dissolve and spin, and I felt my legs giving way and everything went black.

Next thing I knew, someone was hovering above me. A man, fanning me with a newspaper. I tried to get myself up on my elbows but I slipped back down and my head smacked against the flagstone floor. I saw stars. I thought that was made up, for cartoons, but it's real.

And then the man said here, love, let me help you up – and he reached for my hand. The wrong one. I tried to say something but I was too dazed, and as he grabbed it his eyes widened in surprise.

I pushed him away, got up. The man tried to get me to sit down for a minute, but I couldn't bear it, everyone looking at me, so I shoved past him, stumbled through the crowd, managed to make my way out the back.

It had rained and everything smelt fresh and clean. The cold air was bliss. I just leaned against the wall and shut my eyes. I felt woozy. A bit drunk.

After a minute or so the door opened. It was the man.

I hadn't been able to get a good look at him before, the light had been behind him, but now I could see he had curly dark hair and a nice smile. He didn't look like John Travolta. But he was handsome. Very handsome. I suddenly felt self-conscious. Tried to wipe my sweaty hair off my face. Prayed to God my Fresh and Dry was still working and I didn't stink.

Anyway, he'd brought me the glass of water, and I sipped it, and we started chatting. His name's Bobby. Bobby Douglas. He said Martin Adams had been his best friend. They'd been in the Air Force together. Stationed, whatever that means, in the Shetland Islands. Saxo something.

Were you a pilot, then? I said.

He laughed at that. Said God, no. No. Just a lowly mechanic.

And I'm not in the Air Force any more. Left to work on the oil rigs. More money in it, supposedly. Black gold, they call it.

Then he looked at me, and said, what happened to your hand?

Well, that took me by surprise. Most people don't ask that outright. But I didn't mind it, coming from him. He asked it in the right way. Not in that pitying hushed way that gets my back up, but not rudely either. Sort of casually, as if he was asking for the time. I can't really explain.

So I told him. Thalidomide. And he nodded. And that was that.

And because we'd got the hand thing out of the way already, we could talk without me worrying, waiting for the moment he'd notice. He looked at my face the whole time we were chatting. We talked about loads of stuff. About our hometowns (he's from Aberdeen), about music (he likes Crosby, Stills and Nash), about our families (he's the eldest of five siblings) and . . . well, everything. And I felt this feeling. Looking at him, him looking at me. This feeling like there was a change in the air. The sun coming out. Warming me, all over.

And then he offered me a cigarette. I took one. He struck the match, lit mine and his both. His hand being so close to my mouth made me feel a bit giddy. And as I breathed it in, I felt dizzy again. I sort of leaned back against the wall and he said woah there. You still feeling faint? You should go on home.

I can't, I said. The landlady needs me.

Wait here, he said. I'll go and talk to her.

And he went inside, and after a few minutes he came out, with my coat and bag, and said there you go. Got you the evening off. Roped in one of my mates to cover for you. Can I walk you home?

And that was how I ended up walking arm in arm through Crowholt with a Scotsman I'd only just met.

We talked as we walked. He was so easy to talk to. And funny, so funny. He told a story about Shetland, about a bird, something called a bonxie, attacking him, and by the end I was laughing so hard I had tears rolling down my cheeks.

At one point he stopped in his tracks and paused and said, wait a minute.

What? I said.

I just realised I don't even know your name.

Sylvia, I said.

Sylvia. That's a beautiful name, he said.

Sounded even better coming from his mouth than from Monsieur Leclerc's.

I didn't want the walk to end but before I knew it we were on the estate. Walking down the road, up to the conifers, next to the house. I stopped at the gate.

Is this you? he said.

I looked at the house. The light behind the curtains. I could hear the telly on. Playing the theme tune to *Some Mothers Do 'Ave 'Em*, and Mum laughing and Dad coughing. And I was suddenly desperate not to leave him and go in. Back to my old life. I'd felt something, some possibility. As if I'd opened the lid of a treasure chest, just a crack, and seen the gold inside. And now I was expected to slam it shut again.

I looked at the hedge the cow had eaten and felt like crying. Stupid, right? I don't know what came over me.

I turned to him and looked at his face. He looked at me, his beautiful blue eyes shining in the glow of the streetlight. And before I knew what was happening we were kissing.

I've kissed boys before. Ben Norton in third year shoved his tongue into my mouth like a battering ram. David Godfrey at the roller disco in Minehead, who tasted like cheesy Quavers. I never understood kissing. But Bobby. He kissed me, softly, slowly, gently, and it was like he wasn't just kissing my mouth, he was kissing my whole body. I just melted. God. The whole world disappeared. I don't know how long we stood there, on the grass verge, under the streetlamp. It started to rain again and we didn't stop, I barely even noticed the water soaking me. He smelt faintly of shaving foam and tasted smoky, electric. I could have kissed him forever.

And then a stupid moronic cretinous voice said: I'm gonna tell Mum!

I broke away. Looked. It was George, on his bike. With his idiot mate Eddie. Both gawping at us.

Fuck off! I said.

George just stared at me and said you're snogging a MAN!

And I said, oh well done George, your powers of observation are astounding.

I'm telling!

Don't you dare, you little toerag, I said, but he wheeled his bike through the gate, into the garden. I didn't care. I didn't care about anything. I'd just tasted heaven. Nothing else mattered.

George opened the front door and I heard him shout: Mum! Sylvia's kissing a man!

I'd better go, said Bobby, laughing.

I mumbled into his neck. Please come and see me again, I said.

Of course I will, he said. Tomorrow?

Yes.

He kissed me again, briefly, on the lips, then on my forehead, then on my hand, and then he walked off, up the street. He turned and raised a hand before he disappeared round the corner and I was left there in the rain, feeling the spots where his mouth had been, lips, forehead, hand, burning, as if they'd been branded.

Mum opened the front door. Her silhouette against the light. She looked at me for a moment. I thought she was going to kick off. But she just said come in, love. You'll catch your death.

\* \* \*

Jane skim reads the next few entries. Her mother's scratchy blue writing grows slanted, rushing, breathless. *I feel like a butterfly emerging from a chrysalis*, she writes. *Like Bobby's touch has rearranged me, split me apart.*

Jane flips through the pages, trying not to read, but words, phrases, jump out at her. *His mouth. My bra. Felt him. Held me. Very gently, he – it didn't hurt. No blood. I read in* Jackie *magazine once heavy petting, tampons, horse riding – Sally said when she did it with Dean the first time – I want to be close to him always, I love him I love him I love him.*

She comes to six pages which consist entirely of Bobby's name, written over and over. In capitals, in cursive, squashed into the margins, scrawled across the page, surrounded by love hearts. There is a portrait of him, sketched in pencil, scribbled out, a note beneath it: *I could never do him justice. Nobody ever could, not even Michelangelo. His curls are black as midnight. His eyes are chips of blue ice. His lips are living poetry.*

Jane blinks, rubs her eyes. Lifts the bottle of gin to her lips, then realises it's all gone. She rolls a cigarette instead, lights it. Smokes it. Brushes some dropped ash from her leg. Thinks about putting the diary back in the tin, going to bed. But she's hungry, now, for what she knows will come next.

Her.

She flips through more pages, hormone-soaked teenage ramblings, *Bobby, Bobby, Bobby,* until she reaches:


*29 January 1979*


Oh God, oh God, oh God.

This morning as soon as I woke up I had to puke. I ran out of my room and barged straight into Mum. She was carrying Dad's tea and toast up on a tray and it spilt everywhere. I made it to the loo just in time. I was heaving and retching for ages, puking and puking, it was bloody awful. Mum held my hair out of the way, and rubbed my back, and when I was finished I flushed the loo and wiped my mouth, and she took me back into my bedroom and sat me down on the bed. And then she said, Sylvia. Look at me.

I looked at her. Her face was pale, her eyes wide.

What? I said.

What have you been doing with that man? she said.

What are you on about?

Your bloke. Bobby.

What do you mean?

She rolled her eyes. Don't be acting all coy, she said. You know perfectly well what I mean.

I felt myself blushing. Nothing, I said. We've kissed a bit is all.

Don't lie. And don't play me for a fool. I've seen those love bites on your neck. Have you been using protection?

Mum!

Well, have you?

I just stared at the carpet. Shrugged. Most of the time, I said.

Most of the time? Jesus, Mary and Joseph, she said. When did you last have a bleed?

Mum! I squirmed away from her. She grabbed my wrist.

When, Sylvia?

I thought for a second. I had to think back a long way. Months. In fact, I haven't had one since before I met Bobby. And it slowly dawned on me. I stared at Mum and she stared at me and I started to cry.

Mum said oh, you stupid girl. You stupid, stupid girl. You've gone and done it now. I knew it. No towels in the bathroom bin for months – and as soon as I saw you throwing up . . . all my pregnancies: you, George, the two I lost. Each one started exactly like this. Morning sickness. Oh Christ, she said, I should have put my foot down, should have nipped this in the bud right when it started.

And then Dad came in, scratching his belly through his string vest, saying what's all this about? Where's my breakfast?

Oh bog off Alan, said Mum. Make your own bloody breakfast. And he left, grumbling, and Mum looked at me and said oh, you silly girl, you silly, silly girl, but she sat next to me and put her arms round me and stroked my hair while I sniffed and snotted.

Look, she said. We'll manage. Whatever happens, we'll manage. It's not the end of the world. It's not ideal, but it's not the end of the world. Just for God's sake, don't tell your father yet, he'll hit the bloody roof, be round there with a shotgun.

But, I said, but – but what am I going to tell Bobby?

And Mum raised her eyebrows and said: you'd better tell him he's going to be a father.

*30 January 1979*

Sally came over today. She knew something was the matter straight away. She always does. As soon as she came in the room and saw my face, she said, oh no. He hasn't dumped you, has he?

No.

Well what? Has he two-timed you?

No.

Tell me, then, she said. You look like a wreck.

So I took a deep breath and said: I'm pregnant.

It was the first time I'd said it out loud.

Well she went absolutely nuts. Are you joking? she said. Oh my God. Pregnant? You? Weren't you using rubbers?

Yeah, I said, but – but a couple of times we just got carried away. But he always pulled out before he – you know.

She was beside herself. Pregnant! she said. Oh my God. Oh my GOD. What are you going to do? Do your mum and dad know? Does he know?

Not yet, I said. I'm telling him tomorrow.

When she'd stopped freaking out, she sat down and took my hand and patted it and said now brace yourself. Prepare for the worst. Remember Kathleen? Her and Steven? Love's young dream, childhood sweethearts, everyone thought they were gonna get married, and then when she got up the duff he dropped her like a hot potato. Men are pigs.

Thanks, Sal, that's cheered me up, I said.

I'm just telling you the truth, she said. And then she saw how miserable I was and she tried to make me smile, goofing around. She leaned in to my stomach and said coo-ee little baby, it's Auntie Sally speaking, and I gave her a shove and we both ended up laughing. I felt better after that.

But now she's gone, and it's late, and I'm meeting Bobby tomorrow in Exeter to tell him. I'm so nervous I can't sleep.

### 31 January 1979

I woke up this morning feeling like a condemned man about to face the firing squad.

I took the bus into Exeter. The conductor saw my face and said cheer up love, it might never happen! I could have strangled him.

I rested my head against the cold glass of the bus window and watched the fields roll past. It was a beautiful morning. Everything sharp and silvered with frost, glinting in the sunlight, but all I felt was misery. Forty-five minutes, the bus takes. I was willing it to go for longer. Hoping we'd break down or get stuck in traffic or something. But we got closer and closer.

Soon we were pulling into the station, and I got off the bus, hoping maybe Bobby wouldn't be there, that he had forgotten about our date, but no — he was there, waiting by the chocolate machine, in his wool coat with the collar turned up, smoking a cigarette, looking like a film star, so gorgeous I couldn't stand it. Everything seemed in slow motion as he turned and saw me and smiled his beautiful smile, and I thought this is it. This is the moment my life is ruined forever. And I just stood in the middle of the bus station and burst into tears.

God, Sylvia, he said, hurrying over. What's wrong? He held me, looked at my face, and I said:

Bobby — I'm p-p-p-pregnant!

Then I just wailed. Loud enough that the pigeons that had been pecking around the station flew up into the rafters. People were staring, I could tell, but I didn't care, my heart was breaking, I could actually feel it breaking in my chest.

Bobby just looked a bit dazed, and said pregnant? Did you say you're pregnant?

And I nodded, and he ran his hand through his hair and blew out his cheeks and then laughed. He laughed! And he said, God, he said. Pregnant. Are you sure?

Yes, I choked.

And he took me in his arms and held me close. I clung to him like a drowning woman to a life raft, thinking this is it. One last embrace before he says so long Sylvia, nice knowing you but I'm back off to Shetland now, you'll never see me again. And he cleared his throat and leaned back and held me at arm's length and looked at me, and said, Sylvia — and I braced myself for the awful words . . .

I was going to ask your father's permission first, he said. Do it all properly, but I suppose we don't have time for all that.

And I just stood there, stunned.

And my God, he got down on one knee, right there on the filthy bus station concrete, with the fag butts and the pigeon shit, and took my hand in his, and looked at me with his beautiful blue eyes, and said Sylvia Legg, will you marry me?

What? I said. It came out like a squeak.

Will you marry me? he said.

Are you joking?

I'm deadly serious, he said. And I could tell he was, from his eyes.

And I said – I said yes! Yes!

And then he stood up and embraced me and we kissed and the people who had been watching clapped and cheered and a bus beeped its horn and a couple of pigeons flew up into the air. And I was hysterical.

When I'd calmed down a bit he said come on, fiancée. Let's go get you a ring. So we walked hand in hand to Argos and chose a ring, a simple gold band (he said he'd get me a fancier one once he'd saved up a bit), and slipped it on my finger right there in the shop. And then we had hot chocolate and doughnuts from the van in the Guildhall to celebrate and then it started to snow. And we walked across Cathedral Green in it as the street-lamps came on and I thought this is the happiest anyone could ever be. This has been the most perfect day of my entire life.

We are going to be such a happy family. Bobby, the baby, and me.

Jane swallows. Shuts the diary. Looks at the alarm clock, the bright red numbers glowing. It is ten past three in the morning, the caravan milky with smoke. Her gin is wearing off, like a tide going out, leaving her high and dry on jagged rocks.

She puts the diary back in the tin, shoves the tin in the broken drawer. Her foot throbs. She is suddenly hollow with exhaustion, with a feeling of shame, of wanting to wash herself, as if she has touched something disgusting. She shouldn't have read the diaries. She won't touch them again.

She crawls into bed and falls asleep.

Jane wakes to a pounding headache and a dry mouth. She drinks three glasses of water in a row, swallows two aspirin, brushes her teeth. She glances at herself in the mirror. Her eyes are bloodshot. She can smell the gin on herself, the booze leaching out of her pores. She should have a shower but she woke too late.

She opens the caravan door, wincing at the light. Outside, a mist clings to the land, so thick she can hardly see through it. A steekit stumba, the islanders call it.

Jane drives slowly, carefully, her fog lights on, their beams swallowed up in the opaque air. She arrives in the car park, looks at the factory. Smokes a cigarette. Then goes in.

'Are you okay, Jane?' asks Terri, smiling, as Jane puts her dungarees on. 'You look a wee bit worse for wear.'

'Out partying last night, were you?' says Dawn. 'First time for everything.'

Jane ignores her. 'Aye, Terri,' she says, shutting her locker. 'I'm okay.'

Pat comes in, clipboard in hand.

'Morning, ladies, how are we all? Sandra, you're washing today please. Dawn, weighing. Terri, Jane,' she says, checking her clipboard, 'you're on crabs. Shelling.'

'I've not done shelling before,' says Jane, a twinge of pain shooting through her head as she speaks. 'Can't I do summat else? I'm not feeling up to learning something new today.'

'No. You're shelling. Terri'll teach you.'

Jane winces as they step onto the factory floor. She lowers her head against the bright glint of metal, the hiss and clank and hum of machinery. She follows Terri to the chiller, helps her wheel trays of legless, clawless crabs into a room with a stainless-steel table, watches as Terri grabs a tray, tips the crabs out. She takes one, sticks a knife into the carapace, cracks the crown off, pulls out the meat with a series of deft flicks. Jane's stomach rolls.

'You've got to be careful with this bit,' says Terri. 'See these? The darker sort of rubbery bits? They're the gills. Dead man's fingers,' she says.

'What?'

'That's what people call them. Dead man's fingers. See? Look . . .' She fans out the gills; they look like a grey hand, clutching. 'They're tough, taste bitter, so you've got to scrape them out, like this . . .'

'Excuse me,' says Jane. She only just makes it to the toilet in time, vomiting loudly into the bowl.

'Stomach bug,' says Pat. 'I'm not buying that. You're hungover. I can smell the booze on you, you reek of it.'

Jane doesn't reply. Just looks at her boots against the tiled floor of the changing room, feeling like her head's been scooped out and shat in.

'You're not to come to work hungover again,' she says. 'What the hell were you thinking, getting drunk on a Sunday night?'

'I know, Pat. I'm sorry.'

Pat glares at her.

'Is there summat wrong?'

'No. Nothing wrong.'

'Well. Good. Now fuck off home. And make sure tomorrow you turn up for work sober. And on time.'

Jane is wrapped in a blanket on Mike's sofa, watching the TV, when she hears his key in the lock.

'Hi,' she mumbles, when he steps inside.

'Oh!' he says, seeing her. 'You okay?'

'Left work early. Not feeling too good.'

'No?'

Jane shakes her head. 'Threw up. Hungover.'

'Hungover?'

'Mm.'

'Why're you hungover?' He unzips his coat.

'Drank a bottle of gin.'

'What, by yourself?'

Jane nods, grimaces.

Mike looks at her. 'Want a cuppa?'

Jane shakes her head.

'Have you eaten?'

Jane shakes her head.

'Fancy a fry-up?'

Jane shakes her head.

Mike comes in, sits on the arm of the sofa, takes her hand. 'Is there summat the matter?' he says.

But she can't tell him about the arm. To tell him would make it real, somehow. Telling Maggie was okay, because she was there, she's from the past, she knows it all first hand, but Mike – she's told him her past, of course. All the islanders know it. But she doesn't want to bring it into their present. Their future. Not yet.

He looks at her. His kind brown eyes searching her face. I'm a mussel, she thinks, closed up tight. His eyes are the knife trying to crack me open.

She says, 'It's nothing. I just fancied a drink, and I ended up drinking too much. I'll be okay.'

'If you're sure,' he says, and he kisses her gently on the hand. Then he stands up. 'I'm just home for lunch. Then I'm off for that meeting with that fishmonger from Glasgow. Hoping he'll sign the contract today.'

Mike makes himself a sandwich, then sits in the living room with her. They watch the news. There's a story on about the plastic in the ocean. About the Great Pacific Garbage Patch. Jane thinks of her mother's arm floating on the surface of the quarry. She isn't sure what it was made of. PVC, maybe? Vinyl? It's probably still as fresh as the day she got it. All those years ago.

Mike shakes his head. Gestures with his sandwich to the TV. 'They need to do something about this,' he says.

'About what?'

'All this plastic in the sea,' he says. 'Surely there's got to be something they can do. We're wrecking the planet.' He takes a bite of his sandwich, chews. 'I was talking to Roy,' he says. 'You know Roy, the one who runs the birding tours? He was saying the numbers of kittiwakes and terns, they've gone right down. Summat to do with global warming affecting the plankton' – he swallows the mouthful of sandwich – 'and then that affecting the sand eels. And he said all that rain in the spring, you remember the landslip? Blocked that road, the one heading from Norwick to Skaw? That's all cos of global warming as well. That's what Roy reckons, anyway.'

Jane stares at the TV, dumbly. Then she says, 'Have you still got those pickled onions?'

'Eh?'

'The pickled onions, you know. The ones you bought at that market in Lerwick? With the chillis in? I just fancy one.'

He blinks at her. 'Aye,' he says.

Jane gets off the sofa, shuffles into the kitchen. Rummages in the cupboards. Finds the jar, the onions bumping against the glass like eyeballs. She unscrews the lid, fishes one out with her fingers, pops it into her mouth, crunches. The bitterness floods her tongue. She eats three in a row, relishing the vinegary tang, sucking the juice from her fingers. She takes a swig from the jar, vinegar dribbling down her chin.

'Wow,' says Mike, appearing in the doorway with his empty plate. Jane belches. Clamps a hand to her mouth.

Mike raises his eyebrows. 'I won't be kissing you any time soon,' he says.

'Oh,' says Jane.

'Joking. Come here.'

Jane lies awake, listening to Mike's soft snoring. She gazes into the darkness. Turns her head, looks at the clock on the bedside table: 4.30 a.m.

She sighs, shuts her eyes. Flings an arm across her face. But images can't stop playing on the backs of her eyelids. A burning mill. A scum of plastic on the ocean. An arm in a lake.

She rolls over. Looks at Mike, his sleeping face. Then she pulls the duvet off her, gets out of bed and pads across the carpet, hugging herself tightly against the cold. Pulls on her sweatshirt, jeans, coat, trainers. Then eases open the bedroom door, and slips out.

The lights of her car illuminate the road ahead, frost glittering on the grass. Some sheep startle as she passes, their eyes reflecting green in the light from the headlamps. Jane grips the cold steering wheel, her hands in their fingerless gloves numb from scraping ice off the windscreen.

Back in the caravan she sits huddled in bed, listening to the heater tick as it warms up. She looks at the cracker tin in her lap. Hesitates, her aching fingers hovering over the pitted metal. Then she pops the lid open, lifts out the diary, and with a deep breath in, opens it.

*17 February 1979*

I am writing this as a married woman.

I am Miss Sylvia Legg no longer. I am:

MRS SYLVIA DOUGLAS!

The wedding was yesterday. It was tiny, at the registry office.

Hardly any guests, just close family on my side and then a couple of Bobby's friends. His family is all the way up in Aberdeen and couldn't make it in time. He wasn't bothered though, doesn't have much to do with them anyway, as far as I can tell.

I wore a white satin dress with a high ruffled collar. George said I looked like I'd swallowed a plate. Dickhead. I was worried my belly was already starting to show, but Mum said it's still flat as a pancake. I held my bouquet in front of it anyway, just in case. Ivy and red roses and baby's breath. I had my hair loose. A bit of baby's breath stuck in it. No veil.

Bobby wore the same suit he'd worn at the wake and had a red rose and ivy buttonhole. He'd wanted to wear a kilt and a sporran but he couldn't get one sorted in time. Shame. He looked so handsome anyway.

Sally and Judith were my bridesmaids, in matching green dresses, long and velvet. Judith chose them. Sally moaned about hers, said she looked like the bloody Lady of Shalott. Should be strumming a lute, singing hey nonny no. I think they looked nice. At least they were warm in their velvet; I was freezing, the heating in the registry office had broken and I could see my own breath.

The service went by in a blur. Don't remember much of it really, except there was a huge portrait of the Queen looking down from the wall and for some reason Bobby and I both got the giggles at it. We had photos outside. It was so cold Bobby said my lips were turning blue. We did them quick as we could and then drove to the reception at the pub. Moira had decked out the function room really nicely, with flowers and candles and a big banner with 'Bobby and Sylvia' painted on it, surrounded by hearts and horseshoes. Mum had got her friend Doris to make the cake, two tiers with pink roses piped around the edges, and a little plastic bride and groom on top. We cut the cake and Dad made a speech, he was half-cut and only said about twenty words but it's the thought that counts, I suppose. Anyway, we ate and danced and stuff, and halfway through 'Chapel of Love' Bobby put his hand on my back and whispered in my ear, and we snuck out to the room we'd booked upstairs.

One good thing about being pregnant is we don't have to worry about rubbers any more. It's a lot better. They ruin the mood like anything. Plus my boobs have gone up like bloody Zeppelins, which Bobby seems to enjoy, so all in all things are good in the sex department. Bit weird to think there's a baby inside me when we're doing it, but I'm sure it can put up with a bit of jostling around.

Anyway, we did it, and afterwards we lay in bed and Bobby smoked a cigarette and we talked. About the future. I'd been putting off thinking about it, if I'm honest.

Bobby has to go back to work. To Shetland, to the oil rig. He's stayed in Devon too long already, his boss is holding his job open until he gets back, has a man covering for him, but he's getting impatient now. Plus Bobby's been living off his savings, staying on a sofa at an old mate's place, and the money and the welcome are running out, he said.

The plan is that he's going to go back up to Shetland, he's going to find us a place to live, and after the baby is born I'm going to join him.

I asked why I can't go there now, and he said that he's staying in the oil terminal camp at the moment, and it's no place for a woman, let alone a pregnant one. And I'll need my mum at the start, after I give birth, to help out.

I said to him, what's Shetland like? Will I like it? And he smiled and said it's the finest place on earth. It's beautiful. And he told me about where we'll live, on an island called Unst, right at the very top. He said it's rugged and beautiful and wild, and in the summer the grass is like velvet, and there are wildflowers everywhere, and the sea looks Mediterranean, it's so blue. And there are birds, puffins and skuas and bonxies, and animals, otters and seals and orcas, and little miniature ponies with faces like teddy bears. And the night sky so black you can see the Milky Way, like a smear of paint, and some nights, new moon nights, you get the aurora, shimmering down from the heavens, green and pink and glowing.

God it sounds like heaven.

I can't believe my luck. All these years wishing for some stranger to come and sweep me up and take me away from this boring town, and here comes this man, purely by chance, and he's going to take me to a paradise island.

I keep thinking about the paper mill. If a spark hadn't drifted down – if the paper hadn't caught fire – if Martin Adams hadn't gone back in – if he hadn't burned to death – well, I'd still be where I was when I started writing this diary. Nothing would have changed.

Just one little spark. That's it. Life's funny, isn't it.


### 24 February 1979

Bobby left today.

I haven't stopped crying. I don't think anyone could ever cry as much as I have. He nearly missed the train because I was clinging on to him. My heart was breaking, it felt like I was dying. He leaned out of the window and waved and waved until the train disappeared, and all that was left were the cows in the field beyond the tracks, chewing the cud, staring placidly at me as I sobbed.

Dad had driven us to the station and had been waiting in the café. He came out and patted me on the back and handed me an iced bun he'd bought. To cheer me up, I suppose, like I was a child. I was in too much despair to even think about eating but I did nibble at it in the car on the way home and it was quite soothing actually. By the time we got home I'd finished it all.

When we got in, I wanted to go straight up to my room for a good cry, but Mum called to me from the living room. Her friend Esther was over. She's weird, Esther. She lives in the arse end of nowhere, out near Mutterton, in this little old tumbledown cottage, and she has eight cats and straggly hair and wears these long skirts with bells sewn onto the bottom so she jingles as she walks. George has always said she's a witch. I think he's probably right.

Anyway, Mum said, here, Sylvia. Come and lie down on the sofa.

Why? I said.

Esther's going to predict the baby's sex for you.

Well I couldn't resist, could I. So I went and lay down, and Esther said, hello Sylvia, my dear, and she put her hands on my belly and smiled, and then she smoothed my hair back, and then yanked a strand out.

Ouch! I said. Bloody hell.

Give me your wedding ring, she said. I gave it to her – took a bit of twisting, my fingers have puffed up like sausages – and she threaded the ring onto the hair.

I'm going to hold it over your stomach, she said. If it swings in a circle it's a girl. The circle is a feminine shape. Round, like the full moon, like Mother Earth. If it swings in a line, it's a boy. Straight up and down, like an arrow, or the phallus.

Phallus? I said.

Penis, said Esther.

Oh, I said. Mum caught my eye and pressed her lips together, trying not to laugh.

Well, Esther dangled the ring over me, and I stared at the ring, shining there. And in a few moments, it started to move. No mistaking. Back and forth, like a pendulum, in a straight line, across my belly, to and fro, to and fro.

Gosh, that's definite, isn't it, said my mum.

Esther said, yes. Very strong masculine energy there. Congratulations, my dear. You're having a son.

It did seem very sure of itself. And Mum said that Esther's never been wrong, ever, and she's done it for all her friends and relatives throughout the years, hundreds of them. She has Romany blood apparently.

A boy. I can just picture him now. A little chubby baby boy, all dressed in blue, with bright blue eyes like Bobby's.

Knowing it's a boy cuts down on the number of names we need to think of. I've been wracking my brains for names. Can't think of any girls' ones I like. But for a boy, I like the name Charles. Charlie.

Jane sits in bed, staring at the page. Then she shuts the book, gently. She gets her tin of tobacco from the shelf, rolls herself a cigarette.

She opens the caravan door to milky pre-dawn light. Sits in the doorway, lights her cigarette, inhales. Her whole body feels fragile, transparent. She is trembling slightly. She smokes and looks at the dewy grass. Tries not to think. Not to think of that last word, inked on the page in her mother's hand. Don't think about it. Don't. If she thinks about it, she'll start crying and never stop.

A padding of paws. Nell, loping up to her, across the field, out of the mist, her breath curling in plumes. She whimpers, nudges her snout into Jane's hand, her tail wagging.

'Good girl,' says Jane, 'Good girl, Nell,' and then suddenly she's crying, the tears hot and choking. She presses her face into Nell's fur, clutching the scruff of her neck, clinging to her. She sobs. Nell licks her ear.

A clanking, in the distance. From Maggie's house. The sound of a steel bowl being hit with a fork.

'Nell! Breakfast!'

Jane lets Nell go, watches her bound off across the grass in the direction of Maggie's voice. She wipes her eyes, sniffs. Then her mobile phone buzzes in her pocket. Mike. She answers it.

'Are you all right? Where are you?' he says.

'I couldn't sleep,' says Jane. 'I came back to the caravan.'

'Are you okay? Have you been crying?'

Jane clears her throat. 'No. Just hunged up. Look, I'd better go, got to get ready for work. Love you.'

She dresses, her limbs leaden. Brushes her teeth. She still feels the dregs of gin in her blood, the hangover settled in her bones, her stomach queasy. She drinks a coffee and eats a slice of dry toast, then grabs her bag. As she's about to leave, she glances at the diary, open on the bed. On impulse, she grabs it.

She gets to the factory early. Sits in her car, the heater on full blast, looking out of the windscreen at the ocean. She watches a flock of gulls swarming after a boat, seen dully through the sea mist, as if through tissue paper. In her head, like the tolling of a distant bell, is the name. Charlie, Charlie, Charlie.

Jane looks at the passenger seat. On the grey fabric is the diary.

Not a good idea, she thinks. Not now, not just before work. Stop it, she thinks, even as her hand reaches out, picks it up. Why are you doing this to yourself?

She opens the pages, begins to read.


*30 March 1979*


I haven't written in here for a while. I've been putting all my writing into letters to Bobby instead. We've been writing pages and pages to each other. Some of it quite rude. All about what we're going to do when we're back together again. Makes me blush just thinking about it.

He calls me, too, but he's only allowed one phone call a week on the rig, six minutes long. And I've got no privacy here. I have to thread the phone cord under the kitchen door and sit on the floor next to the fridge and talk in a whisper.

Last time he phoned, Mum and Dad were watching TV in the living room, and George was out round his friend's, and he was the last one on the rig to call, so we could talk openly and for longer than normal, and things got quite heated. He said it's torture, he keeps thinking of me, dreaming of me. Asked if I dreamt of him. Actually I've been having strange nightmares, last night I dreamt I gave birth to a goldfish and had to carry it around in a bowl. But I didn't tell him that. I said yes, my darling, I've been dreaming of you, of holding you and kissing you, and he said he can't wait to hold me in his arms. Kiss me, deep and slow. Undress me. God, my heart was pounding and I could feel myself blushing all over. I was sitting there, listening to his voice, and the muffled sound of the telly next door, and the hum of the fridge, and the ticking of the kitchen clock, and he was saying all this stuff, in a whisper. Saying how he would kiss me, lick me, all over. My breasts, my belly, between my legs, touch me, slip his fingers into me. Said how he was hard, how he couldn't stand it any longer. God, neither could I. I was so fired up I thought I might burst into flames. I sat there, barely breathing, looking at the pattern on the lino, threading the phone cord around my fingers. He asked if I was touching myself. I wasn't. But I did, then. I braced my knee against the door, wedged the phone between my shoulder and ear, lifted my skirt. And I began to touch myself while he talked to me, could hear my breathing coming faster, my heart beating, and I felt myself getting closer, closer, and then Mum yelled from next door:

Sylvia! *Dick Turpin's* on! Hurry up!

I was so startled I shrieked and slammed the phone straight down. God knows what Bobby must have thought.

I don't know what the female equivalent of blue balls is but I had that the whole bloody evening. Had to finish off later in the bath. Got into quite an elaborate fantasy about Bobby, dressed in a cape and a tricorn hat, robbing my stagecoach on horseback.

God, I just want to be with him. Every day is one day closer to him. Bobby, I love you, I love you, I love you.

### 14 April 1979

Bobby has found us a house!

He sent me a long letter telling me all about it. The house is a croft (I think that means like a farmhouse?). It's cheap, he said, because it needs doing up, but on the weeks where he's not working on the rig he'll work on it, and have it ready for me and the baby by the time we arrive.

He sent me a map, too, of Unst, and marked the croft's location with an X. It's near a place called Baltasound. The place names up there are funny. Gloup. Yell. Funzie. Houbie.

And he sent a pamphlet about Unst, from the Shetland Tourism Organisation. Information all about the wildlife, and the history, and the geology. Things to do, places to visit. It all sounds really nice. I'm excited to see a puffin, they look so cute.

He sent me some other photos too. One of the oil rig he works on, a black and white photo cut out of a newspaper. It looks kind of scary, loads of legs and bits sticking out, sort of spidery, with a flame coming out of the top. And a little photo of himself, taken in a photo booth. In case I'd forgotten what he looks like, he said. Oh Bobby, how could I ever forget what you look like. Your face is all I think about. The photo of him is drop-dead gorgeous; his hair's got a bit longer and he has a bit of stubble which I like, makes him look rugged. I showed Mum and she sniffed and said he needs a shave, looks like a right scruffbag. She's been in a bit of a mood with me recently. Ever since I told her I'd be going up to Unst with Bobby. Well, she'll just have to get used to the idea.

*15 April 1979*

I had a blazing row with Mum today. About me moving up to Unst. I was chatting away about it over breakfast, telling her and Dad and George about the Shetland words Bobby's taught me, like peerie means little, and smoorikin is kiss, and muckle bosie means a big cuddle.

They speak a different language? said George, dribbling milk down his chin like an idiot. I hate the way he eats cereal.

No, I said. It's just different. It's a dialect.

Oh well that's great, said Mum. She was sewing a button on Dad's shirt, and had a mouth like a cat's bumhole. You won't understand a bloomin' word they say.

Bobby can help me, I said. I'll be fine.

Why can't he come and live down here? It would be much more sensible.

His work's up there, Mum, I said. He's got a good job there.

Doesn't sound much good to me. He'll be away two weeks at a time. How will you cope? Who'll help you with the baby? she said, jabbing away with her needle. Should be your own family looking after the baby. Not a clan of bloody kilt-wearing Highland flinging Scotchmen. And living in some dingy old farmhouse! It'll be damp and cold and miserable. They're building that lovely new estate near the chicken factory at the other end of town. Pat's daughter's getting one. Lovely smart houses, all modern. Play parks for the littluns and nice big gardens. You could get one of those.

I don't want one of those, I said.

Why not?

Because I'm bored of Crowholt, I said. I want to go somewhere new, do something different with my life.

Oh what, live in a mud hut on some godforsaken island hundreds of miles away from us? With some man you've only known a few months? You can barely look after yourself, my girl, let alone a baby. She went on and on, blah blah blah, and I rolled my eyes, and she called me insolent and I called her ignorant and it all got pretty heated. George was watching us, mouth open, head swivelling between us like he was at a tennis match. And it ended up with me saying she was just jealous because she'd had a boring life and never left Devon and her saying how she's mollycoddled me and ended up with a selfish snooty brat of a daughter and I stormed off round to Sally's and we smoked cigarettes (I asked the doctor the other day if I should quit, but he said not to because it helps keep my stress levels down) and we listened to Rod Stewart and I had a good moan until I felt better.

I came home as the streetlamps were coming on. Mum was sitting in the living room, staring at the TV. Said tea's in the oven. I said I've already had tea round Sally's and she said well I'll just feed it to the dog then, at least he shows a bit of bloody gratitude, and I stormed off upstairs and here we are.

I can barely stand to be in this house any longer. I just want to be with Bobby.

6 May 1979

Mum and I have reached a sort of truce. We're both just ignoring the fact I'm moving away.

She's knitting like nobody's business. Booties and hats and blankets. Mainly blue, she trusts Esther's gypsy magic that much, but some yellow as well, just in case. She's been buying up those new nappies too, the disposable ones, from Exeter. Expensive as anything but she's got some coupons and she says she has to, she doesn't know how I'll cope with terry towels and safety pins one-handed. At my last appointment with the occupational therapist they gave me some tips for picking up the baby and feeding him and stuff, and a weighted doll to practise on. George has called the doll Damien after that *Omen* film and keeps making out it's possessed. He's an idiot.

I'm getting so fat. I used some of this month's wages to buy two crimplene maternity smocks, one yellow, one blue. I never knew they even made clothes this big. Dad said I look like a ship in full sail. And not all of it is my bump either, I'm getting fat all over. Need to be careful, because if I get too big my arm won't fit, but I can't stop eating, I just want to eat and eat and eat. And I've got such a craving for sour things. Pickled onions mainly. I hated them before but now I can't get enough of them, the sourer the better. I got through three whole jars last weekend. Sitting in the kitchen, eating one after the other like they were crisps. I even drink the juice afterwards. Isn't that disgusting? Mum says that definitely means it's a boy – for girls you crave sweet things, for boys sour—

Jane stops reading. She sits there, in the car, staring at the page.

'Oh, shit,' she whispers.

She thinks back. Back to Mike. They've always used a condom, always, apart from that one time, a few months ago. And she'd taken the pill, the day after, sitting there in that little room with the nurse, who watched as Jane, feeling like a wayward teenager, had washed it down with water from a paper cone. She remembered the nurse saying it wasn't 100 per cent effective, no method of contraception was, but no. It couldn't be. Couldn't.

She thinks of her tender breasts in the shower, the soreness as the water hit them. She thinks of how nauseous she's felt recently, the bile seeming to sit in her throat, ready to rise.

She sits there, her mouth dry, her heart beating hard. Then she starts the car, reverses, drives out of the car park. Pat, in her hi-vis, is cycling towards her.

*Shit.*

Jane swallows, stares at the road, passes Pat. In her rear-view mirror, she can see Pat has stopped and is staring after her, before she disappears in a cloud of Jane's exhaust smoke.

Jane drives off the ferry into Lerwick, parks up, gets out of the car. The morning mist has burned away, and sunlight gleams off the wet pavements, the seagulls swooping in brilliant white arcs overhead. She turns down onto Commercial Street. It's a cheerful day, the winter air clear and crisp, the sound of a fiddler playing a jaunty reel, Christmas displays bright in the windows, but she feels dread in her belly like a hunk of stone.

She turns into Boots. Walks down through the shop, looking at the signs: haircare, cold and flu, seasonal allergies – and then she sees it. Feminine products, family planning.

Jane stands in front of the shelves, looking at the boxes of tampons and pads, condoms and lubricants. Down at the bottom, there – pregnancy tests. She grabs the cheapest one. Walks to the counter with it burning in her hand.

As she's queueing at the checkout, her phone rings.

Pat.

Jane stares at her phone until it goes silent.

A woman is taking a long time at the checkout, rifling through a sheaf of coupons, counting out change from a little plastic purse. Jane looks around her. She's in the cosmetics aisle, next to the nail polish. Gleaming jewel colours, a whole spectrum of bottles. Maybelline, Max Factor, No7, Revlon.

Revlon. She remembers the shape of the bottle, the cool glassy weight of it in her hand, the care she took as she stroked the brush over her mother's fingernails. She can still taste the pear-drop tang of it at the back of her throat.

Cherries in the Snow.

She looks at the reds. There it is, she's sure of it, that slightly blueish red, like a ripe raspberry.

The woman with the coupons pays, leaves, and the queue moves forward. As if of its own accord, Jane's hand reaches out, grabs a bottle.

Jane arrives at the counter. Places the two items before the checkout girl. Pregnancy test. Cherries in the Snow.

The sound of chatter, the hiss of the milk frother, faint guitar music. Jane listens to the noise of the café drifting through the toilet door as she sits, jiggling her leg.

Three minutes. Three minutes and she'll know. She won't look before three minutes is up. Behind her, on the cistern, is the pregnancy test, white and terrifying as a witch doctor's sharpened bone.

Her mobile phone buzzes in her pocket and makes her jump. Pat again. She watches it ringing, thinks of her boss on the other end, her ear pressed against the phone, a frown line scored between her eyebrows.

The phone falls silent. As Jane puts it back in her pocket, her fingers brush against something smooth and cold. The nail polish. She pulls it out, looks at it. She thinks of her mother's diary entry. *I'm even going to paint the nails. I bought polish with my birthday money, Revlon's Cherries in the Snow.*

Jane unscrews the lid. The tang of it hits her nose, sharp and chemical. She clamps the bottle between her knees, loads the little brush with red lacquer, swipes it onto her thumbnail. Looks at it, glistening wetly. Then she paints another nail, and another, until the whole hand is done.

It looks ridiculous, her dry calloused hands with their bitten nails painted glossy red. Perverse. Her mother's hand, her real hand, was always beautiful, skin kept supple and soft with Pond's Cold Cream, the white jar that sat on her dressing table.

Someone rattles the toilet door and Jane jumps. A blob of nail polish drips on her jeans. She swears, dabs at it with some toilet paper, the lacquer soaking into the denim.

She checks her watch. Three minutes has passed. She screws the lid back on the bottle. Takes a deep breath. Skim reads the instructions on the back of the box one more time. A plus symbol means pregnant. A line means she isn't. Positive. Negative. Positive. Negative. Addition, subtraction. It's got to be a line. Has to be.

She reaches behind her, grabs the test, looks at it.

In the little window is a small blue cross.

She stares at it.

*Shit. Shit, shit, shit.*

Someone rattles the door again.

'Wait a minute, for fuck's sake!' she shouts.

Jane straightens up, shoves the test and nail polish in her bag, looks at herself in the mirror. Her exhausted face. Pregnant, she thinks. Mother, she thinks.

She has an urge to smash the mirror. Raise her fist and smash it. But she doesn't. She unlocks the toilet door, steps out into the café, shoves past the waiting man, and leaves.

Jane waits in the queue of traffic, watching the ferry approaching the dock. Her phone buzzes in her pocket. She hesitates, then pulls it out. She can't ignore Pat any longer; she has to explain.

But it's not Pat. It's Mike.

She pushes the call button.

'Hi,' she says.

'Jane? Are you okay? I just tried to call you at work but they said you weren't there. That you'd turned up and then left . . . where are you?'

The voice is the father of the baby inside her. She thinks about telling him. Oh, I was just doing a pregnancy test. I'm carrying your child right now. Congratulations. But instead she says:

'Just been in Lerwick. Shopping.'

'Shopping?'

'Yeah.'

'Okay – well, anyway. I was ringing because – well, there was a policeman here. Looking for you. PC Barry French. Said he wanted to talk to you.'

'Ah,' says Jane. She grips the steering wheel, watches the ferry come to a stop.

'Is everything okay?'

'Yeah. Everything's fine.'

'D'you know why he was there? Are you in trouble?'

'No. I'm – it's okay. It's – it's probably to do with planning permission for the caravan. Nothing serious,' she says, as the ferry's prow begins to lift, noiselessly, and cars begin to drive off it. 'I'd better go. Ferry's just turned up.'

'Okay.'

'All right. I'll see you later.'

'Jane?'

'What?'

'Love you.'

'Love you too,' she says, her mouth dry. 'Bye.'


When Jane pushes the police station door open, PC French is behind the desk, sipping tea from a mug that says: 'If you are what you eat, then I'm CHEAP and EASY!'

'Oh!' he says. 'Jane. I wanted to speak to you.'

'I know,' says Jane. 'That's why I'm here.'

'Would you like a cuppa?'

'No.'

'Want to take a seat?'

'No, thanks. Please,' she says. 'Have they found anything?'

'Well,' says PC French, 'I had a call from Devon and Cornwall Police this morning. Now the DNA test has confirmed that the, er, the prosthetic arm, is indeed your mother's.'

Jane stares. Nods. 'Aye. Of course it is.'

'They've also run some other tests,' he says, looking at some notes, 'which seem to indicate that the prosthesis has been submerged for quite some time, in deep water. And − are you sure you won't sit down, Jane?'

'I'm fine,' she says.

'Well − there is some material on the arm which would suggest . . . well, they've concluded that − that there is a likelihood that your mother's body is still in the quarry.'

Jane is frozen still.

'Material?' she says.

PC French shifts in his seat.

'Yes. A − a residue. The forensics team explained that in cold, deep water there's very little oxygen, and a body can stay relatively well preserved in those conditions. It's the, um, the fat in the body − at those temperatures it forms a sort of waxy cast, and . . . Well, I won't go into too much detail. But they found some attached to the prosthesis. The technical term is − hang on, I wrote it down − adipo . . . adipocere. Not sure how you pronounce it. Commonly known as corpse wax, they said. That was what they found, on the arm.'

Jane is silent for a moment. Then she turns, steps back out through the door, and retches loudly. She clamps her hand over her mouth, steadies herself with a hand on the wooden gate, gulps the air. PC French appears with a glass of water.

She waves the water away. Clings to the wood. Watches a sheep idle across the grass opposite.

'I'm sorry,' says PC French. 'I just − I get carried away with forensics stuff, I think it's all fascinating.'

Jane doesn't reply.

'Want to carry on talking out here?'

Jane nods.

'So, as you know, the quarry is too deep and too difficult to dive very far down. So the police down there are planning instead to drain it. They'll need to get the permission of the local landowners first, which may take a while. And obviously they'll have to put quite a lot of infrastructure in place, so it'll be weeks, months maybe, before—'

'What, just . . . they're just going to drain it? The whole thing?'

'Aye,' says PC French.

'How?'

'Well, they'll pump the water out onto the fields nearby. And then remove all the debris, the dumped machinery, all the stuff people have fly-tipped over the years. And then they'll have to search through all the muck and silt at the bottom, which is the painstaking bit.'

'They think she's – they really think she's down there?'

PC French nods.

Jane feels sick again. She swallows it down.

'I have a contact number,' says PC French. 'For a Detective Inspector Nadine Sumner. She's said you can call her direct line, ask any questions you like, whenever you want.'

He hands her a slip of paper. She looks at the number. The Crowholt area code, 01884. It rings in her head like a forgotten playground chant.

Jane is cleaning her caravan. She climbs a stepladder, scrubs the green scum and gulls' guano from the roof. Runs a hosepipe from the croft's garden tap, hoses it down, scrubs the moss from the corners of the windowsills with a toothbrush. She has an urge to purge, to scour; she needs to be busy, to be moving, She doesn't want to sit still. Sitting still leads to thinking. To thinking about her mother's corpse, down at the bottom of all that water. To thinking about her pregnancy. Two unfathomable things.

Jane sprays the windowsills with silicone lubricant, then waxes the caravan until the walls are white and gleaming, until her arms are aching. She stops, stands back, wipes her forehead with her arm, looks at her tin can, and out over the glistening sound, the low hills beyond.

She hears Nell barking, up at Maggie's house. She feels a sudden twinge of jealousy; wishes, for once, that she had a pet. A companion. A dumb animal, like her nan's Alsatian, something uncomplicated and loyal to keep her company. Something that could sleep on the end of her bed and be there when she woke in the night. The closest thing to a pet she's had was a cat that made friends with her once, at work, used to hang around the cannery scrounging for scraps; a big tigerish tomcat with a chunk out of one ear. She liked him, used to smuggle him out bits and pieces, salmon heads, chunks of crab meat. But one day he'd got hit by a lorry in the loading bay and that was that. She'd felt responsible, somehow. She shouldn't have encouraged him.

She is bad luck. She always ends up hurting people.

Abort the baby, she thinks. That's what she needs to do. And then she should break up with Mike. And sell Dawn's brother the croft. Take the money and run. Run far away, somewhere hot and bright. Start again. Start afresh.

It takes Jane a minute to realise that Nell is still barking. A high, whining baying. Jane turns, looks at Hamarsgarth, gleaming white in the frigid, sunlit air. She listens to Nell's howls, carrying across the field.

'Nell?' she shouts. Then she drops the cloth and bottle of spray wax, and runs up the field.

She bangs on Maggie's door. Nell's howls turn to high, desperate yips.

'Maggie?' she says. 'Maggie?'

She pushes through the front door, into the porch, and Nell jumps up at her, whimpering. Jane can see Maggie's legs, in their tea-coloured tights and knitted slippers, poking out of the living room. A chair on its side.

'Mags,' she says, and rushes over. Bends down. Maggie is on her front. One hand reaching for the phone, which has been pulled from the table onto the carpet. In the other is a lightbulb.

'She's fractured her hip,' Jane says, fiddling with the telephone cord, perching on the arm of Maggie's sofa. 'They'll have to operate.'

'Oh, poor Mum,' says the voice on the other end of the phone, its sunny Australian twang sitting oddly over the Shetlandic lilt. 'She'll be okay though, won't she?'

'I'm sure she will,' she says. 'But you know. It'll take a while for her to recover.' Jane rubs her tired eyes, says, 'I told her not to go climbing on chairs, changing lightbulbs. I told her, I said that's what I'm here for. But she never listens.'

'She's always had a stubborn streak. Independent. Took pride in doing things for herself after Dad died, you know. Well, thank goodness you were there. I'd hate to think . . . Steve and I, we worry about her rattling around that old house, those steep stairs . . . We've tried to talk to her about downsizing, getting a nice bungalow, but she'd never. Too attached to that place, all the memories of Dad, of Laura.'

Jane glances at the photograph on the mantelpiece. The urn.

'Yeah,' she says.

'But it makes us feel much better knowing you're there, Hannah.'

Jane freezes. 'Jane,' she says.

'Oh – that's right. Sorry, sorry. Jane. I still think of you as three years old, you know. Apologies.'

'It's okay,' says Jane. Although her heart is pounding in her chest.

They talk some more. Dave says he would fly over to visit Maggie, but they have a family holiday booked, been planned for ages, he can't let the kids down. Jane says that she understands, promises to call him if there's any news.

Then she thumbs through Maggie's address book, finds the name Steven, dials the number. Has a nearly identical conversation with a man, only this time the sunshine in his words is Californian rather than Australian. He's sorry to hear about his mum, he would fly over, but he's in the middle of an important project at work, really has to be there for it, it's at a critical stage, and the buck stops with him.

'But keep me updated, yeah?' he says.

Jane puts the phone down. Looks at the photograph of Laura. Jane wonders, if Laura was alive, if she would be the same as the boys, or if she would drop everything, catch the next plane home. A daughter is yours for life. A son is yours 'til he takes a wife. That's what Maggie said, once.

Yours for life. She wonders if she is her mother's for life. It feels like it. She thinks of the wedding ring swinging over her mother's ballooning stomach. A straight line for a boy, a circle for a girl. Perhaps she is doomed to circling, relentlessly, to coming round and round again to the past. If she'd been born a boy, she could have shot off in a straight line, like an arrow loosed from its bow. A linear progression. Would have been able to cut herself off from her history, forge her own path.

Jane is suddenly exhausted. She can't face trudging down across the muddy field to the caravan. Night is drawing in and a cold wind is blowing. Instead, she tips some dog biscuits into Nell's bowl, tops up her water, then climbs the stairs to Maggie's spare room.

Maggie's spare room is Laura's old bedroom. Maggie's redecorated it since Laura died – the walls are a careful magnolia, the chest of drawers and wardrobe empty, the new bedsheets crisp, barely slept in. But there are still signs of Laura – a blob of dried pink nail polish on the bedside cabinet, ghostly Blu Tack stains on the ceiling from ancient posters, a cigarette burn on the windowsill. Jane wonders if there are other traces of her – some of her skin cells, still trapped in the carpet fibres; a stray strand of hair maybe, missed by the vacuum cleaner, glinting secretly in a corner. Jane lies on the bed, looks up at the ceiling. She feels uneasy, in this bed. Like a big ugly cuckoo in the nest. A cuckoo with her own egg forming inside her. But the bed is soft and warm, and the wind is whistling outside, and Nell has followed her upstairs and curled up on the rug, and so she closes her eyes and tries to sleep.

'Isn't it beautiful?' says Mike. 'Look at that sunrise.'

Jane smiles, nods. They are on his boat, chugging gently out over the ocean, between the rows of grey plastic floats from which the mussel ropes hang. The sky is aflame, a wash of rosy pink and lavender, wisps of cloud like golden threads.

Mike cuts the boat engine and drops anchor, the chain rattling down into the calm water, the gentle waves knocking and clucking against the sides of the boat. She watches him working in his oilskins. In the golden light, he glows.

'Mike,' she says.

'Hmm?'

'I love you.'

He smiles. 'Love you too.'

He hooks the line of floats up with a long pole, attaches it to the winch. She feels a jolt in her stomach. Looks down. Her belly is huge.

'Oh,' she says. She puts her hand on it. Feels a thump. Another. The baby. She feels joy spreading through her.

'The baby's kicking,' she says, breathlessly. But Mike doesn't reply.

'Mike?'

She looks up, but Mike's gone. PC French is there, at the tiller.

'Red sky in the morning, shepherd's warning,' he says, and he looks sad.

The winch is working by itself, hauling the line of ropes out of the water, encrusted with its black clumps of mussels. Up they come, dripping wet, from the depths.

As they rise, Jane sees a hand clinging on to one of the ropes, white and thin. Lifting up out of the water, slowly. There is a smell in the air, of rotting meat.

'No,' says Jane. 'No.'

Slowly, slowly, a head of dark hair appears, tangled with kelp, encrusted with barnacles.

Her mother.

Starfish cover her eyes. Her mouth opens, wide, yawning. An eel slithers out, slick and black.

# Chapter Two

It is so hot. So, so hot. So hot you can actually see the heat, the air wavy above the road, shimmering in the sun. There's a hosepipe ban, and all the grass is dead and brown. Mum's fuming about her flowerbeds.

It's been too hot to do anything but stay indoors — can't even walk Rex because the tarmac would burn his paws. I spend all my time sitting on the sofa, watching telly and fanning myself and feeling like a sow in a pig pen. Even if it wasn't thirty-five degrees outside I wouldn't want to go out. Hate the stares I get from people. God, they don't half ogle. I know what most of the village think, they think Bobby's knocked me up and run off. My fingers are so fat now that I can't even wear my wedding ring to prove them wrong. (I wear it around my neck on a chain. It hangs against my heart.)

Well, they can think what they like. Soon I'll be shot of the bloody lot of them, of this whole stupid town. Six weeks I've got 'til the baby's born and it can't come soon enough.

Mum still keeps making little digs about Shetland. Joking about kilts and haggis and bagpipes and stuff. I said to her, as haughtily as I could, actually Mum, culturally, Shetland is more

Scandinavian than Scottish (it was something Bobby said in one of his letters). She said, oh hark at Kenneth Clarke over here. You don't even know what Scandinavia is. I said, yes I do. It's a country near Iceland. Turns out it's not. Anyway, that's beside the point.

### 15 July 1979

I'm not feeling well. Stomach keeps cramping. I knew I shouldn't have touched that potato salad. Judith brought it to the picnic today and it had been sitting out in the sun for hours. I thought it tasted off but I still ate it so she wouldn't get offended. Stupid.

The picnic was good, though. We went to the flooded quarry, in the woods. I remember the first time I went there – it was with George, when we still hung around together, before he turned into an annoying brat. We'd wanted to go for ages. Mum was always saying how dangerous it was, how we must never ever go there, and that was like a red rag to a bull, wasn't it? So one morning we bunked off school, and we took a compass and Dad's OS map (the symbol for the quarry was a wrinkly oval, sort of like a deflated balloon) and set off into the woods.

I'll never forget seeing it for the first time. One minute we were walking through the forest – it was autumn, and the trees were bare and the ground was covered in sodden leaves – and then suddenly we were standing on the edge of this massive drop. Like a huge bite taken out of the earth, a sheer rock face plunging straight down, and at the bottom, all this dark water. Made me feel giddy, looking down at it. We found a way to the water's edge, an old tarmac track, all cracked with weeds growing through it, which led to a rusty gate, and beyond it, a scrap of shoreline.

We spent some good days there. For about a year or so it was our place. We just messed around, really — threw stones at the water and shouted so our voices echoed and examined the little caves around the water's edge. Carved our names into the rock face. Lit a few fires. Once George tried to build a raft, but it didn't work. We never swam, though. Mum had scared us too much for that.

And then one summer day we got there and there was a bunch of teenagers there already. Drinking and swimming and listening to music, and that sort of ruined it then. It didn't feel like our place any more. And then George hit puberty anyway and turned into a knobhead and I wouldn't have hung out with him if you'd paid me.

Anyway, I hadn't been down to the quarry for ages, but Sally said let's have a picnic there, and go swimming. She knew a shortcut to the water, from a gap further down the bridle path. Apparently her and Noel Woodward used to go down there all the time to snog each other, until he cut his hair short and she didn't fancy him any more on account of his big ears.

Sally lent me her old bikini, the red one with the hibiscus flowers on it, because I can't fit my belly into my swimming costume any more. The bikini looked obscene on me. To think I've always wanted bigger tits. When I took my smock off Sally said Jesus Christ, Sylv. You'd give Dolly Parton a run for her money.

The quarry wasn't as big as I'd remembered. The water looked so lovely. Glassy green and still. Sally and Judith swam. They looked so elegant and graceful, gliding through the water, like a couple of mermaids. I felt like a whale, beached on the shore. Scoffing potato salad.

I dipped my feet in the water though. Looked at them, wavering palely beneath me. Thought of how deep the quarry was, plunging down into the rock. Mum had said it was a couple of hundred feet deep. That made my head spin. I looked at my feet dangling there and felt suddenly faint, like I had vertigo. This cold sweat came over me and I felt this awful chill, like the sun had gone in and I was suddenly freezing cold.

I pulled my feet out of the water, feeling shaky and sick. Said to Sally and Judith I wanted to go home. Wasn't feeling well. Sally said God Sylvia, you look white as a sheet.

God I feel awful. Really shouldn't have touched that potato salad.


*16 July 1979*

I'm a mother.
Baby born today 2.45 p.m.
It's a girl.
No name yet.
Don't know if she'll live.


*17 July 1979*

I'm writing this from a hospital bed. The baby is next to me in a plastic tank. She's so small. Covered in wires and tubes. She has pencil-thin limbs and eyes the colour of sloes. Blue-black. Her skin is still bright pink, raw-looking. She looks like a skinned rabbit.

She wasn't meant to come so soon.

I don't know how I feel about her. I can't quite believe she's my baby. My daughter. I feel quite numb. Have done since the birth.

She was born on the living-room floor. It was awful. Sudden and brutal. I just kept thinking I'm going to die, I'm going to die, and I felt so distant from myself. Like the pilot of a crashing plane. Like my brain pressed the eject button, and I was drifting on a parachute, watching the crash, the wreckage below. I didn't feel part of my own body. Everything was far away. And it was so fast. So fast.

I remember pushing one last time and feeling the baby come out of me and I was sure she was dead. I didn't want to look at her.

But then I heard this little wail. And I looked.

She was all slimy and gory. Looked half baked, more like an organ than a baby.

It's all hazy after that – I was losing lots of blood apparently, had a hemorrage (don't know how to spell it). I don't want to think about it too much. It makes me feel faint.

I'm still half convinced I'm dreaming. Like I'm going to wake up any moment and be back pregnant again. Before the quarry. It all went wrong at the quarry.

*18 July 1979*

The baby is doing okay. I'm not allowed to hold her, yet – she's still too fragile. If I'm honest I don't really want to. I know she's mine, but it doesn't feel like it. I have this funny feeling in the back of my mind that her real mum will be here any minute to pick her up. That sounds crazy, doesn't it?

She's not what I expected. I'd expected a boy. A bouncing baby boy with bright blue eyes and doughy cheeks and blond curls. And instead, here is this little scrawny girl. All squashed and red.

They say she's doing well, though. She's got a hole in her heart. Between the ventricles. The oxygenated blood and the spent blood mixing together. But it'll probably knit together with time, the doctor said. If it doesn't, they can operate when she's older.

She doesn't move much. Occasionally she'll move her arms a

bit. Or yawn. So slowly. Looks like she's underwater. And sometimes she'll open her eyes. Just a bit. They're dark, like a shark's.

Mum has been on at me to name her. The little tag around
her wrist reads Baby Douglas. I've tried names on her. Hanging
them on her like a coat on a hook, but they just slip right off.
Sarah. Joanne. Nicola. It feels silly even trying, like naming a
shoebox, or a packet of mince. You name things with person-
alities. With souls. She still looks too raw. Too animal. If
anything, she looks like she should have an alien name. One
in a language that isn't invented yet. A string of numbers or
symbols or something. She doesn't feel like she belongs to this
world.

*19 July 1979*

My milk's come in. I have to use a breast pump, which looks like
a bicycle horn with a bottle on it. It stings, and seeing the milk
squirt into the bottle makes me heave.

This morning was the worst. I'd been pumping for ten minutes,
my teeth gritted, my hand cramping up, my face turned away so
I didn't have to look, and when I finally finished, I held up the
bottle only to see a tiny splash of milk at the bottom. Barely a
teaspoonful. I burst into tears and threw the pump on the floor.
Said I'm not doing it any more. I feel like a bloody dairy cow.

Sylvia, said the midwife. Don't be silly. It's for the baby, she
needs it to grow.

But it hurts!

It'll hurt even more if you don't do it. Your milk will go sour
and you'll get mastitis.

She got another pump. Handed it to me. Look at your baby,
she said. Look at her and think about cuddling her. It'll help the
milk flow. And so I clamped the horrible thing to my breast and

squeezed the horn and looked at my daughter and bit my lip against the pain. And all I thought was I hate this, I hate this, I wish you'd never been born.

I've still not been allowed to hold her. I wonder if that's why I don't feel as if she's mine. I've only touched her skin with a fingertip. It feels so smooth and hairless. Like rubber. For one mad moment I thought maybe my real baby had been replaced with a doll. Like the nurses had come in and swapped her. I haven't touched her since, it frightened me too much.

I talked to Bobby on the phone yesterday. He wants to come down and see the baby. I had a sudden fear of him meeting her. What would he think, of this strange little thing? And what would he think of me, with my saggy belly and my leaking tits and the catgut stitches between my legs? I tore down there, when I pushed her out. They sewed me up. I must look like Frankenstein's monster down below. I can't imagine making love ever again.

So I told him to wait, wait just a bit, until we're out of hospital, there's no point yet because nobody can hold her and we're not allowed many visitors anyway because of the risk of infection, so best to keep away. I said I'll send him a picture.

And he said how is she? Is she bonnie? I bet she's the most beautiful baby in the world.

And I said oh yes, she's gorgeous, just perfect, I love her so much.

*22 July 1979*

The other day I dreamt of a cat prowling around the ward. It jumped up onto my bed and curled up on my stomach. When I woke up, I remembered the one that lived in our garden when I was little. White with tan patches. It gave birth to kittens on the compost heap one spring. Five of them. We found her nursing four of them in the gap behind the shed, but the fifth was off at a distance, lost in the long grass. Mewling and mewling. It still had its umbilical cord attached to it, curling from its belly like a piece of string.

Well we tried to pick it up and give it to the mother, but she wanted nothing to do with it. Hissed at it, her ears flat back as if she was afraid. The kitten kept trying to find her, stumbling forward on its little wobbly legs, calling and calling, but she was having none of it.

So Mum took the little kitten inside. Lined a shoebox with a blanket, fed it milk from an ear syringe. I stroked its soft little head, talking to it, willing it to grow strong, but the next morning we found it dead. I can still feel its little body in my hand. Feather light and soft, its little bones under the fur.

God I was devastated. I wept and wept. I was so angry at the mother cat. At her cruelty.

Mum said the kitten was probably sick. Might've had something that could make the other kittens sick, too, and that's why the mother didn't want it close.

Maybe she was right. Maybe the mother cat knew something. Some instinct telling her something was wrong.

Humans are just animals, aren't we?

*26 July 1979*

The baby's forest of wires is thinning each day. I hold her now. She's so light, just a little scrap of a thing. I'm sweating the whole time I hold her, scared of breaking her. You can see her heartbeat in the soft spot of her head.

She's filled out a fair bit. No thanks to me. I stopped pumping milk. I got mastitis. My breasts taut and hot and burning, the milk curdling under my skin. They gave me tablets to dry it up. God, I'm so relieved to be rid of that pump. I give her powdered milk now, from a bottle with a rubber teat. She didn't like it at first. Crinkling her face up. But soon she got hungry enough to eat it and now she's used to it.

They say she'll soon be ready to come home. Bet you can't wait to take her home, they say, introduce her to everyone, and I say oh yes, can't wait.

But I'm still half waiting for her real mum to walk through the door and pick her up. What's taking her so long?

Mum was on at me again. You've got to name her, everyone's asking what her name is, you'll have to register her soon.

I said, I'm going to let Bobby name her.

Oh, said Mum, don't let him choose! He'll pick some silly Scottish name. Wee Morag or something. She started arsing about then, talking to the baby in a stupid Scottish accent saying oh, halloo Morag, och aye the noo.

And I said stop it Mum, just stop it, and she said oh, where's your sense of humour, and I burst into tears.

And she said Sylvia, what on earth is wrong with you? It's been like walking on eggshells ever since you've had this baby. Can't say anything without you biting our heads off. All you do is sit there with a face like a wet weekend. You're meant to be happy, you're a new mother, you've got a lovely little girl. Yes, she was a bit early, but she's healthy, and thriving, and beautiful. Count your blessings.

And I didn't know what to say. I couldn't explain, how could I?

Rebecca Pert

15 August 1979

I haven't written in here for a while. We brought the baby home and things have been difficult.

She is asleep now. Lying in the corner of her Moses basket, so small she looks like a dropped sock.

I wish we were still in the hospital. With people to tell me what to do. I feel completely lost. I'm just in a constant sweat, imagining all the ways she could get hurt, or killed. All the accidents that could happen. Slips, falls, suffocations, poisonings, burns, drowning, broken bones. And I have nightmares, awful nightmares. I dream I'm giving birth again, only this time the baby is dead, or deformed. I dream that Rex is hunched over her Moses basket, his jaws bloody. I dream things so sick I can't even write them here. My brain is like a cinema playing a horror movie, endlessly.

I can't go into the living room any more, because it puts me in a panic. It still smells of labour, to me, of blood and sweat and flesh and fear. There's a stain on the carpet. An anti-stain, really, a lighter patch where Mum scrubbed away the blood, and when I look at it I feel like I'm going to faint.

Mum is doing lots of the work of looking after the baby. She dresses her, changes her nappies, feeds her. Sings to her. She tells me to rest. I feel perhaps if I did more, I'd bond with her. But it's easier just to lie in bed.

It's for the best. She's safer with Mum anyway. A capable pair of hands.

I'm not capable. And I don't have a pair of hands. I can't wear my prosthesis when I'm looking after the baby. It gets in the way. I have to use my stump. I hate it.

91

*24 August 1979*

I broke down today.

It happened this afternoon, when I went in to feed the baby. She was sitting in her bouncer in the living room, looking at a shaft of sunlight on the wall, with that serious expression of hers, and I felt – I don't know how to describe it. She seemed so absorbed, so self-sufficient, that I almost felt intimidated by her. I didn't want to pick her up, or talk to her. She just gives off the sense of wanting to be left alone.

I thought, don't be stupid, Sylvia. You're her mother. She's a tiny baby.

So I called out, sweetheart, I've got your bottle. And she turned and looked at me, but her expression – she gave me the most withering look. It was as if she was saying, oh. It's you. What do you want?

And I stared at her, and something just snapped. I felt this hot wave of rage sweep over me. I wanted to throw something at her. Isn't that awful. And instead I just swore.

Anyway, Mum came in and said what's wrong?

Her, I said. She's what's wrong. The baby.

Why? What on earth do you mean?

Her personality, I said.

What?

She's so – so . . . aloof, I said.

Aloof?

She's so quiet! It's not normal.

Oh, honestly, Sylvia, said Mum. You're complaining that you have a quiet baby? Count your blessings.

She crossed to the baby, reached down, stroked her cheek. The baby frowned, turned her head away. Mum laughed. I didn't.

See? I said. That's another thing she does. It's embarrassing. I'll be pushing her in the pram, and some little old lady wants to look at her, make a fuss of her and she reacts like that — turns away. She just doesn't like people. Doesn't smile.

Ah, she's just too busy thinking. Figuring out the world. Still waters run deep, that's what they say, said Mum, and the tenderness in her voice made me prickle — with what? With jealousy?

And the floodgates opened then. I started ranting. About the baby. How it's like she doesn't even want a mother, like she doesn't need one. If I'm late feeding her, she just isn't bothered. Looks at me as if, oh, you're here, I wasn't expecting you. How I don't feel like she's my baby at all. How I just wish I could give her away to someone. Someone that would love her. Because I don't, I can't, no matter how hard I try. Isn't that awful? Isn't that the worst thing you've ever heard? And she knows it. She knows I'm not right. I was so happy before she came. And now I'm so sad. So angry. All the time.

She's ruined my life, I shouted. I wish she'd never been born.

Then I clamped a hand over my mouth and burst into tears.

Mum looked at me for a moment, her eyes wide. Then she reached out and pulled me close to her and I sobbed into her shoulder.

What's wrong with me? I said. What's wrong with me? I'm a monster.

She said, you aren't well, Sylvia. You had a shock. The baby was born too soon, and you weren't ready. It's all right. You'll get there. But — maybe you could see the doctor, she said. See if there's anything he can give you. Just to help you along.

Like what? I said.

Mum waved her hand. You know. Tablets, or something. Just to help you settle down a bit. Nora's daughter, up the road. She had it too. The baby blues, they call it; it's nothing to be ashamed of—

Nora's daughter was a lunatic! I said. She tried to give her baby to the checkout girl at Safeway! Do you think I'm going to do that? Do you think I'll hurt her?

Of course not, she said. Of course not. But just please – go and see the doctor.


*26 August 1979*

I saw the doctor today.

I dressed as neatly as I could. Washed and brushed my hair, patted a bit of Panstik under my eyes to hide the circles. I didn't want to come off as crazy. I'm not crazy.

The doctor was very nice. It felt embarrassing talking to him. I was so nervous, half expecting men in white coats to burst through the door. Carry me off to a padded cell. George once showed me a photograph in one of his books of a man getting a lobotomy. They put an ice pick under your eyelid and tap it with a hammer, chop off a bit of your brain. Turn you into a vegetable. I wondered if that was going to happen to me.

Obviously I didn't tell him everything. I only told him that I was feeling a bit depressed, a case of the baby blues you know, and finding it hard to cope with motherhood, and my mum had suggested maybe some tablets could help, something to help me get back on an even keel, just something temporary, to tide me over . . . God I was blathering on like an imbecile. But he just nodded along and then when I ran out of steam he smiled and said of course, Mrs Douglas. Many new mothers find medication useful to regulate their moods. Just something to smooth the rough edges. I'll prescribe you some Valium, a low dose to start with, and we can see how you go.

He wrote out the prescription and chatted to me about the baby. All her immunisations up to date? Any worries about her development? How is she feeding? He weighed her, said she's doing well, considering she was premature. He listened to her heart, said it was fine, despite the hole. Said she's a healthy, happy girl.

As we were getting ready to leave, he made his glasses waggle up and down at the baby and she laughed. A proper chuckle, right from deep in her belly. And I stood there smiling, my face feeling like a mask.

*28 August 1979*

Yesterday morning I sat in the kitchen with a cup of tea, looking at the bottle of tablets in my hand. The bottle is smoky brown, with a white cap, and a label which reads: 'VALIUM 10MG E/C TABLETS. TO BE TAKEN AS DIRECTED. To be swallowed whole, not chewed.'

I shook one of the pills onto the wooden tabletop, poked at it. They're sunshine-yellow, scored across the middle. I picked it up, put it on my tongue, took a sip from my cup of tea, swallowed. Then paused, looking out of the kitchen window at Mum's hydrangea bush, the flowers powder-blue. The colour of the flowers means something about the soil, but what it is, I've forgotten. I sipped my tea, waiting, listening to the distant sounds – birdsong outside, Mum humming as she fed the baby a bottle in the living room, the ticking of the kitchen clock.

So this is what it feels like to be mad, I thought.

I drained the mug of tea and waited some more, wondering how long the pill would take to work, but ten minutes passed and I didn't feel any different, so I got up and went about the day.

It was only an hour or so later, when the baby was crying, and I was rocking her crib and shushing her, that I realised that the noise wasn't really bothering me. It was as if I had invisible earplugs in – not that the sound was any different, but its effect felt muffled. It felt a bit as though I'd had a glass of wine; that warm, blanketed feeling, where everything seems to matter less.

At dinner I took another pill, and that night I slept like a log. Barely remembered getting up to feed the baby in the night.

Mum said I was looking perkier this morning. Said I had some colour in my cheeks.

*4 September 1979*

Every morning, every evening, I pop a pill. Wash it down with a cup of tea. Each time I savour the sensation of it – I imagine it dissolving in my stomach, diffusing its yellowness into my blood, as if I've broken off a little bit of sunshine and it's warming me from the inside. The doctor was right – it smooths the rough edges. Things don't seem as important. So what if I don't feel any bond with the baby? She's fed, and clothed, and alive. I still don't love her, but at least I'm not bothered by her, her stillness, her staring. In fact, I'm pretty still too, and find myself staring – at the pendulum of the clock on the living-room wall, at the lacy pattern in the doilies on the coffee table, at the dimpled Artex on the bedroom ceiling, my mind quiet, my thoughts low and muted, like someone has turned the radio down.

If I forget a dose, I start to feel the irritation creeping back in again, my thoughts getting louder, the volume on the dial slowly turning up, and I'll realise I've been chewing my lips, or gritting my teeth, or jiggling my leg, and I'll head upstairs to the medicine cabinet as soon as I can, take a tablet, swilling water from the tap to wash the pill down, and then I feel able to breathe again.

It's strange, isn't it? Like a magic trick. Who knew happiness was so easy? I feel like telling the whole world about it, about what they're missing out on. Today in the supermarket I saw a woman hissing under her breath at a screaming toddler, her face red, her arms laden with shopping, and I felt like going up to her and saying, 'Have you tried benzodiazepines? You really must, they're wonderful.'

*10 September 1979*

Bobby arrived today.

I was dozing in the winged chair when he arrived. The knock at the door made me jump out of my skin. My head was fuzzy. I'd been feeling the badness creep back in over the past couple of days, despite the tablets. It worried me a bit. I guess it was nerves, about seeing Bobby for the first time in months, about introducing him to his daughter. So I'd taken an extra pill with dinner, and it had worked, perhaps a bit too well. I felt distant, disjointed.

I stood up, steadied myself, one hand on the back of the chair. Mum was asleep on the sofa, the remote in her hand. Hannah was asleep in a Moses basket at Mum's feet, flushed and full with milk. Dad had gone to the pub, George was out at Eddie's. *3-2-1* was on the TV, the volume down low, the audience applauding as Ted Rogers walked down the steps, shaking people's hands.

And through the pills' fog I felt a sense of being on the brink of something – like the feeling of time slowing down just before the first big drop on a rollercoaster, that breathless, heart-stopping pause. My husband. It still felt strange that I had a husband. I looked at the wedding ring on my finger (it's skinny enough again, now, to fit the ring on). A man I barely knew, and he was here, this stranger, and he had come to take me away, with this baby that still didn't feel like mine, to start a new life on an island I know nothing about, hundreds of miles away. I'd tried to remember

Bobby's face earlier, to prepare myself for this meeting, but I couldn't fix it in my mind's eye. It melted, shifted. What exact colour were his eyes? I knew they were blue, but what type of blue? What shape were his ears? I couldn't remember. And here he was, just the other side of the front door. The postcards, the feverish phone calls, the long letters all seemed so stupid now. A silly schoolgirl's fantasy. Play-acting. But now it was real. Too real.

I stood with my hand gripping the back of the chair, swaying slightly. The clock on the mantelpiece ticked. Opening the door would mean setting the rest of my life in motion. Could I just stay standing like this forever? Maybe, I thought dreamily, if I didn't move, he'd give up and go away.

But then he rang the doorbell, and Rex barked, and Mum snorted and opened her eyes, and I had to move. I turned and went to the front door and opened it, and he was there, handsome as ever, holding a bouquet of pink roses and baby's breath, and he held his arms out and I hugged him, and we kissed, and it was nice, but strange – a bit like I was dreaming. And when we stopped kissing, I said: come and meet your daughter.

He scooped her up from the Moses basket, and looked at her face, and said aren't you beautiful. Just like your mummy.

And then he said: we'll call her Hannah.

Hannah. Bobby says it's a palindrome. Same backwards as it is forwards. Something clever about that, isn't there? he said. Seems lucky, somehow. What do you think?

And I said yeah. It's nice. Although it felt just like all the other names in my mouth. Like nothing. Like ash and air.

Hannah, he said, beaming down at her. Hello, Hannah.

Hannah.

Jane, sitting at Maggie's kitchen table, looks at the name, written there in blue ink. She feels her fingers contract slightly with the muscle memory of writing it – on the front of exercise books, on her peg label, on her friends' polo shirts on the last day of school. Not written since then, except on the deed poll five years ago, when she'd written it out of her life forever. Not that she'd been under any illusion that changing her name would disguise her identity on Unst. Everyone knew she was Hannah Douglas. Knew all about her. But it was symbolic, the change. A way of signalling to people that she'd broken ties. A step away from the past.

Jane. Plain Jane. Jane Doe. She took comfort in its sturdiness, its austerity, its neatness, like a piece of Shaker furniture. The teeth closed at either end of the word, sealing it off neatly like a little parcel. Not like Hannah, with its breathiness, its untethered sound, all air. The flap of a butterfly's wings. Same backwards as it is forwards. Duplicitous, like something reflecting in a lake, half sunken.

What would she name this baby if she had it?

Jane pauses. Then shuts the diary.

She's not going to think about that. Not going to begin to think about that. There's no point. She's not having this baby.

Still, as she gets up and puts the kettle on, she feels the thought tugging at her, like a fish hook.

Robert, for a boy. After her dad. Could be Robbie. Baby Robbie.

Stop it, she thinks. Stop.

She switches on the radio. 'Rockall, Malin, Hebrides,' it says. 'Southeast veering southwest 4 or 5, occasionally 6 later. Rain, then squally showers. Poor, becoming moderate.'

Jane turns up the volume as the kettle boils. Makes the tea, sits back down at the kitchen table, pulls a cigarette from the packet. She hesitates for a moment, then puts it to her lips, lights it, inhales. Nell pads into the room, nuzzles her snout into Jane's palm, and she ruffles the dog's ears, looks out of Maggie's kitchen window. There's a bird feeder stuck to it with a suction cup, empty save for a few sunflower seeds at the bottom. She'll fill it later. Beyond it, the grass, then the fence, then the stretch of gleaming water, the brown hills beyond.

She smokes half of the cigarette before stubbing it out, the taste turning her stomach. Then she puts on her coat, boots, and steps out of the door.

Jane stands in the hospital corridor, clutching a bouquet of yellow chrysanthemums, reading the signs overhead. Audiology, Dental, Renal, Theatres – her eyes linger just a fraction too long on Maternity – Ward 1, stairs and lift.

She follows the signs, heads up the stairs, turns into the ward. It takes her a moment to find Maggie. She is asleep in one of the beds. She looks different asleep, much older. Her normally wild hair has been combed back. Her mouth is open, her face slack.

Jane approaches the bed. A nurse is checking the charts and smiles at her.

'Daughter?' she says.

'No. Friend. Neighbour. How is she?'

'Well, she's doing as well as can be expected,' the nurse says. 'Hopefully she'll be back on her feet soon. But healing is going to take a little while. At her age the skin's very thin. She needs lots of rest. Here, let me pop those in a vase for you,' she says, taking the bouquet.

Jane sits down on a chair next to Maggie's bed. She is snoring lightly. Her hands on the crisp white sheet look like bruised fruit on a china plate.

'Hi Mags,' Jane says, quietly.

Maggie doesn't respond. Jane glances around, at the ward, the other visitors talking quietly to the people in the beds. She looks back at Maggie.

'Nell's fine,' Jane says. 'I took her out in the car to Easting Beach yesterday. She had a good run. Swam in the sea a bit. She rolled in a dead gull. Had to give her a bath. I used your lavender shower gel, hope you don't mind.'

Maggie carries on snoring.

'She's good company,' says Jane. 'It's been nice having her there. These past few days. It's been lonely. I haven't seen Mike. Can't face him, really. If I saw him, I don't think I could keep it a secret.' Jane glances at the ward, then looks at her shoes against the polished linoleum. 'I'm pregnant, Mags,' she says, her voice dropping to a whisper. 'I took a test.'

Maggie's eyes move slightly under their purplish lids, and she snores again.

'I've made a doctor's appointment,' says Jane, quietly. 'To – to get me a referral. To get rid of it.' She hesitates, then says: 'I had one once before. I don't think you know that. When I was seventeen, just before I came to Unst. My first proper boyfriend. It was fine,' she says. 'Barely remember it. The nurse held my hand as they gave me the sedative, and the next thing I knew, I was in a recliner chair with a maxi pad between my legs and a heating pad on my belly. I had a custard cream and a cup of tea and two paracetamol, and that was that.'

Jane swallows. Looks down at her lap. She is so aware of her stomach, has never felt so conscious of it before, beneath her ribs, above her hips, under the layers of clothing – thermal vest, cotton top, fleece jumper. It feels separate to her, somehow, carrying its strange passenger.

'I need to get rid of it, Mags,' says Jane. 'I can't . . . I can't pass on any of this – this badness.' She sees, in her mind's eye, the wedding ring circling on its rope of hair. 'I heard on the radio the other day that girls are born with all their eggs inside them. They don't make any new ones. Which means that I – as an egg – was once inside my nan's womb. And the egg that turned into this thing inside me was in the womb of my mother. My mother made this egg,' she says, her voice hoarse, hollow. 'It's one of her cells. It's like – reincarnation, isn't it?'

She hears footsteps approaching. Glances up to see the nurse, the chrysanthemums arranged neatly in a plastic beaker.

'There,' she says, putting them down on Maggie's bedside table. 'Aren't they lovely? Brighten the place up. Ah!' she says, smiling. 'Someone's awake!'

Jane looks at Maggie. She is blinking, looking blearily up at the nurse.

'How are you feeling, Mrs Turner?' says the nurse, patting Maggie's hand. 'You have a visitor.'

'Hi, Maggie,' says Jane.

Maggie turns her head, looks at Jane. She frowns.

'Sylvia?' she says.

Jane feels her stomach drop. Her skin prickle all over.

'No,' she says. 'It's me, Jane.'

'It's your neighbour, Maggie. Your friend,' says the nurse. 'She's brought you some lovely flowers, look—'

'Sylvia,' says Maggie, hoarsely. 'I haven't seen you in – in so long. You – you went away . . .' She frowns.

Jane sits in the chair, her mouth dry, her heart beating hard.

'She's a little confused at the moment,' says the nurse in a low voice. 'A side effect of the medication.'

Maggie is still staring at Jane, with a frown. 'Your little girl. How is your little – Hannah, how is Hannah? Lovely little girl, how old is she – and of course,' she says, vacantly, 'you've got a peerie boy, your boy. What's his name? What . . .'

*Don't*, thinks Jane, *please don't*, as Maggie squeezes her eyes shut, tilts her head – but then her face smooths out, she opens her bright blue eyes and says, 'Oh, of course. That's right. Charlie.'

She looks at Jane. Jane stares back, feeling icy cold, hollow.

'Charlie,' Maggie says, smiling. 'Darling Charlie, oh. How is he? Is he – is he walking yet? Oh. But – but you . . . but Bobby . . .' She frowns again. 'Sylvia, but you went away, and it was – oh,' she says, her eyes widening. 'Oh, no. Sylvia, I'd forgotten. What you did—'

'Mrs Turner,' says the nurse. 'Let's sit you up. Get you a drink. It's time for your medicine.'

'But . . .' says Maggie, lifting a hand, pointing at Jane, 'But she's here, we must call – we must tell someone, everyone is looking for her!' She looks at the nurse, back to Jane.

'I'm sorry,' says Jane, 'I'm sorry, I have to go,' and she stands up, and turns, and walks out of the ward, breaking into a run, through the corridors, down the staircase, out through the doors of the hospital. Into her car. Slams the door behind her, feeling panic swamp her, flood her. She clutches the steering wheel. Gasps for air.

# Chapter Three

29 September 1979

I'm writing this on the ferry. I've just come down off the deck. Bobby's asleep in the chair next to me, Hannah in her pram, parked next to him, gumming on her fist.

I'm so tired that I don't feel solid. All fuzzy round the edges.

We had a little leaving party today. It was nice, I suppose. Sally and Judith were in tears, although Judith asked if I was taking my LPs with me and if not could she have them. Cheeky mare. George was sweet too, gave us a leaving present of a picture of him and Mum and Dad in a frame he'd made in woodwork class. Dad was a bit choked up. Mum was in bits. She held me so tight when we said goodbye that I thought she'd crush me. She gripped my shoulders and looked me right in the face and said to me, so only I could hear, if you don't feel right, if you're struggling, call us. Call me. We'll come and get you. She held my face in her hands and said I'm going to miss you so much, my darling girl.

Dad drove us to the station. I looked at Mum's face as the car pulled away. Watched it until we were round the corner. Felt like a stone sitting in my stomach.

But once we'd said goodbye to Dad at the airport, I felt a bit better. Bobby bought us a drink in the bar to calm my nerves and toast our new adventure, even though legally I'm not allowed alcohol yet. I think sometimes he forgets how young I am.

The plane wasn't as bad as I'd thought it would be. I'd thought I'd be terrified of flying, but the pill and the booze had kicked in and it was quite relaxing, actually – the jingling of the drinks trolley, the hum of the engines, and nothing to do but sit and wait.

We flew over Crowholt. It was funny seeing the village from above. I could make out the estate. The burnt paper mill, the black smudge of it, like a cigarette burn on a map. I could even pick out our house. I knew exactly what they'd be doing inside: Mum clearing up the buffet things, George feeding Rex crisps, Dad settling down with a beer in front of the TV. It made me feel quite lonely imagining them like that. Everything I'd ever known, down there, so small. A collection of Lego bricks. And then it was behind us. Left behind so quickly.

Hannah slept the whole way. I suppose she liked the engine noise. I had a tomato juice from the trolley which was as disgusting as it sounds. I looked out over the tops of the clouds. It was quite amazing really.

It wasn't long before we touched down in Aberdeen. Bobby collected his car and we drove to the terminal and boarded the ferry. We went to our cabin – twin beds, with a cot wedged between them, and an en-suite shower room – and then we had some lasagne and chips in the restaurant and listened to the safety announcement. On hearing the signal, passengers must wear warm clothing and make their way to the assembly stations. I was beginning to feel seasick even though we were still docked in port.

It was dark by the time the ferry set off. I went up on deck by myself while Bobby gave Hannah a bottle. I went right to the back – can't remember if that's the prow or the stern – and stood in the wind and the cold and listened to the rumbling of the engines, and watched the lights of the land receding, and the water falling away behind us.

And I had the weirdest feeling, the same one that I had when I was in labour. That feeling of being distant, being like a passenger in my own body. I gripped the railing tight. Had a feeling that if I let go, I'd just vanish. Disappear into the night and the wind. I watched the lights from the shore shrink slowly to little pinpricks, until they were snuffed out in the blackness.

And then this woman came out for a smoke, and tried starting a conversation with me, so I made my excuses and went back to the cabin. Hannah was asleep again, in the cot. Bobby held me and kissed me. I think he wanted a proper snog but I didn't feel like it. Now he's snoring on the bed next to me and I'm writing this. The ferry's rolling gently, and the moon is shining through the cabin window, and I've taken another pill, so now I'm going to sleep.

*30 September 1979*

I'm writing this in our new home. Sitting in bed, the smell of peat smoke in my hair, the electric blanket warming my legs. It's so cold. Bobby says I'll have to stock up on thermal underwear.

It's so silent here. No sound at all. No low rumble of the motorway, no whoosh of the trains. Only the sound of my pen scratching on the paper, and Bobby's sleeping breaths next to me.

Is this really my life now? I keep thinking I'm going to wake up. Everything since Hannah's birth feels like a dream. Will anything ever feel real again?

This morning I woke up just as the ferry was docking. It was a miserable morning, cold and cloudy, and Lerwick didn't look like much, a load of boxy brown and grey buildings with slate roofs, hills humped against the outskirts of the town, and the sea dull, like beaten pewter.

We had a fry-up in a café – well, Bobby did, I could only manage a bit of toast, I was feeling a bit queasy from the ferry – and then we got in the car and started the journey across the islands.

The road swept in curves across the hills, and I watched out of the window, Hannah on my lap, as the land rolled past. The countryside is moorland, brown and green, with dark patches of heather and black channels of peat which remind me of chocolate fudge. No trees, anywhere. Just fences, and ruined stone houses, and sheep. And the sea. I read the signs as we passed them – strange-sounding place names. Laxfirth. Wadbister. Girlsta.

My eyes got heavy. I tucked Hannah down into the footwell, cocooned in blankets, drew my legs up beneath me and dozed for an hour or so. I dreamt. I dreamt that I'd left Hannah in Devon and had accidentally brought a plastic doll with me instead, one with socketed limbs, eyes that fluttered open and closed. In my dream I decided not to tell Bobby – I'd keep the doll, pretend everything was normal, keep it a secret. Then I woke up, and looked down at Hannah lying in the footwell and sucking her fingers, and I felt a sense of something – disappointment? Dread? – roll over me. I shut my eyes again. And in what seemed like a matter of seconds, Bobby was shaking me gently awake.

We're here, he said. Home sweet home.

I blinked, looked at him. We were parked not fifty yards from the sea – I could see it behind Bobby, grey water and ash-coloured sand. Ahead of us was a white cottage, stuck into a little hillside. The walls were dirty at the bottom, like the hem of a wedding dress that had been trailing in mud. Peerie Hamarsgarth.

Bobby took Hannah in, then carried me over the threshold. Set me down on the sofa in the living room. Hannah was squirming and grizzling, so I gave her a finger to suckle while I looked around me and Bobby brought our things in.

The living room was gloomy, the grey light from the little window reflecting dully off the white gloss walls. There was another armchair, a TV on a little wheeled table. A fireplace. Across the ceiling above it were strung a couple of lengths of rope, from which hung some vests, underpants, and a stained tea towel. The only bit of decoration was the photograph of Hannah and I that Mum had taken, that I'd posted to Bobby months ago. He'd put it in a brass frame and propped it up on the windowsill.

I looked at the photograph. I remembered it being taken, remembered hating it being taken, had felt saggy and exhausted and a hundred years old, had begged Mum to just take a photo of the baby instead, but Mum had said nonsense, he'll want to see you, too. He'll be missing you.

I'd been relieved when the photo had come back dark and indistinct. Mum's thumb had been over the flash and you could barely see me.

It felt odd, sitting in an armchair with a baby, looking at a photograph of myself sitting in an armchair with a baby. This armchair didn't feel quite steady; my body still felt as though it was rocking with the motion of the ferry. I sat very still.

The room smelt vaguely damp, slightly earthy. Black mould speckled one corner of the ceiling. Bobby saw me looking at it, said don't worry about that. It's just the salt air. It wipes off, wee bit of bleach, no problem.

He traipsed in and out of the croft, bringing in the boxes, bags, suitcases. Hannah started to wail, hungry, so I went to the kitchen to make her up a bottle.

I started to fill the kettle from the tap, then stopped. The water was brown, like lightly brewed tea.

That's the peat, Bobby said. Sometimes it'll do that, when the reservoir gets stirred up by gales. Don't worry, it's perfectly safe to drink once you've boiled it. Doesn't taste any different. Best kind of water to put in your whisky, so they say. Occasionally you might get a wee twig or bit of moss in it, but fish it out and you'll be fine.

I looked at him to see if he was joking. I don't think he was.

I fed Hannah the peaty milk, feeling uneasy. She didn't seem to mind. While I fed her, Bobby explained the croft to me. Looks basic, he said, but it's got all mod cons. Washing machine – you have to watch that, it moves about six inches across the room on the spin cycle. Radio, TV – reception's terrible, so bad we don't have to pay the licence fee. Oh, and there's a blown tube which I need to fix, makes the picture a bit green. But it still works, if you get the aerial in the right place. When there's not a power cut, of course. Sometimes when the gales come in they blow down the power lines. But it's all right – if the lights go out we've got a Tilley lamp, which I'll show you how to use, and heaps of candles. Always keep a good stock of candles. D'you like the lino? I got it from a shop on the mainland, they were just throwing out offcuts. This was all just bare earth before, no floor at all. Thought it was nice enough, though I've no eye for interior design . . .

I looked at the linoleum. It was a dirty pink, with a pattern that looked like blobs of old chewing gum.

Thought you might like it, he said, and I saw he was nervous and wanted me to say something nice, so I arranged my face into a smile and said it's lovely, looks great.

Then he showed me the bathroom.

If the kitchen had smelt damp, the bathroom was positively aquatic. The paint on the ceiling was flaking in patches, the grout between the tiles was black.

Not much to say about the bathroom, said Bobby. Same thing with the peaty water; it feels a bit strange bathing in it at first, like you're a teabag brewing. But you'll get used to it.

Then he led me up a steep flight of stairs to the bedrooms. Hannah's room, papered yellow; our room, papered green. Both set into the roof, the ceilings sloping down to about ten inches above the floor.

I sat on our bed with a sigh. Bobby said you must be shattered. You have a lie-down, I'll take Hannah, get things sorted.

But she needs changing, I said.

I can do it, he said.

You know how?

Aye, of course. I practically raised my baby sister, remember? I'm a nappy changer extraordinaire.

I'd forgotten. How many siblings did he have? Christ, I thought. I didn't really know him at all.

I handed Hannah to Bobby, and he took her in his arms, kissed her nose. As soon as he was out of the room, I started writing this.

So much I don't know about him. So much he doesn't know about me. And yet here we are. Husband and wife and baby. In our new home.

I'm trying to shake the nagging feeling this was all a big mistake.


*5 October 1979*


We've been here five days now.

For the first few mornings I woke up and it took me a minute or two to remember where I was. I'd stare at the window over my head, and listen to the wind, and the sound of seagulls, and bleating sheep, and think where the hell am I? But that's passed now. I'm getting used to the place.

We've been for lots of walks around the island. The pram is pretty useless for walks, so Bobby carries Hannah instead, zipped into the front of his coat. We've been to Muness Castle, and to

Sandwick Beach, and yesterday we went to this place up the road called the Keen of Hamar, this expanse of bare rock which looks like the surface of the moon. Bobby was excited about it, telling me there's a plant there that doesn't grow anywhere else in the whole world. Shetland mouse-ear, it's called. I wanted to see some but it doesn't flower in the autumn. Guess I'll have to wait.

In the evenings we make love. I don't enjoy it like I used to. Partly it's the pills, they kill my sex drive, but mostly it's the feeling that my body isn't mine any more. I'm embarrassed by it. My soft saggy stomach with its stretch marks, my deflated breasts, the skin on them slightly crêpey like an overripe peach. My nipples have stretched and gone dark, like the pennies you press in the machines at the seaside. And God knows what I look like down below. All my stitches have long gone but I'm sure it's a mess down there. Not that Bobby cares. Still as enthusiastic as ever. I just let him get on with it. I shut my eyes and hold him, and listen to the wind, and the gulls, and the bed springs squeaking. If I take a pill beforehand, it's easier – the whole thing seems distant, as if it's happening to someone else. Either way, I'm always glad when it's over, when he's soft and sleepy and I can pull the covers over myself and just hold him close.

We've been to the local shop a couple of times. It looks like an old shipping container on stilts. It's like Aladdin's cave in there. Stuff everywhere, piled up to the rafters. The owner's got an accent so thick I can barely understand her. Luckily Bobby can translate. I thought the people here would sound Scottish but they sound more like Polish Pete, the man who lives two doors down from us in Crowholt who came over from Krakow after the war.

We've had people dropping round. Visitors. A couple of friends of Bobby's, the farmer from up the road, a few old ladies from the local church. Bringing presents – homemade cakes, a sack of potatoes, biscuits. They all seem nice. All dress the same, in parkas and rubber boots. They look so outdoorsy, so in keeping with the island. I feel a bit stupid in my polyester blouses and eyeshadow. They look at me with polite interest. None of them have asked about the arm, although I've seen a few of them notice.

They coo over Hannah. Tell me how much she looks like me. I nod along, although I don't think she looks like me at all.

I haven't met our next-door neighbours yet. The ones in the big white house up the track. I've seen the two boys out in the garden, they look about ten or eleven maybe, and I've seen the woman, walking their collie dog, but they haven't come to say hello. I asked Bobby about them. Apparently the mother's called Maggie, and there are three children, a girl and two boys. The father died years ago. Our house belonged to them, apparently. Bobby bought it off them. He says he doesn't know much about the family; they keep themselves to themselves.

Hannah's settled in fine. She's smiled now, a few times. Only at Bobby, though. He's so easy with her, goofing around and pulling faces and playing peekaboo with the tablecloth. When she smiles at him her whole face lights up. I've tried making her smile but she just stares at me like I'm an idiot. But it's okay. The tablets stop it hurting.

*6 October 1979*

This morning Bobby left early to help one of his friends repair a wall on his farm. The day was my own. The sun was shining. I decided to take Hannah out in the pram and call Mum from the phone box. I've called home a couple of times, but only quickly. I fancied a proper chat.

I dialled the number. Pressed the receiver to my ear. Listened to it ring. Looked at Hannah's sleeping face. Looked at the view from the phone box – the road, the low boxy houses, the grass, the glittering water. There was a band of rain coming in the distance and a rainbow appeared over the sound. I thought, I'll tell Mum about that rainbow. But the phone just rang, and rang. I listened to it for a long time. Willing Mum to pick up. But nothing happened, and then the rainbow faded anyway, and I felt so sad.

I put down the receiver. Oh well, I thought. Never mind. I can call back later. I collected my twenty-pence piece and put it back in my pocket. Shoved the pram out of the phone box and started back to the croft.

I managed to hold it together until I got to the turning down the track to our house. But seeing the croft – the strange white building, my new home – I burst out crying. I wanted my mum. I wanted to go home. I wanted the two-bar heater, and my record player, and the sound of the motorway, and Rex, and I stood in the mud by the cattle grid and sobbed and sobbed, feeling like my heart would break.

And then I felt this hand on my shoulder.

I jumped out of my skin. It was our neighbour. Maggie. In a wax jacket and headscarf, frowning at me with these piercing blue eyes.

She looked at me. Said, are you hurt?

All I could do was shake my head. Blurted out something about being homesick. God I must have looked pathetic, snotting and sobbing in broad daylight.

Well, she seemed to hesitate a bit, and then soften, and said – come de wis in.

What? I said.

Come in, she said. I'll put on the kettle.

So there I was. Sitting in Maggie's living room, blowing my nose into a handkerchief while she dandled Hannah on her lap. I apologised for being so stupid. So childish. Said I'd be fine, I just needed time, and the island was lovely, really, just very different. I just needed to settle in, make some friends.

She said she understood. Said her daughter, Laura, had left for university a couple of weeks ago, was sure she was feeling homesick too.

Oh, I said. And she looked at me. As if waiting for something. I felt like I was being tested.

That's her, Maggie said, pointing to a photograph on the mantelpiece. Laura.

I looked at the girl. Long dirty-blonde hair, with a fringe. Big green eyes.

Oh, I said again. But Maggie still seemed to be waiting for something. So I said, she's very pretty.

Aye, said Maggie.

There was an awkwardness in the air. Something unspoken. I couldn't put my finger on it. So I just smiled politely, and made some excuse about having to get Hannah home, she needed changing. And I thanked Maggie for the tea, and left. She watched me leave from the doorway. Felt her bright blue eyes on me all the way up the path.

That evening, Bobby came back, cheerful and knackered from lugging stone all day. I poured him a beer and heated up some dinner and while he was eating, I said:

I met our neighbour today. Maggie, at Hamarsgarth.

Oh, he said.

Yeah. She seems nice.

He just nodded, made a noise in his throat. Something seemed off. I wanted to ask him more, but then Hannah started grizzling for a bottle. But I kept thinking about Maggie, all evening. About our meeting. The sense of something unspoken, hanging in the air, invisible, like a spiderweb. And me the fly that blundered into it.

*7 October 1979*

Bobby and I have had our first row and it's all my fault. I'm so bloody stupid. It's our last day together before he goes back to the rig, and I've ruined it.

It started as soon as I woke up. Today was Sunday, and Bobby shook me awake and said hey, Sylv. Wake up. It's time for church.

Well, I thought he was joking. I've never met a less God-fearing man. But it turned out he was being serious.

It's not really about the religion, he said. It's about showing your face. Being a member of the community.

I haven't been to church since I played a donkey in the nativity at primary school, I said. I don't know what I'm meant to do.

Just sit there and listen, Bobby said. And then have a chat to people after. That's all there is to it.

So we got up, and dressed, and I stuck Hannah in the pram, and we walked to the church. It's an ugly little grey building, not like the one in Crowholt, with its arched ceiling and brightly coloured screen and stained glass. It's so plain inside.

Well, we got in and sat at the end of a pew near the back. I felt faces turning to look at us. Some I recognised, some I didn't. There were some whispers. One or two smiled, but lots didn't. Bobby looked ahead, his chin up. Sort of defiantly. I saw his Adam's apple bob as he swallowed, and he was drumming his fingers on his lap. Nervous.

And then the vicar stood up. He's one of those old men who still somehow looks like a little boy, even though he's bald and wrinkly. Something about his eyes. And he started talking about us. Me and Hannah. Welcoming us to the island and that, saying that he was sure we'd soon agree it's the best place in the whole world to live, a peerie slice of heaven, and the whole village was thrilled to have us here, that the island is used to welcoming incomers, they breathe new life into the place, they enrich the community, and he was sure everyone would give us a very warm welcome. Some people nodded and smiled but some of them just stared. Glanced at each other. I was starting to feel really uncomfortable.

And then, the vicar started a sermon about welcoming people – for you were strangers in the land of Egypt – but Hannah started to cry. Really going for it. Her hunger cry. It's like an air-raid siren, rising and falling. I didn't mind. Gave me an excuse to get out. I took her out into the fresh air, gave her a bottle. She fell asleep again but I didn't feel like going back into the church, just sat out the back by the bin bags and empty Calor gas bottles, rocking the pram and thinking about what the vicar had said, and the stares from the pews in front. The nudges and whispers.

After the service people started to come out of the church, and Bobby found me hiding round the back. He wanted me to go and meet the vicar and thank him for the sermon, but all I wanted to do was go back to the croft.

Come on, he said. Just come and shake his hand. Won't take two seconds.

I want to go home, I said.

Sylvia, he said. Just quickly, come on. It's rude not to. He wrote that sermon just for you. To welcome you.

Well I don't feel welcome, I said. And I want to go home. I could feel tears coming, pricking the backs of my eyes, and I saw some people glancing over at me, and – well, like a petulant child, I took the pram and walked off. I thought Bobby would follow me, but he stayed behind, and I got home before him and sat in the silent croft, stewing.

By the time he got in I was in a right sulk. We didn't talk for hours, avoiding each other, until I couldn't bear it any longer, and then, when Hannah was napping, and he was packing his stuff ready for the rig, I stormed into the bedroom and said:

Why do they hate me?

Who?

The people. Here. They were glaring at me, whispering.

Bobby sighed. Then he came over and drew me into a hug. Kissed me on the top of the head. People here, he said, they're a close-knit community. Suspicious of outsiders. It's not personal.

It felt personal, I said.

It's not, he said. And trust me, they'll love you once they get to know you. How could they not? He lifted my chin so I was looking him in the eyes, and said: I asked the vicar to give that sermon today. To give you a special welcome. Because I know how intolerant people can be up here. And I wanted him to set them straight. To let them know that I won't stand for that. You're my wife. This is our home now.

Oh, I said. Oh, Bobby. You asked him to do that?

He nodded.

Well, I could have cried. But he just kissed me, and held me, and said it was all right, but I still feel so stupid for having acted so childishly. Picking a fight like that, after such a kind gesture. I'm an idiot.

*8 October 1979*

Bobby left this morning. I walked to the airstrip with him. I was hoping there might be a freak gale, to delay him leaving, but it was a still morning. Not a breath of wind. There were a few other families there. The other women said goodbye cheerfully, casually, their children waving. I tried my hardest not to cry, I really did, but when the helicopter blades started whirring I couldn't help it. Hannah started screaming fit to burst at the noise and the wind, which gave me an excuse to fuss over her, bending my head, so the others wouldn't see me blubbing. Still, two women came up to me after the helicopter had disappeared

117

into the sky. Said, oh it's always hard the first time, especially with bairns, but it gets easier, and would I like to have a cup of tea with them, but I said no, no thanks, I've got to get on.

I walked Hannah home. By the time we got back to the croft she'd fallen asleep in her pram. As I shut the front door and stood there in the porch I felt the silence close in around us. Just me and her now, I thought. Alone. For two weeks.

I looked at her sleeping face and felt this wave of panic. Christ, I thought. What if I have an accident? What if I trip and bang my head and pass out? What if I choke on some food and die and nobody finds us for days? I had a vision of myself, slumped at the kitchen table, flies buzzing around me, Hannah stuck in her bouncer, screaming and screaming in the silent house.

Don't be stupid, I told myself. I put Hannah in her playpen and tuned the radio to a pop music station and set about cleaning. I swept and mopped the floors, washed up, scrubbed the oven, changed the bed (Christ, that was difficult. A continental quilt. Bobby got it on a trip to Norway – he says it's much better than heavy layers of sheets and blankets – but it took me ages to change the cover on it. You need two hands, really. I was sweating by the end). I tried to tackle the mould in the corners of the room with bleach but it was no good, the speckles stayed there no matter how hard I scrubbed. I wiped down the surfaces, cleaned the bathtub, put a load of laundry into the washing machine. Then I fed Hannah, and fed myself, and changed her, and stuck her in the pram, and went out to the shops.

The weather had turned. A wind had got up. God, the pram is a struggle when it's windy. Mum and I chose it so carefully when I was pregnant, spent ages testing them all out in Mothercare, finding one with a handle I could use with my arm, one as light as we could find, that can fold up easily. But pushing it up the road, I wish I'd gone for a heavier one; I felt like one strong gust could snatch it clean away, send it hurtling into the sea. I gripped so tight my knuckles were white. By the time we got to the shop I was sweating.

People had been stocking up. There were gaps in the shelves. I picked up a few tins of powdered milk, and some flour, and there was one loaf of bread left, and no disposable nappies at all, but we've got some terry towels that'll do in a pinch. I got the last packet of cheap loo roll. I wanted some sausages for tea, but I couldn't see any.

Anyway, I got to the counter. Usually it's an old lady at the till, but this time it was a man with a face like a bulldog and huge horned eyebrows. I asked him for three packets of Marlboros, please, and did he have any sausages, and he pulled the wire basket towards him and looked at me like I was an idiot, and then let out this stream of Shetlandic nonsense. I couldn't catch a word of it. It's all ws and ds and oos. Wi da widdir biggin up. Da Earl. Dunna hae fags. Nae til damorn. I blinked at him and shook my head and said, I'm sorry, I don't understand. I'm new here, I'm not very good with the accent. And he glowered at me and started punching the prices into the till.

'We don't . . . have . . . cigarettes,' he said, slowly, like he was talking to an idiot. 'And there'll be no fresh meat until the mornin', if the ferry's runnin', which I doubt it will be, due to the gales which have been forecast.'

Right, I said. Well, thanks anyway, and I pushed Hannah out of the shop.

Well just as I was going down the ramp, the bloody bag split. The bag of flour burst on the floor, the tins of milk rolled off down the slope. So I swore, and put the brakes on the pushchair, and was scrambling around in the wind and rain trying to pick it all up, and just when I'd managed to stuff everything into the basket under the pushchair, the bell tinkled. This man, who'd been in the queue behind me, was unwrapping a fresh packet of Marlboros, three more packs tucked under his arm.

I looked at him.

Did you just buy those? I said.

Aye, he said.

The man in the shop told me there weren't any.

Oh, he said. He musta been mistaken.

Well, I turned right back around, jostled the pram through the door, pushed back into the shop. There were two old women at the counter, and I could pick up some of what they were saying.

They're all da same, incomers. Greedy, said one.

You go right fae da walk to da shops and some soothmoother has bought da last loaf.

I felt myself turning bright red.

The shopkeeper saw me. Cleared his throat. The old women turned. Had the decency to look embarrassed. I stood there, dripping on the carpet, covered in flour, Hannah grizzling in the silence.

I just saw a man who'd bought some cigarettes, I said, trying to draw myself up, look dignified. You'd said you didn't have any.

The shopkeeper shifted on his feet.

He'd reserved them, he said. In advance.

I stood there for a second. I wanted to say that it wasn't fair, but I realised how childish I'd sound. So instead I gritted my teeth and pushed Hannah out of the shop, pulling my hood up against the rain, cursing this stupid island and all the stupid people on it.

Anyway, we got home. I tried to get the fire going, and managed it eventually, but it was bloody hard work and seemed to throw out so little heat it hardly seemed worth the effort.

I'd been planning to save my last cigarette for the following day, but I was so fed up I decided to smoke it. I lit up and looked at Hannah. She was on the playmat, gumming on a rattle.

I thought about her, her life, growing up on this island. Wondered if she'd grow up with a Shetland accent like those people in the shop. Or if she'd grow up feeling like an outsider. If she'd be picked on, called a soothmoother. If she'd end up hating me for bringing her here.

I felt this weight in my chest, this dull ache. I wanted Bobby here. To wrap his arms around me and to tell me it would all come right, that we'd be fine. But Bobby wasn't here. He was hundreds of miles away, in the middle of the ocean, and would be for another thirteen days.

I took a pill. They don't seem to be working quite as well as they did. I wonder if they go off, have a best before date? I'll have to get some more. I'm starting to run low anyway.

Well I was sitting there, feeling pretty bloody sorry for myself, when there was a knock on the door.

It was Maggie. In an anorak, holding her hood tight against the wind.

I've brought you some things, she said. In case there's a power cut.

She handed me a plastic bag. Candles, a bottle of heating oil, batteries, a torch, matches.

I invited her in and boiled a kettle (the water was brown again) and made us a cuppa each, and we sat down, and we drank our tea, and smoked. Listened to the wind. She looked sad, somehow. Kept looking around the place with an expression I couldn't quite read.

Then she said: so. What do you think of Unst?

It's – lovely, I said.

You don't sound convinced.

Oh, no, it's just . . . It's very different.

The weather's not doing it any favours, she said. And the nights are only going to get longer now. I wish you'd come in spring, she said. It's brally pretty in spring.

I know, I said. Bobby told me. About the wildflowers and stuff.

She tapped her ash into the ashtray.

How did you meet Bobby? she said.

I hesitated. Then said, well, it was at a wake, actually. One of his friends had died.

Ah. Martin Adams, she said.

I looked at her. Yeah, I said. Did you know him?

Knew of him. Bobby mentioned him.

Oh, I said. You know Bobby well?

Pretty well. Through Laura, my daughter. They met at the oil refinery. She worked in the camp canteen.

Oh, I said. Sitting there, trying to think, my brain fogged a bit with the Valium. Trying to think if Bobby had ever mentioned Laura before. I was sure he hadn't — had never told me anything about her.

And then Maggie waved a hand and said, anyway, you were telling me about how you met Bobby. Martin Adams' funeral?

So I told her. All about the wake, the fire. Devon. Finding out I was pregnant. The proposal. Kind of hurried through it, because she was looking strange, kind of disapproving, and I didn't know if I was saying too much. Maybe it wasn't the done thing to talk about this sort of stuff. So I kind of petered out, and said, well, I had the baby in August, and then Bobby came down to get me, and now . . . here I am.

Then she nodded, and took a drag on her cigarette, and didn't say anything.

And I felt awful, like I'd blundered again into something, and I sat there feeling my cheeks burning, and suddenly I blurted out:

Is there something wrong with me?

What?

It's just — I get the sense everyone up here hates me. The islanders. The man in the shop today wouldn't sell me some cigarettes. And in the church people were giving me filthy looks.

I know I struggle to understand the accent. And I don't have the right clothes, and I don't do the right things. But I'm trying, I really am. I'm trying to fit in . . . And then I had to stop talking else I was going to cry.

Oh, she said. No, no. No.

Well, what is it?

It's not you.

Isn't it?

No. It's just – well, some people don't like outsiders. Especially some of the older folk. They don't like change. There's been lots of change here, since they struck oil in '71. And then of course there was that big tanker spill, last December – the *Esso Bernicia* – well, that caused a lot of bad blood between the locals and the oil folk. So it's not you. It's incomers, in general.

I sat there, looking at the carpet, trying not to cry. And Maggie came over and put a hand on my shoulder, and said don't worry, dear. Folk will get used to you. Don't take it to heart. Things will be better in spring.


## 11 October 1979

Disaster.

I'm out of pills.

I took my last one this morning. Then battled through the wind to the health centre, clutching the pram, my prescription in my pocket. Only for the pharmacist to tell me I needed to order in advance. Five working days, she said. I asked her if I could have something – anything – just to tide me over. She looked at me like I was a junkie. Said she couldn't just dole out drugs willy-nilly. I could take the ferry to Lerwick, try the pharmacy there.

The ferry's not running, I said. The gales.

She shrugged.

So I came home.

No cigarettes. No pills.

I'm not feeling great. Been sitting here watching TV, but I can't concentrate on the programme. Feel jittery. My hands are shaking.

I keep looking out of the window. Watching the sea, the iron-grey waves with their heads of white foam rolling and crashing on the shore, the grass rippling in the wind. The horizon has disappeared, sky and sea blurring together in one wash of grey.

It makes me feel trapped. Claustrophobic. No way off the island. No way out, no way back.

The power's out.

Night's drawing in. Still the power's out.

I'm writing this by candlelight. Couldn't get the Tilley lamp working. Lit the fire but it keeps dying.

I'm still not used to the nights here. In Crowholt I was never scared of the dark. The nights seemed friendly enough. There was always the orange glow of streetlamps, the low rumbling of cars passing, the trains in the distance. And of course, the knowledge that we weren't alone, we were surrounded by neighbours, all asleep in their own beds.

But the nights here are different. When the moon isn't out, the darkness is total; it's so thick it feels like it has an actual weight to it, like you could pinch it between your fingers. And the only sound is the howling wind. There's no comfort in that.

I'm trying not to think about how vulnerable we are here. A one-armed woman and her baby, all alone, with just a few candles to keep the night at bay. No car, neighbours a minute's walk away, nearest telephone a ten-minute walk away. If some mad axe murderer came creeping up on us . . .

Don't be stupid. There are no mad axe murderers here. Bobby told me; said there's barely any crime on the island, people leave their doors unlocked all the time. Crime's so rare here that a few years ago someone stole a wallet from a house in Yell and it was the front page story of the local paper for three whole days. He laughed when he told me that. We both laughed. We're safe. I know that. But still, the croft is eerie in the candlelight, and the wind is moaning and rattling, and I daren't look into the shadows in the corners of the room in case something is lurking there.

I feel like I'm going insane. I'm frightening myself. I'm frightened.

Hannah started crying as I finished writing that last bit. Made me jump, the sudden noise. I went to her room, got her out of the cot. Took her into the kitchen, held her on my lap in the pool of light cast by the candles, trying to ignore the darkness.

I gave her a bottle. Sang to her as I fed her – mainly to comfort myself, if I'm honest. I sang 'Loch Lomond' to her, like Bobby does, but I couldn't remember the lyrics, and my voice sounded thin and frightened, so I stopped. The silence that flowed in after it was worse than before.

I looked at her sleeping. I thought about the hole in her heart. I could see it, in my mind's eye, a rip in a pink membrane. I put my fingers on her chest, felt her heart beating there, quick, light, like the wing-beats of a moth. And I imagined it sputtering, skipping, stopping. Her dying in my arms.

Why does my mind do this? Why does it throw up these horrible images? All the time I think of her dying.

Is it because, deep down, I want her to?

If I could click my fingers and make her disappear, would I?

I thought back to her days in the tank, when she was born. To how revolted I'd felt. How I'd wanted to get rid of her, abandon her, like the mother cat in the long grass.

I looked at her sleeping face. Her mouth slightly open. In the light of the candles, the dark shadows under her eyes made them look sunken, like she was dead already. And my mind started oozing these black thoughts. Spilling out like oil from the seabed.

The wind had nearly torn the pram from my hand the other day – all it would take would be a clifftop path, a freak gust . . . nobody would know it had been deliberate. But no need for something so elaborate, so violent. Cot death. It was ever so common. I glanced at the sofa cushion. A few seconds, held over her sleeping face. That's all it would take.

I was horrifying myself but in a distant way, like I was outside my mind looking in. I stared down at her face in the candlelight, and wondered if I could really do it, if I had the capacity to, if I could, in fact, do it right now, and I sat there with my hair hanging over her, cradling her, until I was suddenly aware of a movement out of the corner of my eye. I looked up.

Someone was staring in at the window.

There was a second or so where my lungs wouldn't work. I just stared at this face, this horrible white face, and it stared back at me – and then I sucked air down my throat and I screamed, God I screamed, and Hannah jerked awake and started wailing, and the face looked in impassively – and I realised it was a sheep. A fucking sheep.

Jesus Christ. I clutched Hannah to my chest, and I breathed, and then I laughed. I couldn't help it. Only a sheep, a stupid sheep. The fence must have blown over in the gales, it must have escaped from the field. I laughed as Hannah wailed, but it was a laugh with an edge to it, and it sounded wrong, and so I stopped, clamping my hand over my mouth. I looked at the sheep, and it looked back at me, its face like an ancient mask, long and white, and it seemed, suddenly, as if it knew what I'd been thinking, as if it was a judge, sent by nature to witness the most unnatural thing – a mother that would kill her own child.

I shushed Hannah, dandled her on my lap. There there, I said. There there, mummy's here.

And after a few seconds the sheep turned its face away, and the windowpane was filled with darkness again, and Hannah fell back to sleep, and I'm sat here, feeling like a monster.

This morning I woke up to the whole ceiling shimmering. I thought I was going mad.

Took me ages to realise it was just sunlight reflecting from a puddle outside. I was in the living room, on the floor, curled up on the rug. Hannah was asleep on her playmat next to me. And the washing machine was whirring too. The power was back on.

I got up and looked out of the window, the one the sheep had looked through. The storms had blown themselves out overnight and the sea was blue and calm. There were sheep everywhere, a few right down on the beach, practically standing in the surf. The fence which borders their field was lying in a big tangle on the grass, and two men and a collie dog were trying to round the sheep up, the men shouting, the dog circling, pacing.

I got Hannah on the first ferry to Lerwick. Went to the pharmacy. Got the pills. I took two straight away, swallowing them dry. I bought some fags too. Then just sat in the town, near the harbour, smoking and looking at the huge ferry docked in the port, the one we'd arrived on. I tell you, I was this close to buying a ticket and getting on it. Going back home. I could have done it. Rang Mum. Got her to wire me the money. Just left. Sorry, Bobby, this was all a mistake.

But I didn't. I came back here. To Unst. To Baltasound. To Peerie Hamarsgarth. To this horrible old damp lonely croft on this island where I'm miserable and everyone hates me. Why? Why am I doing this to myself?

I'm going to talk to the doctor. Up my dosage.

Jane looks out of the steamed-up windscreen, the rain hammering on the glass. She's in the health centre car park.

She looks at her watch. 10.29. As she watches, the numbers change. 10.30.

*Go*, she thinks. *Come on. Go.*

But she doesn't move. Her muscles resist, her body a dead weight.

*You're just here to get a referral*, she thinks. *Nothing's happening today.*

She takes a deep breath. Gets out of the car, hurries through the rain into the pebble-dashed building.

'Oh, hi Jane,' says the woman at the desk. It's Lucy Fleming. She used to work at the cannery.

'Hi Lucy,' says Jane, lowering her hood, dripping rainwater onto the carpet.

'How are—'

'I've got an appointment at half past,' says Jane. 'Doctor Mouatt.'

Lucy types something into the computer. Clicks around. Frowns.

'Huh,' she says. 'I can't see you here.'

Jane waits, drumming her fingers on the counter, as Lucy clicks some more. Maybe, she thinks, the appointment didn't get booked. Maybe she'll have to go home, try again another day. But then Lucy says:

'Oh – there you are,' says Lucy. 'You're down as Hannah.'

Jane swallows. 'That's my old name,' she says. 'Can you take it off the system, please?'

'Of course. No problem.'

'Thanks.'

Lucy clicks some more.

128

'Hannah,' says Lucy, and she makes a face. 'Doesn't suit you, somehow. I never felt Lucy suited me either. Always wanted to be an Elizabeth when I was little. God knows why, something to do with the Queen, I think. Delusions of grandeur.' She laughs. 'Righto,' she says, breezily. 'That's all done. take a seat. Doctor Mouatt won't be long.'

Jane sits down on one of the chairs. Looks around the waiting room. There is a baby, on the floor next to his mother. He is playing with a toy, wooden beads on wires, fat fists bashing at it, lower lip stuck out in concentration. He has a fine thatch of blond hair on his head, one little curl at the nape of his neck.

Charlie's hair was blond like that. White blond. Jane can still feel the texture of it, feather-light, warmed by his scalp. She can still smell its faint baby-shampoo scent. She always wondered if it would stay that blond or if it would darken as he got older.

The baby's mother is watching him, smiling. Taking photos on her phone. Jane watches her, pressing her fingertip to the screen. Trapping this moment like a fly in amber. A perfectly normal moment. Photos when Jane was young were only of special occasions. She remembers a few – her christening, a little wizened face in a froth of white lace. Her first birthday, staring fat-cheeked at a cake on the kitchen table. Her first day of school, in a gingham dress, squinting into the sun. All taken by her dad on his Olympus camera. She hasn't seen them in years. Has no idea what's happened to them. A blessing, Jane thinks, in a way. Growing up before the internet and all that. When she ran, she could leave it all behind. Had something physical to run away from, all those photographs kept in their paper pouches in her nan's cupboard. She couldn't do that now. They upload the photos to the internet and they stay there forever and ever, accessible by anyone, following you wherever you go. It makes Jane panic just thinking about it.

Of course, there are the online newspaper archives, she thinks. But they only ever used one photograph of her, a school photo.

She was an afterthought. Charlie and her mother, they were the star attractions—

A door opens. Doctor Mouatt pokes his head out.

'Douglas?' he says. 'Hannah Douglas?'

Jane flinches at the name. She follows the doctor down the corridor, into a little room.

Jane sits down. Looks at him. He's aged a lot since she last saw him, about ten years ago, when she got that infection in the cannery. A split in her gloves, a cut on her hand, the water so freezing she was too numb to notice.

'Oh, yes,' says the doctor, clicking on his computer. 'I remember. Fish-handler's disease, wasn't it?'

'Yes,' Jane says. Her hand aches at the memory. A huge purple lesion festering on her palm. She still has a scar, a silver seam of puckered skin, left after the abscess was drained.

'Still working at the factory?'

'Yup.'

'And no more problems since?'

'No.'

'Good. Good. Now. How can I help you today?'

'Well,' Jane says. 'Erm. Well, it's . . . I'm pregnant.'

The doctor just nods.

'It's unplanned,' Jane says. 'And I – I don't want a baby. So, could I – could you – could I arrange a termination, please?'

The doctor's face is carefully neutral. 'Okay,' he says, and turns to his computer. 'Let me just make a few notes here.'

He starts typing. Jane looks around the office. The bookshelf, with volumes on clinical dermatology, paediatrics, ocular pathology, and, for some reason, a Jilly Cooper novel. A photograph in a frame, of a small child. A granddaughter, perhaps. A plant on the window-sill, a weeping fig. It could do with a water, Jane thinks, looking at the leaves curling in on themselves.

Doctor Mouatt keeps typing, pecking at the keyboard with his index fingers. Jane realises she's sitting on her hands like a schoolgirl. She untucks them, folds them on her lap.

'Right,' he says. 'When was the date of your last menstrual period?'

'Um . . . I can't remember. I think a long time ago, about a year ago. My periods,' she says, awkwardly, 'they're quite irregular. Really irregular. That's why I left it so long. I only found out I was pregnant the other day. But, I think – I think I know when I might have conceived.'

'And when was that?'

'About three months ago.'

'I see,' says the doctor.

'I didn't know – I'd taken the morning-after pill, you see, and I didn't – if I'd known, I would have come to you earlier.'

The doctor clicks some more, types something. 'The clinic will call you to arrange the appointment,' he says. Then he opens a drawer in his filing cabinet and rifles through. He pulls out a sheet of paper, photocopied so many times the print is going fuzzy. Its title is 'Abortion – your choice, our support'. He hands it to Jane but doesn't look her in the eye.

Jane, sitting on Maggie's sofa, unfolds the leaflet, begins to read. 'We will prepare your cervix . . . sedation or anaesthetic . . . gentle suction . . . slender, specialised instruments . . .'

Jane swallows, her throat clicking. Then crumples up the leaflet, drops it on the sofa next to her. Draws her feet up, hugs her knees.

On the rug, Nell whimpers. She is asleep. Her paws twitch. Jane wonders what she's dreaming about. Chasing rabbits, perhaps.

She looks at Nell. The descendant of the dog her mother wrote about in her diary – her granddaughter, perhaps. Great-granddaughter. She looks at the room she's in. The room her mother sat in, drinking tea with Maggie, after she'd been crying from homesickness. She can't help it, now, seeing the past everywhere, like a set of transparencies laid over her life.

There are photos all around Maggie's living room. On the mantelpiece, the bookshelves, the walls. Wedding photos, baby photos, graduation photos. Each subject bearing a vague resemblance to all the others. The cant of the chin, the colour of the eyes, the curve of the nose, repeated, over and over. Echoes, repetitions. It makes her dizzy looking at them. Like being in a hall of mirrors.

Once, after a couple of sherries on Christmas Eve, Maggie had said: 'Shetlanders, you know. Their favourite pastime is coontin kin. Going back and back over the family history, working out cousins, second cousins, third cousins once removed, on and on, as far as they can go. Everyone is judged by who their family is. Everyone is a part of this huge web. As soon as you meet someone, it's oh, your mother was a cousin of my wife, and she lived at so and so, and they did such and such. I always found it claustrophobic, truth be told.' She took a swig of sherry, looked thoughtful. 'I understand why, though. It's about feeling you belong. Like you're a part of something. And it's a handy way to make sure there's no inbreeding.' She'd laughed, and then looked at Jane. 'But I want you to know, Jane – you're your own person. Don't let yourself feel judged by what happened in the past. You know people say "blood is thicker than water"? Well, that's wrong. That saying, it really means the exact opposite. The original was "the blood of the covenant is thicker than the water of the womb."'

*The water of the womb*, Jane thinks. And she leans back against the sofa and shuts her eyes.

As she's pulling on her overalls in the changing room, her mobile phone chirrups. Jane draws it out, expecting Mike, but it's an unknown number.

'Hello?'

'Jane Douglas?'

'Yes.'

'This is the sexual health clinic at Gilbert Bain hospital. I'm calling to discuss booking you in for a termination.'

'Okay,' says Jane, pausing, half dressed. She sits down on the wooden bench that runs along the wall of the changing room, stares at her feet.

The woman on the end of the phone talks, and Jane listens, barely breathing. Needed at the clinic the whole day . . . won't be able to drive home . . . a family member or friend to collect you . . . Jane nods along, makes noises to say she understands.

'We could fit you in next Wednesday,' says the woman. 'How does that sound?'

'Yeah,' she says. 'Fine.'

'Have you been given a number for the counselling service?'

'Yeah.'

'Great. We'll see you at eight forty-five on Wednesday.'

'Thanks.'

Jane finishes dressing, her hands fumbling with the buttons on her overalls. Pat comes in.

'Jane,' she says. She glances at her, then does a double take. 'Christ, Jane, you look terrible. Your eyes are like pissholes in the snow.'

'Yeah,' says Jane. 'Just . . . didn't sleep well last night.'

Pat looks at her, then shakes her head.

'Right,' says Pat. 'Come with me. I need a word.'

Jane follows Pat into her office, a little white room populated by a desk, a filing cabinet, and an ancient photocopier. On the wall is a poster of an exotic beach. A hammock strung between two palm trees, white sand, blue sea. Pat sits behind the desk, motions for Jane to perch on a kick stool.

'So,' she says. 'I heard about Maggie. Her accident.'

Jane nods.

'How's she doing?'

Jane thinks of Maggie in the hospital bed. Her wizened hand, pointing. Her horrified face.

'She's okay,' Jane says.

'Good. Glad to hear it. Now. I still haven't had an explanation as to why you missed work last Friday.'

Jane looks at Pat.

'I – I wasn't feeling well,' she said.

'Well, you know the sickness procedure,' said Pat. 'You ring me, or one of the other supervisors, as soon as you can. You don't turn up for work, sit in the car park, then drive off at the last minute and ignore our phone calls all day.'

Jane looks at her shoes. 'Sorry, Pat.'

'Was it an emergency?'

Jane shrugs.

Pat leans forward in her chair, says: 'Jane – look. I know summat's going on with you. You've always been one of my best workers. Never sick, never flaky, always kept your head down and got on with the job. Now, suddenly, you're boozing. You're turning up hungover. You're fucking off with not a word of explanation. And you look like shit,' she says, gesturing to Jane's face. 'What's going on?'

Jane doesn't reply. Pat leans in closer.

'It's not your fella, is it?'

'What?'

'The trawlerman. You know.' Pat drops her voice. 'He's not mistreating you, is he?'

'God, no,' says Jane. 'No.'

'Well, what then?'

'It's – it's personal, Pat. I can't explain.'

Pat leans back in her chair, sighs. 'Well, is there anything I can do? Any way I can help?'

Jane shakes her head.

'Right. Well,' Pat says, picking up her clipboard, clicking her pen. 'This is a warning, Jane. Okay? An official one. Any more of this shite . . .' She shakes her head. Looks at the clipboard. 'Today,' says Pat, 'I want you stripping roe.'

Jane thinks of it. Digging out the orange gelatinous eggs with her fingers, tossing them into a pile. Her stomach roils.

'Summat wrong?' says Pat.

Jane swallows. 'I'm sorry, Pat. I just – not roe. Please. Just put me on summat else. I'll do anything. I'll wash fillets, even.'

Pat looks furious, for a moment. Then mutters under her breath, 'All right – fine. Heading, then. But this is the last time I'm giving you special treatment. Okay? After this – enough.'

'Thanks, Pat,' says Jane, and gets up from the kick stool, walks out of the office, feeling Pat's eyes on her.

Jane takes her place at the slime line, places her foot on the pedal. She grabs a fish, heads it, passes it on. Grabs a fish, heads it, passes it on.

But something's wrong. She can't get into the rhythm of it, can't let her mind wander. Each time the blade cuts the head off the fish, she winces. She can almost feel it. The separation. The blade slicing through flesh, bone, arteries, fat, tendons, muscle. Everything seems bright, loud, hideously clear – the blood, the cold, the steel cutting blade. She feels herself sweating. She fumbles a fish, only nicking the tip of it, slicing straight through its eyeball, severing the front of its mouth.

She looks at it and feels a wave of nausea.

*I can't do this,* she thinks. *I can't, I can't.*

She drops the fish on the steel and turns. Hurries across the factory floor. She sees the others, slitting, gutting. And she can't help but look up as she passes the section where they suck the fish guts out. The rubber hoses are attached to a frame overhead, and the vacuum nozzles shoved into the split bodies of the salmon, run up and down. Blood and guts sucking up the tube.

Jane turns her head away, but can't help it, picturing herself, her legs in stirrups, a nozzle on a black tube like that shoved up into her. *Oh God*, she thinks. *No. No, get the image out of your head, that's sick. Sick.* But she can't stand the place any more, can't stand the smell, the noise, the bright blinding steel, and she breaks into a run, skidding on the slippery floor, barges past Pat, slams out through the door, out into the air, out over the car park. She fumbles for her keys, gets in the car.

She grabs a cigarette from the packet in the glove box, lights it, winds the window down. Tries to start the car.

'Ah come on,' she says. 'Come on, you piece of shit.'

Just as Pat slams out of the door, the engine starts. Jane shoves her foot on the accelerator, screeches out of the car park, rattling over the cattle grid, leaving a puff of exhaust smoke behind her. She turns the radio on, the volume right up, to drown out her thoughts. It's loud rock music. That's good. The pounding drums and wailing guitars. She can feel her heart racing. Not good for her heart, all this stress. Imagines it sputtering, skipping, stopping.

She pulls up outside the shop. The same grey shipping container where her mum was denied cigarettes all those years ago. She drops her cigarette on the ground outside the door. The door where her mother passed the man thirty years before. She goes up to the counter. The woman glances at her, at her head, and Jane realises she still has her hairnet on. She snatches it off, and says:

'A bottle of Gordon's, please.'

Then she drives to Maggie's. Lets herself in. Nell leaps up at her, licking her face, sniffing at her shoes, the smell of the factory. Jane empties some dog biscuits into her bowl, lets her out in the garden.

Her phone vibrates in her pocket. She draws it out. WORK, the screen says. She imagines Pat at the other end of the phone, fuming. She lets it ring, the phone buzzing in her palm like an angry insect.

Then it falls silent. She shoves it back in her pocket, then gets a glass from the kitchen cupboard, pours herself a gin.

As she lifts it to her lips, she hesitates.

*The baby*, she thinks.

'There's no baby,' she mutters, and takes a gulp of it, screwing her face up at the bitterness.

*The water of the womb*, she thinks. She imagines the alcohol filtering through, into the amniotic fluid. Poison.

*It doesn't matter*, she thinks. *In a week's time it'll be gone anyway.*

Her phone vibrates again. Jane ignores it, feeling the buzz against her thigh. After a minute, it stops.

Jane looks out over the garden. Down the track to the croft, its boarded-up windows, the dirty whitewashed walls, the slipped roof tiles. Imagines her mother in there, in the candlelight as the wind raged around her. She feels sick, suddenly, of the past, of these echoes. Has a fantasy of taking a sledgehammer to the place. Hiring a bulldozer. Setting a fire, burning the croft to the ground. A fire wouldn't work, though. The place is so damp, mouldering, nothing would catch. She feels cold, and damp to her bones. Hot and dry, that's what she needs. Again, in her mind's eye, she sees Spain. Brown hills.

Nell comes back in. Jane shuts the door behind her, takes another gulp of gin. And then she catches sight of the computer in the corner of Maggie's sunroom – what she calls the sitty-oot – the cream-coloured monitor sitting on the occasional table, the tower tucked beneath. Maggie's password is written on a Post-it note, stuck to the top of the screen, along with instructions for getting onto the internet, and her sons' email addresses.

Jane goes into the sunroom, slumps in the swivel chair, switches the computer on. Listens to the ghostly whirring and bleeping of the dial-up modem.

She swallows some more gin, then types into the search bar: 'Emigrating to Spain'.

Websites load. She clicks through them, randomly, haphazardly. Looking at pictures of whitewashed houses, cypress trees, rows of sun loungers on golden sand. She skim-reads paragraphs about visas, work permits, the healthcare system. She finds a map, clicks on it. Sits back in the chair, drinks her gin, looks at the place names. Salamanca. Toledo. Jaen. She looks at the topography, the dry brown mountains, the green coast. She types in 'Beginner Spanish phrases'.

*Hola*, reads the page. *Mi nombre es . . .*

'*Hola*,' Jane says. Nell, lying at her feet, pricks up her ears. '*Mi nombre es* Jane.'

But maybe she should pick a new name. A clean slate. She mulls it over.

'*Hola. Mi nombre es . . .* Kate.' *Kate*. She thinks about it. No, too similar to Jane.

'*Mi nombre es . . .*' – she thinks of Lucy, the doctor's receptionist – 'Elizabeth.' *Too long*.

'*Mi nombre es . . .*' But she can't think of anything.

'*Hola, mi nombre es* Jane,' she says again. She looks at the map on the screen. Sighs, runs a hand down her face.

'No,' she says. '*Mi nombre es* Hannah.' The word feels awkward, wrong in her mouth, like the word 'pregnant' did, earlier. She tries it again.

'Hannah,' she says. 'Hannah Douglas.'

The clock in the sunroom ticks. The computer fan whirrs. Jane slumps in her chair, staring at the screen, swirling the gin in her glass, thinking.

Her phone starts buzzing again. She groans. Pulls it out, looks at the screen.

MIKE.

She hesitates, then answers.

'Hi,' she says.

'Jane. Are you okay?'

'Yeah.'

'The factory called me. A woman called Pat?'

'Oh.'

'Jane, she was livid. Said you weren't picking up – she got my number from one of the trawlermen.'

'What did she want?'

'Well – she said to tell you not to bother coming back in again. To the factory. Wanted me to tell you that – well, you're fired.'

There's a silence. Jane sips her gin.

'Jane?' says Mike. 'You there?'

'Yes,' says Jane.

'She can't do that, surely. She can't just call me up and tell me—'

'It doesn't matter,' says Jane. 'I don't care. I wanted to quit anyway. I can't do that job any more.'

'What? Why?'

Jane shrugs. 'I don't know. Just sick of it. Of everything.'

'Where are you now? Do you want me to come and get you? I'm out on the boat right now but I'll be back in an hour or so.'

'No. It's okay.'

'Jane, can't you tell me—'

'No! I can't! Stop *asking*, everyone keeps fucking *asking*!' Heat rises to Jane's face, a wave of fury. 'I just want everyone to leave me alone!'

She hangs up. Sits there, breathing.

Then she sits forward, clicks into the search bar and types, rapidly: 'Crowholt quarry investigation Sylvia Douglas'.

She hits enter, and the results load. Hundreds of them.

The top one is from the *Mid Devon Gazette*. The story only a few days old.

Jane hesitates, then clicks on it.

She stares at the headline, sandwiched between an advert for 'The Retirement Options You Never Knew You Had' and 'One Weird Trick for Nail Fungus!':

'Police to drain Crowholt quarry as part of historic missing person investigation.'

Jane scrolls down, her heart beating hard. There is a photograph of the quarry taken from the air. A huge dark oval in the centre of woodland, like a blank eye.

'A flooded quarry is to be drained and forensically examined . . . a bid to discover the body of missing Crowholt woman Sylvia Douglas . . . shocked the nation in 1986 . . .'

There is a photograph of Jane's mother. The same one that was stapled to lamp posts and taped up in the windows of the newsagents. Her face, startled-looking, washed out by the flash. It was taken on her wedding day, her head above its ruffled collar, as if being presented on a platter. She looks so young, Jane thinks. So impossibly young. She reads on:

'. . . her prosthetic arm was discovered in the quarry by a dog-walker . . . her husband Bobby . . . daughter Hannah, seven years old at the time . . . horrific tragedy . . .'

Jane knows that if she keeps scrolling she is going to see a photograph of Charlie. She drains her glass, sets it down on the table, braces herself, but still, when it comes, it's like a punch to the stomach.

His face. His smiling face. He is sitting on their nan's sofa in a pair of red dungarees.

The same photo they showed on the news. Over and over. Jane hasn't seen it in years.

She sits there, looking at him. As if waiting for him to talk.


*23 October 1979*

Bobby came home yesterday.

I spent all weekend cleaning. Scrubbing and mopping and dusting, changing the sheets on the bed. I did a food shop too, stocked the cupboards. I gave myself a scrub as well. Put mousse and Elnett in my hair and mascara on my eyelashes for the first time in days.

He was happy to see me, though he looked exhausted. Had the shadow of a beard and smelt like saltwater and engine oil. He picked Hannah up, covered her face in kisses, hugged me tightly. I clung to him. Solid, safe Bobby. Here to save me.

How have you been? he said.

Oh, fine, I said.

After we went to bed I woke up to him shaking me, gently.

What's the matter? I said.

Nothing. Just want to show you something. Come on, this way. Come with me.

He led me into the kitchen and said, put your wellies on. We're just nipping out for a sec. And he handed me a coat, and I put it on, and he led me out of the door into the cold night air.

Look, he said, pointing up. Look at that.

I stared. In the sky, rippling across the blackness, were veils of light – a phosphorescent green, but higher up, a deep fuchsia pink, a teal blue. Huge, magnificent curtains of it, ruffling, shifting, stretching up into the darkness. Bathing the whole landscape in this eerie glow.

Bobby put his arm around my shoulders. The Mirrie Dancers, he said. Aren't they beautiful?

Yeah, I said.

It's the best I've ever seen it. Woke me up, the light.

We stood there, together, watching, and it was stunning, but after a bit I was starting to get pretty cold, and wanted to get back in bed, and I turned to say as much to Bobby – and then I noticed he was wiping tears from his eyes.

What's wrong? I said.

He sniffed and said nothing, my darling. Nothing's wrong,

everything is perfect – I'm just overwhelmed, I'm just – it's so beautiful, and I'm so lucky, to see this, with you by my side, and our daughter sleeping in the bed just there . . . I'm just so happy, he said. I'm so happy. Are you happy, too?

Yes, I said. Yes, love. Hoping he wouldn't hear the lie in my voice.

And I leaned my head on his shoulder, and he kissed my hair, held me tight. And we watched the aurora for another ten minutes or so, until my teeth started chattering, and then we went back inside, and then Bobby made love to me, with the green glow bathing us through the skylight. I looked at the patch of night sky and felt very distant. Cold and far away.

### 28 October 1979

I'm sitting here in bed, fuming. Bobby's downstairs. He's got mates round. Five of them. Desmond, Keith, Tony, Harry and Roger. They're so bloody loud, and the floorboards are so thin, I can hear every word they're saying. They're singing now, let me transcribe some of the lyrics, they're practically Shakespearean:

> *The first mate's name was Carter.*
> *By God he was a farter.*
> *He could fart anything*
> *from 'God Save the King'*
> *To Beethoven's Moonlight Sonata . . .*

Hilarious.

Incomers, said Bobby. Just like us. Three Scotsmen, a Welshman, a Brummie. A couple I knew in the RAF, the others are from the rig. They're a bit rough around the edges, but they're good blokes.

Well, I sat with them for an hour or so. Smiled politely. Refilled the bowls of Twiglets and cheese balls. Served them beers, emptied the ashtrays. Listened to them reminiscing about their drunken exploits. Then it was Hannah's bedtime, so I took her up. Stood in the lamplit nursery, rocking her crib as she drifted off.

I could hear their conversation through the floorboards. And I heard them talking about Laura. Maggie's daughter.

Do you remember that lassie who worked in the canteen? one of them said. The one with the . . .

There was a pause, then laughter.

How could I forget, said another one. When she leaned over to dish up the food, Christ, you got an eyeful. Highlight of my day.

What was her name again?

I heard Bobby saying shh, lads—

Laura, said another.

Aye, that was it. Frigid as you like, though.

She wasn't frigid, Kev, you're just ugly.

Wasn't frigid when it came to Bobby. Eh, Bobby?

I heard Bobby mutter something, and there were some whispers, stifled laughter again. A silence. A throat clearing. Before one of them started up again – so, did you see the game on Wednesday . . .

Well, I just sat there rocking Hannah's crib, my skin prickling, my heart thudding.

I kept playing their words over again. Laura. Frigid. Eh, Bobby?

Hannah fell asleep but I stayed there, my hand on her crib, feeling sick. Thinking of the strange atmosphere with Maggie. Her testing me, seeing if I knew anything. Pointing at Laura's photo. Gauging my reaction. I've been played for a fool.

The men are leaving. I can hear the door opening downstairs, drunken goodbyes. One of them just complimented me. You've got a cracking wife there, Bobby.

Hands off, Desmond.

Bet she goes like a rabbit.

Pigs.

Now I'm waiting for Bobby to come upstairs. I feel hot all over. Do I ask him? What do I say?

Well, Bobby's explained. Apparently Laura used to have a thing for him. A crush, he said, a silly schoolgirl thing. She kissed him once. He didn't kiss her back. Told her no way, he wasn't interested. That was it. That was all.

He stood there, arms out, beer on his breath. Swaying a bit. Saying I promise you, sweetheart. I swear. It was nothing. It was long before I met you.

And I sat there in bed with my arms crossed. And I interrogated him.

Why didn't you tell me? (Because I didn't think it mattered.) Does Maggie know? (Yes. She doesn't like me because I upset her daughter.) Are you sure it was only a kiss? (Yes, she was drunk, it was at a party, it was only once.) You don't have feelings for her? (No, my darling, you're the only woman I've ever had feelings for, you're the light of my life, blah blah blah.)

Eventually I sighed and flung back the covers and said switch the light off and get in.

He's asleep next to me now. Snoring fit to wake the dead. And I'm lying here, stomach churning. Wondering.

*29 October 1979*

I saw Maggie this morning. When I was hanging out the washing. We chatted for a bit, talking about the weather. About Hannah.

I asked how Laura was doing at university. And then I took a deep breath and said:

Speaking of Laura . . . Maggie, I know about – her and Bobby.

She looked at me. You do? she said.

Yes. Bobby told me, last night.

I see.

I thought there was something I didn't know. There seemed to be a bit of – awkwardness, I said. I'm sorry I didn't know before.

No, said Maggie, and she seemed flustered, fiddling with her headscarf. No, it's – well, it's been difficult for her, but she'll be okay. I'm sure she'll meet a lovely lad at university who'll take her mind off Bobby.

Yes, I said. I'm sure.

Well, she said. I'm off to the shop. Need anything?

I shook my head. And watched her go, her dog trotting ahead.

When I came back inside, Bobby was drinking a coffee, looking the worse for wear, wincing as Hannah shrieked on her playmat. I have to admit I shut the door just a bit too loudly. Watched him flinch.

Just spoke to Maggie, I said.

Oh?

Yeah. I told her I knew about you and Laura.

Bobby looked at me. His face pale.

You did?

Yeah. Thought it might clear the air a bit. She seemed relieved, actually. Now it's all out in the open.

I set about clearing away the remnants of the party. Emptying the ashtrays, dropping the tins and bottles into the bin bag. Clanking loudly. Bobby took two aspirin and looked pained. Good.

*2 November 1979*

The weather has been odd, this week. Can't make up its mind. We've had sunshine, then driving rain, then drizzle, then more sunshine, then a sudden hailstorm. Been a nightmare for getting the washing dry. But I'm getting better at spotting the weather coming. It's easy when you know where to look. You can see the clouds moving in; the distant smudge of rain falling. It's funny; I still can't get used to the space of the island. The fact there's nothing to break up the view. On a clear day you can see for miles and miles. Oh, you think, there's Maggie's car, driving five miles away, the sun glinting off the windscreen as it winds over the hills. I wonder where she's off to. Or oh look, there's the bus coming, it'll be here in ten minutes.

I feel exposed, sometimes. Nowhere to hide. Like an ant under a magnifying glass. I never thought I'd miss trees as much as I do. Never noticed them much at home, but now I'd give anything to sit under a tree. A big ancient oak tree, looking up at the green canopy. Here there's nothing but grass.

We haven't been up to much, this past week. Had fish and chips on Wednesday – they do things called 'chippy nights' in the village hall once a month, where the people who run the fish and chip shop on the mainland come up and use the kitchen. It was nice not cooking for once.

Bobby's been working on fixing a leak around one of the windows.

Hannah is fine.

I still don't feel like she's mine. Still don't feel connected to her.

The other day I tried to make her laugh. Or at least smile. If I could do that, I thought, maybe things would change, maybe I'd start feeling warmer towards her. Start to feel the way a mother should.

So at first I tried to pick her up, bounce her on my lap. But she just sort of went floppy, like you see the strikers doing on the news when the policemen handcuff them. Passive resistance. So I gave up on that.

I tried pulling faces at her. Bent over her, crossing my eyes, blowing raspberries. She just looked at me like I was an idiot.

So then I sighed and gave up, and as I stood up I whacked my head on the shelf. Hard.

Fuck! I said.

And guess what. She laughed.

She hates me, you know. I'm sure of it.

I'm dreading it being just us two again. Bobby going back to the rig. Just me and Hannah. And the long dark nights.


*5 November 1979*

Bobby's gone again. It was bad saying goodbye but I was determined not to cry this time. I stopped in for a cup of tea with Maggie on my way back from the helipad. She gave me some booties she'd knitted for Hannah. Her two boys were there, reading comics on the living-room floor. They reminded me so much of George, their gangly limbs and scuffed knees. I felt like crying.

I looked at the photos of Laura around the room and tried not to think of Bobby and her. Kissing. I looked at her blonde hair. Did he run his hands through it? Her green eyes, did she cry when he rebuffed her? Her skin, did he stroke it tenderly?


*8 November 1979*

I went to the doctor's today. Asked him to up my dosage of Valium. He prescribed it, no problem. And some sleeping pills, too, for good measure, because I told him I sometimes have trouble drifting off. We'll see if they work.

9 *November 1979*

Slept like a log last night. This morning I had another pill with my morning tea. The new dosage is great. Felt that warm feeling spread over me again. I found myself humming while I brushed my teeth. Not any tune in particular, just a sort of made-up tune. Caught myself in the mirror and smiled at myself. I can't remember the last time I hummed.

10 *November 1979*

Another nice day. Sunny and cold. Took another pill, then went to the phone box, called Mum and Dad. Dropped in to Maggie's on the way back. Had a nice chat. So tired now, going to have a nap.

18 *November 1979*

Bobby's home tomorrow. I've got to tidy up before he gets back, the house is a bit of a pigsty. I've been too shattered the past few days to keep on top of the housework. The bins and ashtrays are overflowing and the floor needs a hoover and there's damp laundry still in the machine. Each evening I mean to catch up on it but I end up nodding off in front of the telly instead.

*20 December 1979*

Haven't written in here for ages. Don't really have the attention span to be honest, feel like my brain's gone on holiday a bit. That's the only thing with these new tablets, they do make me a bit scatterbrained. The sleeping pills seem to leave me half asleep in the daytimes, too. Keep making cups of tea and leaving them. Getting halfway up the stairs and forgetting what I was going up for. Burning food in the oven. The other day I was in the middle of ironing one of my blouses and I drifted off into a sort of daydream, and it was only the smell of the fabric singeing that snapped me out of it. I'd burnt a big patch on the front. Bobby thinks it's funny. Dolly Daydream, he calls me. Asks me, what are you thinking about, when you get that faraway look in your eyes? I think he thinks it's something romantic. But I'm just sort of zoning out. Like if you could see inside my head it would just be a big INTERMISSION screen with gentle music playing over the top.

But it's worth it. God it's worth it.

I've been busy getting ready for Christmas. I've put up our decorations, spent a small fortune on them, from a catalogue. Bobby picked them up from Lerwick the other day. We've got a plastic tree (the largest tree I've seen since we came to Shetland), baubles – some red, some gold, some covered in tiny styrofoam balls to look like snow – a packet of lametta, and an angel with a china face and a white satin dress to go on top.

In the corners of the room I've pinned up these foil things. I don't know how to describe them. They came flat-packed but then open out into these mesh garlands. They're nice; they bob a bit when the fire's lit, I guess from the warm air currents. Hannah loves them, stares at them for hours. I've put our cards up, too, on the windowsills. A few from Devon, a few from Scotland, signed by people from Bobby's family who I've never met, never even heard of. Martin and Kathy, Edith and John, Uncle Wilf and all the family. In the new year, he's said, we'll go to Aberdeen and see them all.

I've got Bobby a Swiss army knife for Christmas, and a bottle of Brut. I've got Hannah a set of stacking rings, and a little cardigan with velvet trim. I know what Bobby's got me because I saw it in the wardrobe the other day – a nightie, peach satin with lace on the top and bottom, and a bottle of Badedas bubble bath. I'm getting Maggie a bottle of advocaat and some chocolate Brazils.

I'm a bit nervous about cooking Christmas dinner though. Bobby's going to do all the peeling and chopping, all I'll have to do is stick it in the oven, really.

We're having duck. I've never cooked duck.

### 25 December 1979

I ruined it. I ruined the whole day.

It was going well. We unwrapped the presents in the morning. Bobby was pleased, I acted surprised, Hannah was more interested in the wrapping paper than her toys, but at least she was happy.

We cooked dinner, and ate it, and the meat was overdone and the potatoes weren't crispy enough and the bread sauce was full of lumps, but Bobby said it was a triumph, and anyway, the Christmas pudding was perfect because I bought it from the shop. After dinner we walked to the phone box, and stood in a queue, and I rang Mum and Dad, and Bobby called his dad in Aberdeen and spent most of the time saying aye, Dad. I know. Yes. I know. Yes, you just said that, and rolling his eyes at me, twirling his finger next to his temple. Crazy.

Then we went for a drive to the beach, and had a stroll there, and then came back and played card games for a bit, and then I gave Hannah her bath and put her to bed, and I snuck two tablets when Bobby wasn't looking – it was Christmas, after all – and then we sat in front of the TV and drank – Tia Maria for me, Tennent's for Bobby – and ate dates and nuts.

Well, the Tia Maria slipped down so smoothly that I didn't notice, at first, how drunk it was getting me. It was only when I was watching Legs & Co twirling around on *Top of the Pops* that I realised I wasn't feeling well. It was making me feel dizzy, watching them spinning about like that, and my vision was going blurry, strange. I tried to get up from the sofa, but my body suddenly wouldn't do what I told it to. I remember thinking: oh shit. And then I passed out.

I woke up with a gasp. Bobby was kneeling over me, shaking me by the shoulders, and I was wet all over. He was about to splash more water on me when I yelled stop, no!

Thank Christ, he said, and he pulled me up to him, held me. I realised I was on the kitchen floor. My mouth tasted sour, and I saw that I'd been sick all down myself.

And Bobby said what the hell happened? My God, I thought you were dying.

And I told him, I was half awake and not thinking straight, and I said, oh, it's probably the pills. I took an extra one – and I shouldn't have drunk with them—

What? What pills?

The Valium, I said.

Valium?

Can I have some water, please? I said.

I drank some water, then stripped off my clothes, had a bath, brushed my teeth, got into bed. I was exhausted, just wanted to sleep, but Bobby came and sat on the end of the bed.

Valium? he said. Sylvia, what are you taking those for?

I was finding it difficult, with Hannah, that's all. After she was born. I didn't know about mixing them with drink, I said.

There was a silence.

I don't like it, he said.

Like what?

I don't like the idea of you being – doped up.

I'm not doped up, I said. I'm still myself, I'm just calmer. The tablets, they just . . . I tried to think of the phrase the doctor had used. Smooth the rough edges, I said.

Bobby looked at me. He looked so sad.

We're newlyweds, he said. We've got a gorgeous wee baby. We live on this beautiful island, in a cottage by the sea. It's paradise. What rough edges?

I looked at him. He really did believe it was paradise, I could see it in his face.

You said you were happy, he said.

And I tried to squash down the words which rose in my chest: I'm not happy, I'm miserable, I feel trapped, I want to go home – and instead I held my arms out to him and said I am happy, my love, of course I am. They're just for a little while, just until winter ends, and I'll be careful, I won't drink with them again.

Bobby said okay. Just for a while. But when spring comes, I want you to stop taking them.

Okay, I said. I will, darling.

I've always been a good liar.


*1 January 1980*


A new decade.

Maggie had a New Year's Eve party last night. Bobby wasn't keen, he wanted us to go round to one of his mates' instead, but I said oh come on Bobby, please.

All right, he said. As long as you don't drink. I don't want a repeat of Christmas.

Well, it was a good night, even if I couldn't drink. Hannah

slept upstairs and we kept popping up to check on her. She slept pretty soundly. And I met Laura.

She was fine. A laugh, in fact. And the pills squashed down any flickers of jealousy. We had a good chat. She likes the Bee Gees too. We talked about John Travolta's new film, *Grease*. I haven't seen it yet. She said oh you must, the music's brilliant.

Bobby hung back while I chatted to her. I think he's still awkward about me knowing him and Laura kissed once. But I wasn't worried. Laura barely looked at him the whole evening. Water under the bridge.

### 30 March 1980

Haven't written in here for ages. Sort of lost the urge. All the angst and anguish and whatever, the pills have sorted that.

Spring has come to Unst. Finally. Wildflowers everywhere. The air smells like honey. The seabirds are here, in huge flocks, and the noise is incredible. Bobby and I went for a walk with Hannah today and we found a hooded crow's nest. Right on the edge of a cliff, nestled amongst the sea pink, four pale blue eggs. Nothing between them and the fifty-foot drop but some strands of dry kelp and tufts of wool. It gave me a bit of vertigo seeing them there. We watched from a distance, waiting to see if the mother came back, but she didn't.

Things feel like they've eased off a bit. It's nice to hang the washing out on the line again instead of over the fireplace; it always makes the croft feel damp and sweaty when we do that. And I can get outdoors with the pram without wind or rain battering me, can get out for some fresh air and focus my eyes on somewhere further than the distance from the armchair to the TV. The long, dark nights are getting shorter, too.

Hannah's coming along well. Her eyes have changed, all their blue-black has gone, and now they're brown. She's got long eyelashes, like Bobby. She's quite cute now. Very quiet. I still feel like I'm taking care of someone else's baby, but at least it's a well-behaved baby.

Bobby still wants me to come off the pills. I've lied to him. Said I have, but really, each morning while I make breakfast, I take one. I've put them where he won't find them, up in the highest bit of the kitchen cupboards, behind the icing sugar and glacé cherries. Unless he suddenly discovers an interest in baking, they should be safe there.

I'm nearly at the end of this diary now. Don't think I'll buy a new one.

What to write on the last page?

The End, I suppose.

THE END.

Jane takes a gulp of gin and tonic. Looks out of the steamed-up window. It is warm in the hotel bar. They are playing soft jazz music – Norah Jones, something like that. She looks down at her hand, sees a salmon scale shining on her skin. She turns her wrist, watches the scale catch the light. She realises she's quite drunk.

There is a blast of cold air as the bar door opens. In comes Dawn. She spots Jane, holds a hand up in greeting. Jane nods back.

Dawn comes over, unbuttoning her coat.

'Jane – I have to tell you, I can't stay long. Magnus has football practice. Are you all right? Your answerphone message said you had something urgent—'

'Sit down,' says Jane.

Dawn pulls the chair out, sits, stares at Jane. Then she says:

'Pat said you'd been fired.'

Jane shrugs. 'Apparently.'

Dawn goes to speak, but Jane holds up a hand and says:

'Dawn – I want to sell your brother the croft.'

Dawn looks at her. 'Eh?'

'I want to sell your brother the croft,' says Jane, her voice slurring slightly. 'You're right. It's stupid of me to hold on to it.'

Dawn blinks. 'But I thought – but you – really?' she says.

'Yes. For the price he offered me before. As soon as possible.'

'Well. That's – that's great,' says Dawn, a smile spreading across her face. 'That's great news. That's brilliant. But what will you do? You moving in with your man, are you?'

'No,' says Jane, looking into her glass. 'I don't know. I'm thinking of emigrating.'

'Emigrating? Where to?'

'I don't know. Somewhere hot and sunny. Dry. Spain, maybe.'

'Oh, lovely. Spain's nice. My cousins live there. Torrevieja. Great expat community . . .' She trails off, then sits forward in her chair. 'So – have you got a solicitor yet? No worries if not, but if you need someone, I've got the details for a chap in Lerwick, really good guy, low fees but very thorough, shall I give you his number?'

'Sure,' says Jane.

'Great. Well! Let me get a drink first – we'll have a toast,' says Dawn. 'To new beginnings! By the way,' she says, breaking off, 'you've got fish guts in your hair.'

Jane wipes her head with a paper napkin as Dawn goes up to the bar.

*New beginnings*, she thinks. She doesn't feel new. She feels ancient. In her pocket the diary rests against her leg, with its old ink, the past heavy as a stone. She takes another gulp of gin. Feels the alcohol warm her blood.

Another blast of cold air. Someone is pushing the door open. Someone with a rust-coloured beard.

Jane watches Mike as he looks for her. A second passes before their eyes meet. He smiles. A sad smile. Her heart beats hard in her chest.

'Hello,' he says, coming over.

'Hi.'

'What are you doing here?'

Jane gestures to the bar. 'Meeting Dawn,' she says.

'Oh.'

'You?'

'Well. You know. Just going for a pint.'

'I see. Not looking for me?'

'Of course not.'

She smiles.

'Cigarette?' he says.

Outside, the cold air hits her like water. She tries to light her fag but the wind keeps blowing the flame out. Mike digs in his pocket, draws out his Zippo, lights it, the flame steady.

She inhales deeply. Breathes out. Leans against the wall, her head swimming.

Mike lights his own cigarette.

'Thought you were giving up?' she says.

'I've given up giving up. For now, anyway.'

They stand in silence for a minute, smoking. Then, Jane says: 'I'm selling Dawn's brother the croft.'

Mike looks at her.

'Why?' he says, softly.

'Because,' she says, shrugging.

'Because?'

'Because it's my croft and my life and I'll do what I want with it. Mine,' she says, jabbing a thumb at her chest. 'Not yours, not my mother's. Not Maggie's. Not this—' She almost says 'this baby's', but stops herself. She leans against the wall.

'I just,' she says, waving a hand. 'I need to run away somewhere, get away.'

'From me?' says Mike. 'If you want some space, just say, Jane. I understand.'

'No,' says Jane. 'No, I want you, I do, I want to be with you. I want – but now, things have happened, are happening, and it's like, the universe is warning me . . .'

He looks at her, his forgotten cigarette glowing at his side. 'Is there someone else?'

She laughs. And then thinks, yes, there is. There are a few some-ones. Someone rotting at the bottom of a quarry. Someone forming inside me right now. And me. I'm someone else. I'm not Jane. I'm Hannah.

'Don't be stupid,' she says.

'You're talking in this – this cryptic way, Jane. I don't understand what you're telling me.'

'I'm no good. I'm not good for you. For anyone. I need to . . .' Jane pauses.

'Need to what?'

'I need to puke.'

Mike rubs her back as Jane throws up. When she is done she sniffs, wipes her mouth with her sleeve, looks up at him. He is so good, she thinks, so kind. And she leans against him. Buries her head in his shoulder. He holds her tightly.

'Jane?'

A woman's voice. Dawn, stepping out of the door.

'Oh,' she says, seeing Mike. 'Hi. Jane and I – we were just talking business.'

'She's in no fit state to be talking business,' says Mike. 'Come on,' he says to Jane. 'I'll walk you home.'

Mike is mending a lobster pot in Maggie's front garden. Jane, fuzzy with hangover, stands watching him for a minute, his rough hands working dextrously, livid with the cold, knotting the twine. He notices her. Sits back.

'Hello you,' he says.

She steps over to him. Wordlessly hands him some sheets of paper, folded.

'What's this?' he says.

'An explanation.'

He looks at her. She gestures to the paper.

Mike unfolds it. Rests it on top of the lobster pot. The newspaper article she was reading yesterday on Maggie's computer. She printed it this morning.

'"Police to drain Crowholt quarry as part of historic missing person investigation . . ."' He glances at Jane. She looks away, out over the sea. He carries on reading, in silence, his lips moving slightly. Jane hears him turn the page. She watches the sunlight and shadows on the ocean. A seal bobs near the shore, its slick grey head turning this way and that. To be that seal, she thinks. Weightless and shining in the vast ocean. Not a care in the world.

She hears Mike fold the papers up again. She turns to him. Wonders what he will say. *Why didn't you tell me?* perhaps. Or *Don't worry, it'll be all right.* Both of which would make her want to scream.

But instead he takes her hand and squeezes. And looks at her, with his kind eyes, his eyes bracketed by laughter lines, carved into his skin even when he's not laughing, his eyes that make her feel safe.

'Let's go away for a couple of nights,' he says. 'Somewhere nice. Just you and me.'


Jane, in the soft lighting of their hotel room, examines herself in the full-length mirror. Turns sideways. She's wearing a black dress, one she hasn't worn in years, not since a funeral for one of her old colleagues. She looks at her belly. There's a slight bump, just a small one. She grimaces. It's still small enough to pass off as bloat, perhaps.

Mike comes out of the en-suite. Jane jumps, sucks in her stomach.

He is wearing a shirt and tie. Golden cufflinks gleam at his wrists. His hair is neatly combed. He smiles at her.

'You scrub up well,' she says.

'You too. You look lovely.'

'Makes a difference from overalls and a hairnet, I guess,' she says, turning away. 'What time's the meal?'

Mike checks his watch. 'Forty minutes. We've got plenty of time.'

'Okay. I need to put some slap on, and I'll be ready.'

'You don't need any slap.'

'I do,' says Jane, pulling a face in the mirror. 'I look like the living dead. I need some blush on at least, I'll frighten the other diners.'

Mike looks at her. 'Come here,' he says.

He embraces her. Holds her. Strokes her hair. She shuts her eyes. Breathes him in, his smell. Usually he smells of a mixture of damp wool, salt, engine oil, Swarfega, but now he's wearing some sort of aftershave, warm and woody.

'I love you,' he says.

'I love you too,' she mutters. He takes her hand in his. Kisses it. Then recoils.

'Oh,' he says.

'What?'

'What happened to your nails?'

Jane looks at them. The cuticles look ragged, bloody. Cherries in the Snow. She'd tried to wipe it off with some acetone she'd found in Maggie's bathroom, but there are still traces of it next to the skin. It looks as though she has a horrible disease.

'It's just nail polish,' she says.

Mike laughs. 'Oh, right,' he says, and kisses her hand.

Before long, that hand is opening and closing on the clean starched sheets, her other hand down, knuckle-deep in Mike's hair, as he presses his mouth against her. Her eyelids flutter.

She gazes, distantly, at the hotel room, clean and neat and anonymous, the polished wood, the kettle, the complimentary chocolate on the pillow next to her. She could be anyone here, anyone. None of her past is here. She can let herself be in the present, for once; the present, where Mike is pushing his fingers inside of her, the fingers she watched knotting the ropes of the lobster pot, and as she raises and lowers her hips, moving in sync with him, as she flings one arm out, braces her hand against the cool white wall, she feels a tidal wave of pleasure, building, building, until it breaks, tumbling over her, drenching, leaving her gasping.

They lie together, on the bed. They kiss. She can taste herself on him, her underwater taste. She shuts her eyes.

Then he looks at his watch, sighs. 'We'd better leave in a minute,' he says, then lets his arm flop. 'I kind of fancy just staying in and ordering a pizza.'

'Me too,' says Jane. 'Would be a waste of your nice suit, though.'

'Aye.'

'I won't be a minute,' Jane says, hauling herself up off the bed. 'Just need to freshen up a bit.'

She smooths down her dress, grabs her hairbrush and deodorant from her suitcase, and opens the door to the en-suite.

She pulls the light switch, and as the room is illuminated she stops, her blood running cold.

The bathtub is full of water. Still, clear water. The chain trailing down, the black plug at the bottom, the stopped mouth.

She freezes. Stares at it, the water, clear as glass, still as death, and cold, she can tell it is cold, ice cold.

Jane stands there, feeling as if all the blood has drained out of her. And then she backs out of the room.

'Jane?' Mike says.

'Mike—'

'What? What's wrong?'

'Why would you do that? Why the fuck would you do that to me?'

'Jane, what are you—'

'The bath! The . . .'

And she looks back at the bathtub. It is empty. Dry as a bone. The plug chain hooked neatly over the tap.

She stares at it. Mike comes over to her, looks at where she's looking. She wipes a hand down her face.

'Jane.'

'I thought I saw – just a second ago, it was . . .'

'It was what?'

'Full of – of water,' she says. 'I could have sworn . . .'

Mike goes over, examines the bath. Runs his hand round the inside, around the dry tub. Shakes his head. Jane leans against the wall, runs a trembling hand through her hair.

'I'm going mad,' she mutters. 'I'm going insane.'

'You're not. Come on,' he says. 'Let's go out. Let's go.'


'Mushroom risotto, please,' Jane says to the waitress. Mike looks at her.

'They've got lobster,' he says. 'Or steak. You don't have to have risotto.'

'I just can't stomach the thought of meat at the moment,' Jane says, unfolding her napkin. 'Or seafood. Makes me feel ill.'

'Oh,' says Mike. 'In that case, I'll have the same.'

'No, you have what you like.'

'No, it's okay. I don't want to put you off your meal.'

'Anything to drink?' says the waitress.

'Uh – white wine for me, please,' says Jane. 'The Chardonnay.'

'I'll have the same.'

The waitress smiles, takes their menus.

'Thanks,' says Jane.

'Why do you think you've gone off meat?'

Jane fiddles with her napkin, shrugs.

He reaches for her hand across the table. 'Feeling better now?' he asks.

'Yeah,' says Jane. 'Yeah. Must have been – a trick of the light, or something.'

He squeezes her hand gently.

'It's okay. It's just the stress of everything. You're exhausted. A few good nights' sleep and you'll be all right.'

Jane nods.

At the table next to theirs a waitress deposits a steaming plate of mussels. Mike looks at it.

'Yours?' says Jane.

'Of course,' says Mike.

He glances at the couple as they eat, cracking open the shells. They make noises of satisfaction. Mike smiles.

Jane can smell the mussels as strongly as if they're right under her nose. Between them, on the table, a candle spills its wax, and she can smell that, too. She can smell the lilies in the vase by the restaurant door, twenty feet away, their sweet, slightly faecal scent. Her body, she supposes, sniffing out contaminants, poisons. Trying to keep the thing growing inside her safe.

Their risottos arrive, two huge plates of brown and grey gruel. Mike looks sceptical.

'Excuse me,' Jane says to the waiter. 'Have you got any vinegar?'

'Balsamic?'

'Any will do.'

Jane shakes the bottle over her risotto. Tastes it. Adds more. Mike chews his food, watches her. She catches his eye.

'Just really like sour things at the moment,' she mutters.

They have desert. Mike has chocolate fudge brownie. Jane has a lime sorbet, the tartness flooding her mouth.

'Don't like the wine?' says Mike, looking at Jane's nearly-full glass.

Jane shrugs. She's had a couple of sips, but each one she's had to force down, her throat closing at the taste of alcohol.

'Been drinking too much recently,' she says. 'Need to cut down on the booze.'

They finish their meal and step outside. It's a still evening, the air cold and crisp. The sun is setting across the harbour, the sky apricot, lavender, a deep inky blue. Jane breathes the air. Mike offers her a cigarette. She pauses, then shakes her head. 'Don't fancy it,' she says.

'Huh,' he says, lighting one for himself.

'What?'

'Not smoking, not drinking . . . weird cravings, wanting to smother everything in vinegar,' he says. 'Is there something I should know?'

Jane looks at him. Her stomach lurches. 'What? No, God no. Just – like I said, just been overdoing things a bit with the fags and booze. And they aren't *cravings*, I just—'

'I was only joking,' says Mike, laughing. 'Don't worry.'

'Right. Yeah. I mean, no. That would be ridiculous,' Jane says. 'It would have to be an immaculate conception. We've always been so careful.'

'You know, you'd be a great mum.'

Jane looks at him. 'What?'

Mike shrugs. 'I dunno. I just think you'd be a natural.'

She stares at him. 'No I wouldn't.'

'Sure you would. You're patient, and calm. Hardworking. And you can laugh about stuff – that's important, you know. You can laugh at yourself.'

Jane feels like she hasn't laughed in months. She shakes her head.

'No. No. Mike, I – I could never . . .' She falls silent.

'Why not?'

'You know why.'

Mike looks at her.

'You *know*,' she repeats.

'You're not her, Jane,' he says. 'Your life isn't going to be like hers.'

Jane looks out over the water. And then she says: 'You know what I heard on the radio once?'

'What?'

'They did an experiment. These scientists. With mice. They took some mice, and they put them in a cage, and they wired up the floor of the cage to an electric current.'

Mike frowns.

'And then,' says Jane, 'they puffed the scent of cherries into the cage. Each time they did that, they'd switch the current on. They'd zap the mice. So they repeated this, over and over. Cherries, zap. Cherries, zap. And so the mice came to associate the scent of cherries with pain.'

Mike looks at her.

'And then, they *bred* the mice. And, get this: their babies – even though they had never been zapped themselves – still got jumpy and frightened when they smelt cherries. Somehow, that fear had been passed down to them. In their DNA.'

Mike thinks for a moment.

'But,' he says, 'surely they'd just picked it up from their parents. They'd seen their parents getting jumpy when they smelt cherries, and—'

'No,' says Jane, with a hollow laugh. 'No. See, they'd thought of that, the scientists, and they'd had the babies raised by *other* mice. Ones that hadn't been zapped. And then the *babies'* babies were *still* frightened of the smell of cherries. The fear, the trauma of it – somehow it had got written down in their cells. That pain, that fear. Passed on through generations.'

She stops. Looks at Mike. He has a line between his eyebrows. He says, 'Jane, that doesn't mean—'

'What if it does?' says Jane. 'What if her – her badness has been passed down to me? In my cells, my bones. What if the same thing happens? What if – what if giving birth is like that scent of cherries? It triggers something, some – some madness . . . I'm already hallucinating, Mike, already losing my grip, just like she did.'

Mike stops, takes Jane's shoulders in his hands.

'Jane – forget about cherries, and mice, and whatever. Your mother – she was ill, you told me she had a bad birth with you, and then she moved far away from everyone, and then with everything that happened . . . it just – it was circumstances, it's not destiny. It's not fate.'

'It *feels* like fate,' says Jane, feeling panic rising in her chest. 'It *feels* like destiny. Everything – everything is happening at once, like it's planned. Like bad omens. Like I'm being punished.'

'For what?'

'For everything! For, for loving you, for letting myself think I could have a new life, a normal life. For what I've done, and who I am. And that's why I thought I could – I thought I should run away, but then I thought, it'll just catch up to me again, I can't escape it, this badness, it'll haunt me for the rest of my life.'

She is breathing fast, shallow. She swallows, clutches her coat tightly around her.

'Please can we go back to the hotel,' she says. 'Please can we not talk about it any more. Please.'

They get back to the room. Jane unwinds her scarf, Mike takes off his coat.

'Shall I find us something to watch on the telly?'

Jane nods. As he turns away, she says: 'I'm sorry I ruined it.'

'What?'

*Everything*, she thinks. 'The evening.'

'You haven't. Come on. Sit down.'

They watch a film. An action movie, a thriller. Mike falls asleep halfway through, and Jane looks at him, the flickering light from the TV playing across his face.

He would make a good father, she thinks. He is strong, and calm, and dependable. He can knot ropes and sail boats and start fires. He has thick skin. Broad shoulders. She can picture him, pushing a toddler on a swing. Crab fishing off the pier with a daughter. Teaching a son how to put on a tie, his first day of big school . . .

She shakes her head. Sentimental shite, she thinks. But she feels something. A tug. A pull. An ache.

Maybe he's right, thinks Jane. Maybe everything will be fine. Maybe mice and cherries have nothing to do with it. Maybe she doesn't have to have the abortion—

*No*, she thinks. *No*.

*But what if*—

*No. Stop it. It's not going to happen.*

*But*—

*Read the diary.*

She grabs her bag. Opens it, pulls out the two diaries. Looks at the two final words of the purple one, written in tall block capitals, in black biro.

THE END.

Jane stares at it. Wants to leave it there, their family, with the spring sunshine, the honey-scented heather. The hope of happiness just beginning to form.

But she can't.

She looks at the second diary. It is hardback. Granite grey. Embossed letters. DIARY 1985. Like a tombstone.

She doesn't want to open it. Doesn't want to pick the scab, rip open the wound. But she has to. If she doesn't, she'll never understand. If she doesn't, she might convince herself to have this baby.

She opens the diary. Starts to read.

I'm starting a diary again. To distract me, to focus my mind. Writing, it's like a way of talking to myself. Keeping focused. Keeping sane. Hopefully.

I'm coming off my pills, see. Shook them down the toilet last night. Watched them dissolve, fizzing yellow at the bottom of the bowl, before Bobby flushed them.

What happened is this. Two weeks ago, when Bobby was off on the rig, Hannah got into my bottle of tablets. Don't ask me how. The cap's meant to be childproof. Somehow she worked out how to open it and she swallowed a few before I noticed.

We went to hospital. She had her stomach pumped. They kept her in overnight for monitoring. She was fine. Completely fine.

Anyway, I didn't want Bobby to know. He hates me being on the pills anyway, always nagging me to come off them. I knew he'd go spare if he found out. I swore Hannah to secrecy. But some blabbermouth – a relative of one of the paramedics – bumped into him when he was at the shop, asked him how his daughter was, and the whole story came out.

I should know that you can't keep any bloody secrets on Unst. Gossip and rumours are the lifeblood of the place.

Anyway, Bobby came home absolutely fuming. Said I should have told him. He had a right to know. She could have died, for God's sake. How the hell did it happen? Where was I? Why wasn't I watching her?

Well I got defensive. Said are you saying I'm neglectful? It was two seconds, my back was turned for two seconds. She managed to open it, God knows how, the cap's meant to be childproof.

He said: I hate those pills of yours.

Oh, don't blame the pills, I said. It could have been anything! The paraffin for the lamp. The bleach in the bathroom. Your aspirin for your bloody hangovers. Anything.

Aye, he said, but she probably went for those ones because they're the ones she sees you popping all hours of the day. Like a bloody junkie. She was just copying her mother. I want you off those tablets, Sylvia. You don't need them.

I do, I said. I do need them. Bobby, you don't know how much I need them.

Please, he said. Please. Try. I hate seeing what they do to you. I swear to God, they numb you, they turn you into a zombie. You just sit in front of the TV like a vegetable. Can you at least try? he said. For me? Just try to come off them?

So I said fine. Okay. I'll try.

So here I am. Trying.

After we flushed them this morning he gave me a hug. It'll be horrible for a day or two, he said. Just like it was when I quit smoking. But I managed, Sylv. If I can do that, you can do this.

Thing is, I'm not sure I can. Whenever I'm late for a pill I feel bad. Awful. It's like – the pills, they make things bearable. The fact I don't really love my daughter. The long, dark nights in winter. The fact that the croft is cold and damp, and the power keeps cutting out, and the shopkeeper still looks sourly at me, and I'm hundreds of miles from my family, and my whole bloody existence seems to consist of housework, or going to bloody Women's Guild meetings or fiddle concerts or church services – it's all okay, when I take my tablets. But when I don't take them, when I miss a dose, it's as if a black tide is slowly rising, lapping around my ankles, then my knees, then my hips, each day getting higher. This awful panic, this dread, threatening to drown me. The pills are like my life jacket, keeping my head just above the water. Although it seems to be a life jacket that's deflating over time – I've had to up the dose a fair bit; I guess I'm building up a tolerance.

Bobby – I think he takes it personally, you know, that his wife needs tablets to be happy. He wouldn't understand. I've never met anyone less gloomy. He's always looking on the bright side. He just has this sort of confidence to him, that everything is manageable, that the world has a place for him, that everything will work out in the end.

I've tried to feel that way. God knows, I've tried so hard to be happy, to be really happy, not just to feel the numb contentment of the Valium. I try not to complain. I try to count my blessings, to see things through Bobby's eyes, to take pleasure in the things he takes pleasure in – the seabirds, the ocean, the solitude – but it's such a bloody effort. And sometimes I lie awake at night, Bobby snoring next to me and the sheep bleating from their winter hollows in the hillsides, and I examine it, my true self, my true feelings, the loneliness, the wrongness, even though it hurts, like pressing a bruise, and I just lie there in the darkness and cry and cry until I fall asleep.

How on earth am I going to manage without my pills?

Jane, in the hotel room, can still taste the bitterness on her tongue. The bottle hadn't been hard to open. The tablets had looked a bit like the Haliborange vitamins she took with her Rice Krispies every morning. They were yellow. She guessed they'd taste like banana. They didn't. They tasted bitter, bad.

She can only remember impressions, after that. Her mother's white, scared face. A light in her eyes, a stethoscope on her chest. Her cheeks hot, tingling. She remembers drinking a gritty black liquid, gagging and crying as a tube was shoved up her nose, down her throat. She remembers the pattern on the hospital curtains. Farm animals. She remembers sticky tabs on her body, a hospital gown, and her mother, asleep in the chair next to the bed. A smell came from her: sour sweat, the smell of panic.

She remembers, clearest of all, stopping in at the shop on the way home from hospital to buy an angel cake as a treat, for being such a good girl and promising to keep it a secret. She remembers sitting at the kitchen table, eating a huge slice of it with a cup of milky tea, but the memory of the gritty black liquid and the wormy sensation of the tube down her throat had made her vomit it all up again.

Jane swallows, and reads on.

*17 June 1985*

Twenty-four hours without a tablet.

I felt all right, at first. I went to bed early. Bobby gave me a kiss and said he was proud of me. That we'd do it together. He's home for the next seven days, says he'll look after Hannah, do all the cooking and stuff, help me get over the hump.

It can't be that bad, he says. They're only tiny little tablets. A lot of it is probably the placebo effect, just all in my head, he reckons.

He thinks he's being helpful.

I'm feeling a bit strange now, though. A bit on edge. Black tide rising.

*18 June 1985*

Forty-eight hours with no pills. Have the chills. Am under the duvet in my dressing gown but can't get warm. And feel sick. I keep staring at the crack in the ceiling plaster. It irritates me, that crack. It looks like a lightning bolt, zig-zagging over my head.

The light is getting on my nerves too. It's nearly midsummer, the Simmer Dim, and the sun won't set properly for another week or so. The orange twilight is leaking in around the edges of the curtains, annoying me. I just want darkness. I just want to sleep.

*19 June 1985*

I got it wrong, earlier. My metaphor. It isn't a tide rising, it's a tide going out. I've been floating on the surface of the ocean, ignoring all the stuff lurking underneath the water. And now the tide's gone out and I'm here. On the jagged rocks. The stinking seabed. I can't stand it. I can't take this. I can't.

*20 June 1985*

Last night was awful. I was sweating and shaking and threw up a couple of times. Bobby said it was just all the crap leaving my system, better out than in, but even so, he looked a bit worried.

And everything aches. I feel like I've been hit by a bus.

I saw Hannah peeking round the door earlier.

Daddy says you're not well, she said.

I just nodded.

She looked at me with her solemn face and her big dark eyes and said: are you going to die?

No, I said. I'll be better soon.

Oh, she said. That's good. And she looked at me, and then she did something that surprised me. She leaned forward and gave me a kiss on the forehead, the lightest of pecks, like a little bird, and then she propped a card up on my bedside table. She'd made it herself, bright red flower in felt tip on the front.

That red flower is too much. That bright solid block of colour. It's making me feel ill. That and the feeling of her kiss on my head. Two bright red bullet wounds. I'm not making sense but that's how they feel. Why does she love me? I'd hate me if I was her. I hate myself.

171

Jane remembers. She remembers filling in the flower with red felt tip, her tongue stuck out to help her concentrate. She remembers the feeling of her mother's skin against her lips, the febrile clamminess of it, the way she'd wanted to wipe her mouth afterwards but didn't. She remembers the stale air, the smell of sweat and sick.

Her mother had stayed in bed for another week, sweating in the feverish midsummer light. Her dad had tried to clean, to cook. She remembers the meals he made, overboiled porridge, undercooked oven chips, peas like pebbles. 'I'm sorry, pal,' he'd say, grimacing at whatever was on his fork. She hadn't minded. She'd liked being alone with him.

Soon enough, her mother emerged. White-faced and thin. She'd spent most of the rest of that month in her dressing gown. Lying on the sofa chain-smoking and watching TV. Her mouth drawn down in a frown.

Hannah spent as much time as she could outside. Her skin grew hot and tight with sunburn, her hair got matted for lack of brushing. Her nails were grimy and her knees were grazed. One day she found a dead sheep by the loch, its eyes pecked out, and she'd looked at it for ages, watched the flies swarming around it. On another day she'd collected driftwood, and piled it on the beach, and set fire to it, and scorched her hair on one side, so her dad had evened it out with the kitchen scissors at home and she'd looked like a boy. Another day she climbed the ruins of a croft with Timothy, a classmate, and he'd pulled his pants down and showed her his thing, tiny and pink like a shelled prawn. He'd wanted Hannah to show him hers but she'd run away instead. He's the postman for the island, now. Each time Jane sees the Royal Mail van, she thinks of him there, standing on top of the crumbling stone wall with his pants down.

*15 July 1985*

Finally feeling a bit better. I cooked for the first time in ages tonight. Didn't eat much of it though, can't stomach it. I looked in the mirror and was quite shocked at how much weight I've lost. Valium makes me stuff my face. I'd noticed the fat but hadn't really minded it. I guess it's nice to be a bit slimmer. Even my arm fits again. I haven't worn it for years, not been bothered about my appearance, and then I got too fat and it started to chafe. But I've got it on now. Feels like an old friend.

Hannah seems to have grown up in the past month. Got a suntan. Brown as a berry. Makes her look healthier, you know. She's a bit pallid, usually. Happiest indoors. Reading under the coffee table. She's always been the quiet type. I thought she might be slow, at first. She didn't speak for ages and ages. Still doesn't, much. Other kids her age yammer away nineteen to the dozen, but she just sort of watches. Observes. With her big dark eyes. But when she does talk, she'll come out with words I don't even know the meanings of, and I'll think where on earth has she picked that up from? Probably books. She's always got her nose stuck in one. Anything she can get her hands on. She's asked for an encyclopaedia for Christmas.

Still waters run deep, Bobby says. You mark my words, he says, one day that girl will win the Nobel Prize. She's a genius.

Before I had a baby, I think I had this idea that children were kind of — yours to shape. You know? You bring them up a certain way and that's how they turn out. And you know them better than anyone. You made them, after all, they're your flesh and blood. But Hannah's always felt so separate. I still can't quite shake the feeling she's a changeling.

*1 August 1985*

Went for a walk today, for the first time since I came off the pills. I felt quite fragile. Kind of unbalanced. Like I'd just stepped off a ship onto dry land and I'm wobbly. Don't know whether I'm going to laugh or cry half the time. But it was okay. I'm okay.

*8 September 1985*

Bobby and I made love today. Hannah was out, at Sunday school, and Bobby gave my bum a pat as I was bent over taking my shoes off in the porch. Well, I felt a fire down below. I wanted him, suddenly wanted him, just like I did when we first met. I turned and gave him a snog and before I knew it he was tearing off my blouse and I was fumbling with his belt and he shoved me up against the window, my bum on the sill, and we did it right then and there, in the porch, in amongst the wellie boots and the bags of peat and the tomato plants, the condensation on the glass wet against my back. God it felt good, I wanted him deeper, harder, I was like an animal. At one point I shoved him to the floor, right onto the welcome mat, and rode him, so hard it felt almost violent, like I was devouring him, like a vampire. And I came, a roaring great orgasm. I didn't think I still could, you know. Thought that fire had been totally extinguished by the Valium. But there must have been an ember there, still glowing. Just needed a bit of oxygen.

Well, afterwards we just lay there, on the porch floor, and burst into laughter. Thinking about what if Maggie had looked out of her window. What if the postman had come.

We didn't use protection. I've always been so careful, since Hannah. Always. The thought of having another baby terrifies me. I know Bobby would like one, but I've always said no.

Over my dead body. But I'm sure it'll be fine. I'm sure nothing will come of it.

Jane skips through the next few months. Desperate to know. Desperate to see the first glimpse of him. Hungry for every scrap of his life. Her mother is all over the place. Raw, exposed, without the Valium:

*20 September 1985*

The rough edges catch and snag me. I can't stop crying. Great waves of anger. I smashed a plate against the wall today. But then there is beauty, too. God, the weather was beautiful today. Air like champagne. I watched Hannah reading her book the other evening and felt this tug deep in my chest. Pride, maybe. Perhaps just love.

> I said to her: Hannah.
> What? she said, her dark eyes wary.
> And I said: I'm sorry.
> For what?
> For everything, I said. And then I felt sad, so sad. And I said to her: can I have a cuddle?
> She put down her book and came over to me. And I pulled her onto my lap and hugged her. She was a bit stiff at first. All bones. When did she get so tall, so skinny? Like a bundle of sticks. But then she softened a bit. Rested her head on my shoulder. Six years. Oh, Hannah. I wish I could start you all over again. I wish I could do right by you.
> She sat there and let me sniffle on her for a while. Then she said quietly, Mum, I need a wee, so I let her go.

Jane stares at the page. Reads it, over and over, feeling something aching deep in her chest. Then turns the page.

A blank page, but for two words, written small: *I'm pregnant.*

### 13 October 1985

For a few days I was terrified. Absolutely terrified. Didn't tell Bobby, didn't even want to admit it to myself. I took five tests. I thought about it. Agonised over it. What to do, what to do. And then one morning I woke up and thought, well, you wished for a clean start. And here it is.

I'm going to do right by this baby. It might be too late for Hannah but I've learned from my mistakes. I'm going to be a decent mother. A loving one. I have a chance to do it right. To redeem myself.

I told Bobby. He was over the moon but he was cautious. Said, are you sure? Will you be okay?

I said, I think I will be. But I told him, I'm not going back on the pills again. Not after all the agony of coming off them. So the slightest hint I'm struggling, he's quitting the rig and we're moving to Devon. And I'm not risking a premature birth this time. I'm not lugging sacks of peat around or doing any DIY or whatnot this winter. I'm going to be as horizontal as possible. Hannah and you will have to take on some more chores. I have to rest.

Deal, he said.

### 15 October 1985

Told Hannah about the baby today. In typical Hannah fashion she didn't react one way or the other. Just said okay and looked thoughtful for the rest of the evening.

Jane remembers her mother, reclining in the easy chair, her feet in their tartan slippers up on the pouffe, swelling up throughout the winter, the dome of her stomach growing above her supine body like an egg in an eggcup. She was nervous any time her mother stood upright, thinking the baby would fall straight out.

The whole house smelt of oranges. Her mum craved them, and Bobby bought them by the bagful, fat and round like suns. He'd place the bag with a plate, knife and tea towel next to the recliner chair, and Sylvia would slice the oranges into quarters and tear into them with her teeth, a towel under her chin to catch the drops. The citric smell was Christmassy. Exciting.

Jane flicks through the pages.

*16 January 1985*

Bobby thinks it's a waste of money buying all new baby things. But I can't stand to use any of Hannah's stuff. I had a look in the loft at it — there isn't much left, we gave away most of it — there's her Moses basket, her swaddling blanket, her mobile, but looking at it all made me feel awful, like this great weight had settled on my chest. All the memories came flooding back.

And he said we can borrow things from other people on the island. But I don't want anything second-hand. I want everything new. New and clean. Untainted.

*28 January 1986*

They did a scan of my belly. It was so strange, seeing the baby on the screen. Just an outline of it, ghostly white, its spine like a string of beads, its little heart pulsing. They asked me if I wanted to know the sex. I said no. I want to keep it a surprise. And more than that, I don't want to start loading it up with meanings, with baggage already. I want it fresh and new.

*2 May 1986*

One month until my due date.

*2 June 1986*

Due date today.

*5 June 1986*

Bobby's meant to go back to the rig tomorrow. I said no bloody way, I'm not giving birth alone on the living-room floor again. You're staying right here. He's pulled some strings, sweet-talked his boss. He has one more week off.

*6 June 1986*

Still no baby. What if they have to cut me open?

Maggie brought round a tub of curry puffs. Said the spice in them will get things moving. I ate four of them in a row. Christ they were hot, made my eyes water. But nothing.

The farmer up the road told Bobby I should take castor oil. A spoonful in the morning and evening. Greases everything up, helps the baby slip on out. I tried some of that, too, but all it did was make me feel sick.

Bobby said, you know what they say: lovemaking helps speed things along. Well, we tried it. We haven't done it in a long time,

I've been so huge and uncomfortable. But we did it, gently, side by side on the bed. It was quite nice. But still nothing.

*7 June 1986*

Charles Robert Douglas. Born at 6.32 a.m. 8lb 8oz.
   He's perfect.

Sellotaped into the diary is his hospital bracelet. Pale blue with a white popper. 'Charles Douglas' written on the tag. A bloodstain, brown and faint, on the plastic. Jane touches it gently. It is so small.
   Charles.
   Charlie.
   She remembers him coming home from hospital, her mother, exhausted, milk-stained, beaming, carrying him into the porch in a wicker Moses basket. She'd crouched down and peered at his sleeping face as her dad said, mock-seriously: 'You're a big sister now, Hannah. That's a big responsibility. You've got to set a good example. Look out for him.'
   'I will,' she'd said.

Jane, sitting on the wooden bench, slides her feet into the paper slippers. She puts her socks and boots into the plastic tray, along with the rest of her clothes. Stands up. Breathes deeply. Adjusts the thin gown she's been given.
   A knock. A voice. 'You ready, love?'
   'Yes.'
   The nurse pokes her head around the door. Smiles. 'Good. Just leave your clothes there, sweetheart, they'll be waiting for you when you come round. Follow me.'
   Jane follows the nurse through the door, into a white room.

A man and woman in scrubs are busy preparing instruments. Jane feels her heart beating hard.

The nurse puts a hand on Jane's back, gestures to the two doctors. 'This is Mr Alvi,' she says, 'the surgeon, and Dr Carter, the anaesthetist.' They look up at her briefly, smile over their surgical masks. Jane nods back.

'Now then,' says the nurse. 'When you're ready, you just pop yourself up on this bed – that's it, there you go. Slide yourself down a little bit, love, just wiggle your bottom a bit lower. Now, legs up – I'll just put them in these supports, here.'

Jane does as she's told. With her legs in the air, she looks up at the ceiling. White polystyrene tiles. On a radio she can hear a faint tune, a cheerful bossa nova rhythm.

'Now then, my love. When you're ready, I'll tuck your gown up. Okay?'

Jane nods. The nurse neatly tucks her gown around her waist, leaving her exposed. Her bare skin shivers in the sterile air.

Dr Carter comes over, smiling.

'I'm just going to put a needle in the back of your hand,' she says. 'You'll feel a sharp scratch. Then when you're ready, I'll administer the sedative. I'll count you down from ten. Ready?'

Jane nods, gulps. Looks away. Dr Carter takes one hand. The nurse takes the other. She pats it. 'Good girl,' she says. 'You're doing really well.'

There is a silence. Then:

'Ah,' says Dr Carter. 'There seems to be a slight problem.'

Jane looks at Dr Carter.

'What's wrong?' she asks.

'Well, I'm having trouble, here – finding a vein . . .'

Jane looks down at her hand. It is smooth, shiny, beige. A plastic prosthesis.

Jane stares at it, numb with horror.

'Ah,' says the nurse. 'That's no good.'

'No,' says Dr Carter. 'No good at all. Well,' she says cheerfully, 'we'll just crack on without the sedative. No time to waste.'

'No,' says Jane.

'Mr Alvi?' calls Dr Carter. 'Would you start the operation, please?'

Jane looks over to Mr Alvi, whose surgical scrubs and cap have changed to a set of orange overalls and a blue hairnet. Unsmiling, he hits a huge red button on the wall with the flat of his hand. The bed drops from beneath her, and Jane screams as she hurtles down a metal chute, landing heavily on a pile of packing ice. A pair of hands grab her, shove her across a cold steel surface – she sees a face looking down at her, her own face, as a gleaming blade plunges towards her neck—

'Jane? Jane?'

Jane gasps. Hands holding her, grabbing her. She tears at them—

'Jane, it's me! It's me,' says Mike. 'You're dreaming, Jane. It's okay.'

She blinks. She's in the hotel room, the lamp lit, the television on, muted.

She breathes. Buries her head in Mike's chest. He holds her, strokes her hair.

Jane watches through the windscreen as the prow of the ferry lowers. She yawns, rubs her eyes.

'Sorry you didn't get much sleep,' says Mike, turning the ignition. 'I was hoping a break would give you some rest. Do you think it was the parmesan in that risotto? Cheese always gives me weird dreams.'

'Maybe,' says Jane.

As they drive off the ferry, her phone rings. An unknown number.

'Hello?' she says.

'Hi. Jane?'

'Yeah.'

'It's Pete. Pete Duggan, Dawn's brother?'

'Oh. Hi.'

'I was just calling to ask if I could take a look at the croft today. I'm up on the island visiting Dawn. Thought I'd take the opportunity.'

'Um,' says Jane. 'Sure. From the outside, you mean? I don't know what sort of a state it's in, internally . . .'

'Well, if I can get inside, I'd like a look. If you've got a key.'

'Aye. Okay. Sure.' She hesitates. 'I thought – you were planning on demolishing the place?'

'Well, it depends how much I can salvage. If the basic structure's sound, that'll save me a bit of money. I can extend from that. How would two o'clock be?'

Jane swallows. 'Okay,' she says. 'Yeah. Two's fine.'

'Great. See you then.'

'Bye.'

Jane hangs up. Mike glances at her.

'Dawn's brother. Wants to see the croft. Today.'

'I gathered.'

Jane brings her hand to her mouth, nibbles at a nail.

'Want me to be there?'

She shakes her head. 'No. It's okay. Thanks.'

They drive for a while. Near the turning for Uyeasound, a man shepherds a flock of sheep over the road. Mike slows, stops, the engine idling. They watch the sheep trot, bleating, over the tarmac, their yellowish wool splotched with pink spray paint, hauling themselves up onto a grassy bank.

'So – you still sure you want to sell the croft?' says Mike.

'Yup,' says Jane, not looking at him.

'Will you go inside with them? Today?'

'Nope.'

'Why not?'

Jane shrugs. 'Don't want to. Not interested. It's just a rotten old croft. Nothing to see.'

The last sheep lollops over the road. The man nods at them, closes a gate. Mike drives on.

Jane watches out of Maggie's window. Checks the clock on the mantelpiece.

'Come on,' she says. 'Before I change my mind.'

Then Nell pricks her ears up, starts barking. Jane, through the net curtains, sees a green car turn down the lane.

'Shush, Nell,' says Jane, putting a hand on her head. 'It's okay.'

She steps out into the weak sunshine, waits, her hand in her pocket gripping a set of keys, as the car pulls up, stops. Dawn and a man get out.

'Thanks for doing this at such short notice, Jane,' says the man. 'Much appreciated.'

'No problem,' says Jane. 'You must be Pete?' *Be calm*, she thinks. *Businesslike.*

'Aye,' says the man. He sticks out his hand and Jane shakes it.

They follow Jane up the path to the croft.

'So how long's the place been abandoned for?' asks Pete.

'Well,' says Jane, 'it was last – inhabited, I guess, in 1986. After that, Maggie – my neighbour – took care of the place for a decade or so. Patched up the roof, fixed smashed windows, got rid of birds' nests, you know. My nan wired her money for maintenance, repairs. But since I've been back, and took over . . .' Jane looks at the croft. 'Well, I haven't really touched it for thirteen years. Haven't been inside. Anyway,' she says. 'Here are the keys.'

She hands them to Pete. He looks at his sister, then at Jane.

'You're not coming in with us?'

'I'd rather not,' says Jane.

'Fair enough.'

Jane stands, hugging herself, as the pair walk up to the door. Pete looks at the building, walks around it, peering at the guttering, pressing the window frames with his thumbs, toeing the grass which laps at the walls. Then, jingling the keys in his hand, he goes to the front door.

He puts the key in the lock, turns it, pushes. Pushes again. The door doesn't budge.

'Stuck,' he says. He shoves it, hard, once, twice, three times, the wood swollen with damp.

'Ah come on,' he says.

'Here,' says Dawn, and she goes up, joins her brother in pushing against it, but it stays stuck fast.

'Jane,' says Dawn. 'Could you give us a hand?'

Jane looks at them. Then at the croft. She opens her mouth, closes it. Then goes over.

'Here,' she says, holding out her hand for the key. She puts it in the lock. Turns. Then barges the door with her shoulder, throwing her whole weight against it, once – again – and on the third time it judders open, squealing on its hinges, and Jane stumbles into the porch. She blinks.

Inside, the croft is silent, like a held breath. It smells of dust, of rot, of something animalic. Mice, maybe. Their droppings. The plaster on the ceiling bulges with water, paint has crumbled in scabby patches from the walls. She looks around the porch. Realises she is standing on the welcome mat, now black with mildew, that her mother and father made love on all those years ago – where Charlie was conceived.

Dawn clears her throat behind her. Jane stands back, lets them come in, walk past her. They stare. Dawn wrinkles her nose at the smell. Jane stands, frozen in place, as the pair move through the glazed door into the house. Dawn moves left, Pete right.

Jane hears Pete mutter something; Dawn exclaim. 'Look at this,' she says. 'It's like a time capsule.'

Jane swallows. Hesitates. She turns to leave – to step back out into the fresh air – but finds herself moving forward, into the croft, turning left into the living room.

It is all there. Sofa. Coffee table. Armchair. Welsh dresser. Television. All coated in a layer of dust, fallen plaster, a green creeping algae. The wallpaper – she remembers it, her dad put it up himself, the pattern of powder-blue flowers – hangs in peeling strips.

Jane puts a hand on the doorframe to steady herself. She feels a strange sense of vertigo, seeing everything from adult height, as if she has suddenly grown three feet. She stares at the room. The coffee table, which she used to lie underneath, the tablecloth draped over the top, pretending she was in a tent in the jungle – she scratched her name on the underside once, her mum never found out – the television; she remembers the exact feeling of the oblong power button under her index finger, the static fuzz which clung to the screen when it switched off; the Welsh dresser which held the cutlery and crockery; each evening she'd set the table, she remembers the feeling of the cork placemats in her hand, the sliding of the cutlery drawer, which always got stuck halfway . . . the sensory impressions ping against her skin, like bubbles in a simmering pan.

Dawn grimaces. 'Creepy,' she says.

'Look at this,' calls Pete from the kitchen, opening the cupboards. 'There's still tins of stuff in here – look. Marmite, Angostura bitters, baby formula . . .'

Jane turns. Sees the tin of SMA in Pete's hand, the smiling baby on the front. She remembers the malty smell of it, adding the scoop of powder to hot water, testing the temperature on her elbow. She remembers cradling Charlie on her lap, offering him the rubber teat, the way his blue eyes looked at her—

'Put that back,' she says, but her voice comes out quiet, hoarse. Pete doesn't hear.

Jane looks on helplessly as Dawn and her brother stare up the narrow stairs.

'I wouldn't,' says Dawn. 'I bet those floorboards are rotten through.'

'They look sturdy enough,' says Pete. 'I'll be careful.'

Dawn shrugs. 'It's your funeral.'

Pete starts up the stairs, gingerly, gripping the banister.

Jane, her heart beating hard in her chest, doesn't want him going up there. Poking around the bedrooms – Charlie's bedroom, his nursery, with his white slatted crib, the wallpaper with its pattern of toy trains, his teddy bears—

'Stop!' she says.

Pete turns.

'I'm sorry,' says Jane. 'But no, I – I don't think it's safe. Those floorboards – like you said. Rotten, maybe. It's too dangerous.'

'I want to see the roof,' says Pete. 'See what state it's in.'

'Please. No.'

Pete glances at Dawn, raises his eyebrows, shrugs, and climbs back down. He brushes his hands free of the dust which was coating the banister.

'I'm sorry,' says Jane. 'The surveyor can go up there if he wants, but . . .'

'Nae bother,' says Pete. 'Come on, Dawn, we'd best be going.'

Jane locks the door behind them with trembling fingers.

'Well, it's about what I expected,' says Pete. 'A lot of junk to clear out, though. I was hoping it'd be empty. Ah well,' he says, jangling his car keys in his hand. 'I'll be in touch once the surveyor's set a date. Hopefully we can get all the paperwork done this month. I want to get the work started as soon as spring comes.'

Jane nods. Shakes Pete's hand, Dawn's, a tight smile on her face. Watches as they get in the car and drive off. Then she turns, looks at the croft. Stands there, staring at it, the scent of the place in her nostrils. She thumbs the key in her pocket, over and over again.

In Laura's bedroom, Nell curled on the rug beside her, Jane stares at the ceiling.

*I don't want to sell the croft*, she thinks.

*You have to. What else are you going to do with it?*

*I could clean it up. Live in it.*

*Don't be stupid. It's a wreck. Go somewhere new. Somewhere different. Somewhere hot and dry. Remember?* Hola, mi nombre es—

*I need to face up to the past. Clearing out the croft – it could be a way of making peace.*

*You're deluding yourself.*

*I could raise the baby there—*

*See. See? You're turning out just like her. You want to live in the same house. Make the same mistakes. You're losing your mind already, and yet you're still thinking about having this baby.*

*I'm not losing my mind, I'm just under stress, not sleeping. And I'm not her. I'm my own person, like Mike said.*

*Read the diary. Read it.*

*I don't want to. I know what comes next, I don't need to read any more.*

*Read it.*

Jane sits up in bed. Grabs the diary. Nell looks sleepily at her, then stretches and shuts her eyes again.

Jane opens the book to Charlie's hospital bracelet. Runs her finger over it once more. Then, reluctantly, turns the page.


*9 June 1986*


I finally feel like a mother.

As soon as I held him, I loved him. I got that rush of love you hear about. I just held him and gazed at him and cried.

I love everything about him. Everything. I love his smell, like hay, like milk, like clean laundry. I even like the eggy, buttery smell of his poo. I love his blue eyes, so bright and clear. They look newly minted. He is not an old soul. Not like Hannah. He is new, brand new. All mine.

And the birth was fine. Slow, and gentle, compared to Hannah's. I had an epidural, which was bliss. I didn't even tear this time, even though he was a big baby. And when he came out he was beautiful, clean and pink and plump, fully formed. My gorgeous boy.

*10 June 1986*

Each day he opens up a little bit more. His body uncurling from its froggy newborn pose. His eyes getting more and more alert. I feel so full of love for him it actually hurts. Like an ache. Bobby says he's a bonnie wee lad. Adores him, too, but is cautious about showing it too much, says he doesn't want Hannah to get jealous.

Everything's so different to last time. I didn't hold Hannah for weeks. But I'm always cuddling Charlie. He likes to sleep on my chest, his little head resting just below my collarbone, listening to my heartbeat. It's bliss.

*11 June 1986*

I feel on top of the world. I'm not even tired or anything, I feel so full of energy and life. Last night I stayed up and cleaned the kitchen while everyone slept. Gave it a thorough scrub, inside the cupboards, the fridge shelves, everywhere. Bobby woke up at about two in the morning and came and told me to get back to bed, I need my rest, but I wasn't tired. I'm just buzzing with energy.

*12 June 1986*

Sometimes I look at Charlie and I just weep at how perfect he is. How pure and beautiful. And then I feel so scared. What if something happens to him? I couldn't sleep last night for worrying about nuclear war. We watched *Threads* on telly last year and it's been in the back of my mind ever since. We should be safe up here, we're far away from everything, they'd never drop a nuclear bomb on Shetland, surely? But what if there's fallout? A gale could sweep it over to us; if they dropped a bomb on Norway, a westerly wind could bring the radiation over. We could have a nuclear winter. I don't think anyone would bomb Norway, but you never know. I asked Bobby, I shook him awake, said Bobby, do you think they'd ever drop a nuclear bomb on Norway? I said, do you think we should think about building a shelter? Maybe we should get a stockpile of tins just in case we have to stay indoors for a while, hide from fallout. He said go back to sleep, Sylvia.

I might just start buying a few more tins on our weekly shop.

*14 June 1986*

I couldn't stop crying yesterday for how cruel the world is. How frightened I am for Charlie. I wish I could swallow him down again, into my belly, keep him safe. In a way I wish he had never been born, because now he has been born, one day he has to die. I created his death by creating his life. Isn't that awful? I love him more than anything.

I see death everywhere. It's the height of summer but I can only think of how it will turn to winter again. I look at the lambs in the fields and I start to cry because I think of them in the slaughterhouse. The Lamb of God. Sacrificial lamb. Last night I dreamt Charlie was the second coming of Jesus. He was bathed in a heavenly golden light, and there was music in the air, and I wept for how beautiful it was.

*16 June 1986*

Bobby took me to the doctor's today and I am back on the tablets.

*17 June 1986*

I am feeling better now.

Jane swallows, then flicks through the next few pages. There are some pressed flowers, labelled neatly: 'Kidney Vetch', 'Frog Orchid', 'Moss Campion', 'Self-Heal'. A few scribbled notes, shopping lists. A drawing, of a house and a family, stuck in, labelled 'Hannah, aged 7'.

And then, a lock of hair.

A wispy C-shaped curl, sellotaped in. The tape is browned and brittle, but the hair is still as bright as ever, pale and gleaming like spider's silk. Jane's breath catches in her throat. She reaches out and touches it, her eyes filling, and then lifts the diary, presses it to her lips, hugs it to her chest. As she does so, something falls from the diary onto her lap. A piece of paper.

She looks at it.

A wedding invitation.

*You are cordially invited to the wedding of Neville Shergold and Katherine Pratt. 19. 07. 86, St John's Church, Baltasound. Reception: Baltasound Hall.*

Doves, horseshoes and hearts border the page. Jane feels a weight in her stomach like a ball of ice.

*20 July 1986*

Nev and Kath's wedding yesterday. Nice day for it. Everyone was there, Maggie's two boys, back from university, and Laura. She was playing fiddle in the wedding band. She's had her hair permed – it looks lovely.

Nice service in the church. Kath looked gorgeous.

Reception at the hall. I was shattered though, the pills were making me drowsy, and Charlie was getting tired, so I took him home early. I was in bed by the time Bobby and Hannah got back.

Bobby had a terrible hangover today. Been pale and quiet. Too much punch, I think.

*21 July 1986*

Bobby still not himself today. Hannah's not feeling well either. I wonder if it was the hog roast. Can't be all that hygienic, having meat sitting outdoors in the sun like that. I'm glad I didn't eat any.

At least Charlie's his usual happy self. Still smiling. My ray of sunshine.

*22 July 1986*

This afternoon I took Charlie to the doctor's for his check-up, and came home to a big bunch of flowers, freesias and roses, in a vase on the kitchen table. What's this in aid of? I said to Bobby. He said, just hadn't bought you flowers in a while, that's all. It's a massive bunch, must have cost a pretty penny. Smells gorgeous.

Hannah's still a bit off. Spent all day playing with her sea glass collection, arranging it in patterns on the carpet. Hours and hours she spent doing that. Frowning with concentration. Funny girl.

Jane remembers. She remembers that afternoon. She felt so full of the secret, choked with it, stretched out with it, like her skin might burst.

In a book, once, she'd read about Buddhist monks making mandalas, gently blowing coloured sand through thin golden pipes, making patterns to help clear their minds. That's what she wanted to do. To clear her mind. So she made mandalas, with the sea glass.

It worked, for a bit. She went to bed that night without saying the secret, although it nagged at her all night and stopped her from sleeping.

The next morning her dad left early, to help a friend on his farm. Her mother settled on the sofa to feed Charlie, and Hannah ate cornflakes with sugar on and watched *ThunderCats*.

She remembers looking at her mother feeding Charlie, in her quilted nightgown, her feet propped on the pouffe. She watched her mother look down at the baby, stroke his hair with a fingertip, smile at him. Say some words only he could hear.

Was she jealous? Was that why she said it? She doesn't remember feeling jealous.

Maybe she said it just to see what would happen. The impact. Like seeing a perfect sheet of ice, and throwing a rock at it.

So she said it. Through a mouthful of cornflakes, into the room, she said the secret. And then glanced up at her mother's blank face, and instantly wished she could take it back.

The wedding reception. The slanting evening sunlight striking the baby bath full of bottled beer and ice. The roasted pig on the spit, its flesh orange and shiny, its eyes seared shut.

Music spilling from the hall. Yazoo, ZZ Top, Duran Duran, coloured lights swinging across the dancefloor. Lukewarm cherry

Panda Pops fizzing on her tongue as she watched couples dancing. Her dad, Laura, laughing together, Laura's permed hair framing her face in a golden cloud.

The groom, his trouser cuffs slick with fat after he'd stepped in the tray of grease from the hog roast, was shrieking around the dancefloor, tailed by two yapping sheepdogs who were snapping at his ankles. Everyone howling with laughter as he hopped around the hall, the bride bent double in fits of giggles.

Jane remembers looking for her dad to see if he was laughing. She couldn't see him. Or Laura.

Out of the hall. Down a corridor, dark in the dusk. An open door on her left – the kitchen, empty of people, the half-eaten wedding cake sitting on the counter. Layers of sponge and cream under the fizzing fluorescent light.

She stepped into the kitchen. Nobody there. Hannah reached out, scooped up some crumbs, popped them in her mouth. Snapped off an icing flower, nibbled it. Then she saw a butter knife on the counter, and cut a slice.

Whispered voices. Someone coming. Hannah crouched down, in the corner, behind the bin, her heart pounding, cake clutched in her hand.

Someone crying. A woman.

'Shh. Shh. It's okay. Have some water.' Her dad's voice.

The sound of a tap running, a glass filling.

A silence.

'I'd better go,' he said. 'Hannah will be looking for me—'

'No. Please.' Laura's voice, thick with tears and booze. 'Please stay with me. Just for a bit.'

'I've got to get back to Sylvia.'

'Please. Can't you spare me five minutes?'

Silence. Hannah felt the icing melting between her fingers. She could see the reflection of their legs in the oven door: her father's black trousers, Laura's shiny tights.

'Laura . . .'

'Each time I come back to the island I pray you've moved away. It's like a knife in the heart. Coming home. Seeing you.'

'Don't drag all this up again. Please. It's been years. Please – oh, please don't cry again. Don't.'

Hannah's legs were beginning to ache from squatting. She was barely breathing. Molten buttercream dripped from her hand onto the floor. She listened to the sound of Laura sniffing.

'It's like torture,' she said. 'I keep reading our letters—'

'Laura. Please.'

'It's painful. It's painful, Bobby. It hurts. After all this time it still hurts.'

Hannah peered out. Just in time to see Laura stumble forward, kiss her dad on the mouth.

And then Hannah saw something moving.

She looked down.

A fat black spider was scuttling towards her foot.

Hannah screamed. Laura screamed. Hannah exploded out from behind the bin, rubbish tipping onto the floor, scrambled over the counter, ran out, back through the kitchen, down the corridor.

'Hannah!' called her dad, but she carried on running, slamming into the hall with its music and lights, shoving past the dancers, bursting out through the fire exit, into the cool evening air, into the silence.

She stopped. Leaned against the pebble-dashed wall, next to some bins. The two collie dogs were licking the tray of hog fat clean.

She realised she was still clutching a crushed slice of wedding cake. She threw it to the dogs, wiped her hand on her dress.

The fire exit opened.

'Hannah,' said her dad, breathless.

She looked at him, his face pale.

'What were you doing,' he said, 'hiding in the kitchen?'

She didn't answer. Just walked over to the sheepdogs. Crouched next to one of them, started petting it.

After a second, her dad came and squatted down next to her. Through the windows of the hall came the strains of 'Lady in Red'.

'Hannah,' he said. 'Are you angry at me?'

Hannah nodded.

'Why?'

'Because you kissed Laura,' she said. 'And because – you shouldn't kiss Laura. You should only kiss Mum.'

Her dad sighed, sniffed. Looked up at the sky and whispered, 'Fuck.'

Hannah felt strange. It was the same feeling she'd had when she'd fallen off the monkey bars in the park and landed on her arm. She'd known something was wrong, badly wrong, but it didn't hurt. When she'd looked down, she could see the jagged bone jutting through her skin. That was when the pain had flooded in.

She kept stroking the dog's fur as it nudged its tongue into the corners of the grease tray. The smell of pig fat was making her feel ill.

'Hannah,' said her dad. 'I don't want you to tell your mum what you saw. Or heard. Okay? Because she – because it would make her sad, and she's a bit fragile at the moment, because of the baby. I'll tell her, one day, in my own time. I'll say sorry. But not just yet. Can you promise? Can you keep it a secret?'

It was then that Hannah saw Laura peering through the window at them. Their eyes met. Laura hesitated, her green eyes wide, and then she stepped back and disappeared.

*23 July 1986*

How could he? How could he betray me like that? After I gave up so much for him – after I gave up everything to follow him

195

to this godforsaken island. I gave up my friends and my family and my home to come and live in this hovel and bear his children. I gave him all of myself and all of my trust and it was all built on a lie.

I bided my time until this evening. After Hannah and Charlie were asleep. Then I switched off the TV and looked at him and said:

I know, Bobby. Hannah told me.

He looked at me like a condemned man.

Tell me the truth, I said.

So he did.

A kiss, I thought. A drunken kiss. That, I could have forgiven. Little did I know.

I can barely write it. It makes me want to scream.

Bobby and Laura – they were engaged.

He told me, and I just sat there, feeling like a bomb had dropped on me.

He'd proposed to her a week before he came down to Devon for Martin Adams' funeral. They'd been courting for about a year.

He says he thought he loved her. But when he met me, he realised he'd made a terrible mistake. That he fell in love with me instantly. Like a bolt from the blue.

But did he write to Laura, break it off? Did he hell. He made excuses to her. Lied about why he couldn't leave Devon. Travel problems, money problems, some cock-and-bull story about Martin's will.

And then I fell pregnant. Still he didn't tell her. We married. Still he didn't tell her.

Why? I said. Why on earth did you not break it off with her?

Because, he said, Laura was in the middle of her exams, and the shock of it, of telling her he was finishing with her because he had a secret pregnant wife, that would have devastated her, and her whole future depended on those exams, so . . .

He came back to Unst. Back to work. Back to her.

The coward two-timed us. His pregnant wife and his peerie Shetland fiancée. Kept up his act until Hannah was born.

And this croft. This house. It was meant to be their marital home. He'd already bought the place before he met me. Maggie was furious when she found out. He said he had to beg her, plead with her not to say anything to me.

Well, I felt like a fool. An utter fool. This whole time. What an idiot all the islanders must have thought me. That's why they all hated me, at first. All the mutterings, the sour faces, the stares. What they must have thought of me. A naïve fool at best, a homewrecking Jezebel at worst.

That's why he roped in the vicar to give that sermon. All that stuff about welcoming me. It was to try and save his own skin.

I sat there for a moment feeling like I'd been concussed. And then I walked to the front door and opened it on the night and told him to get out.

He didn't try to argue. Just put his boots and coat on silently while I stood there, shivering in the night air. I couldn't look at him. He reached out to touch me but I shrank away from him. And then he stepped outside and I shut the door on his stupid lying face.

I've been sobbing ever since. I don't think I've got any tears left.

We're leaving this island. I can't stand it here any longer. With or without him, we're leaving.

'How is she?' asks Jane, hovering by the entrance to the ward.

'Much better,' says the nurse. 'The confusion was a side effect of her medication. She's much more lucid now we've changed her prescription. Go ahead, she'll be glad to see you.'

Jane takes a deep breath, steps into the ward. Sees Maggie in her hospital bed, her wiry hair brushed neatly back.

'Jane,' says Maggie, and smiles.

Jane sits down next to the bed, hunching forwards in her baggy fleece to disguise her swollen stomach.

'How are you feeling?' Jane asks.

'Fine,' says Maggie. 'Just fine. Bored to tears and want to get home, but otherwise okay. Stupid woman. Clambering about on chairs at my age. I should've listened to you, I know.'

Jane tries to smile. Looks at her shoes.

'Jane,' says Maggie softly. 'The investigation. Any news?'

Jane shakes her head. Then she looks at Maggie. Opens her mouth, closes it. Opens it again and says –

'Mags – why didn't you tell me they were engaged?'

'Who?'

'My dad and Laura. You never told me. All this time I thought they'd just kissed.'

Maggie looks at her, then breathes a deep sigh. She nods. 'Yes. They were.' She shifts in the bed, smooths the sheet with her hands. 'I – I never thought to tell you. Never found the right moment, I suppose. Didn't want to dredge up the past.'

'Can you tell me now? About them?'

Maggie turns her bright blue eyes on Jane, then sighs.

'Laura was besotted with your dad,' she says. 'I didn't think he was right for her. They didn't have anything in common. I thought she'd end up with a writer, or an academic. An artist. She liked poetry, books. Things like that. Not that your dad was stupid, God no. But she loved him for his looks. It was lust, I think. Not love.' She shrugs. 'But when you're young, the two are easy to confuse. He made her happy. Who was I to stand in the way? So, when he asked . . . I gave them my blessing.'

She raises her thin hands, lets them fall.

'And they were going to live in the croft? In Peerie Hamarsgarth?'

'Aye. He bought the croft from me. I was selling it anyway. She was going to stay on Shetland, not go to university, live with him. It wasn't what I wanted for her, but who was I to say no? And then his friend died, and he just . . . disappeared.' The corners of Maggie's mouth turn down. 'Poor Laura. She was a wreck. Waiting for his letters, his calls. All these excuses he made . . . I knew something was going on. She did too. But she wanted so desperately to believe him, even after he came back and was acting so strangely. And then one day, just after Laura finished her exams, he told her. He'd met a woman and got her pregnant and married her, and now there was a baby, and they were coming to live with him.' She laughs, a hollow laugh. 'I could have happily killed the man. Seeing Laura's face . . . But he begged us, pleaded with us not to say anything to his new wife. She's innocent, he said, it's me that's been the coward. Please, think of my baby daughter. She doesn't deserve to start her life like this. Punish me, not them.'

Maggie shuts her eyes briefly. Jane can see the threadlike purple veins in the thin skin of her eyelids. She opens them, turns her piercing gaze on Jane.

'If it wasn't for you, I think Laura would have been hell-bent on vengeance. She could have a ferocious temper. But you, this sweet innocent baby, born into this sordid love triangle . . . she wasn't that cruel. So, she did the decent thing. Rose above it. Held her tongue. She liked your mother, once she'd met her. Felt sorry for her, could see she was a fish out of water. And over the years we made our peace with Bobby, and put it all behind us. But she carried a flame for him all that time, even after he treated her so appallingly. And that night at Nev and Kath's wedding she got drunk, and stupid, and . . .' Maggie shrugs. 'You know the rest.'

Jane looks at Maggie, then down at her shoes.

'I should never have told Mum,' she says. 'If I'd only kept my stupid mouth shut, none of it would have happened.'

'What do you mean?'

'My dad, my mother . . . Charlie . . . It's all my fault. All my fault.'

Maggie stares at her. 'My God, Jane. None of this is your

fault. None of it. Don't you dare think that. Your mother was very unwell. I always worried about her. About you. I wanted so desperately to protect you. And when your mother took you away – God, I was bereft. I'd grown so fond of you. And I knew, I just knew something bad was going to happen. That awful summer . . .' Maggie shuts her eyes, briefly, a muscle ticking in her jaw. 'And in the years afterwards, I always wondered about you, how you were doing. And then I lost my Laura,' she says, her voice cracking slightly, 'and the boys left home . . . and I felt for years like I was all alone in the universe. Everyone gone.'

She looks at Jane. 'And then you came back. Older, and sadder, and with a new name – but you were back. And I was overjoyed. I wanted to look after you. Keep watch over you.' She smiles, a smile that's half-grimace. 'Turns out, I was the one that needed looking after.'

Jane swallows. The lump in her throat refusing to shift.

'I'm so proud of you,' says Maggie. 'After all that's happened to you. All the pain you've suffered. You're doing so well. A lovely partner, a steady job . . .'

Jane shakes her head. Maggie stops.

'Ah, I can see I'm embarrassing you now. Never been one to take praise. We'll stop, then, for now,' says Maggie. Reaches her hand across the bedspread. Jane takes it; Maggie's skin is dry and thin as tissue paper.

Jane remembers. Her dad's absence was normal. Two weeks at a time for the whole of her life, after all. But this absence had a different colour. This was a bad absence, like the dead sheep's eye socket after the crows had been at it. It was an absence full of ominous silences.

At first, her mother was pale and the corners of her mouth turned down. Then she spent a lot of time on the telephone. They had a phone in the house by then, and she sent Hannah outside while she talked on it. Hannah would sit on the drystone wall that bordered the garden, squashing the little red mites that scuttled over the stone, her fingertips speckled with blood.

She caught snatches of conversation sometimes, through the window. This whole time, Mum. I can't stand it. So ashamed. No, he's on the rig. Another ten days. I just – I want – I don't know. I don't know. I just – this stupid island. I can't bear it. I want to see you. And Dad. And George. Okay. Okay. I'll see. No, I can't. Well maybe in Lerwick. Okay. Love you too.

Her mother began talking about Devon. Do you remember Nanny and Granddad's house? How much you liked it there, when we went one summer? Do you remember the beach? We went to Sidmouth and saw the donkeys, and we had an ice cream. Do you remember? And we went on the steam train and had a cream tea?

Hannah thought she remembered. She remembered anemones in rockpools, their jelly bodies glistening red like organs. She remembered choc ices from her nan's chest freezer, sweating in their paper wrappers. She remembered her Uncle George's earring, winking in the sunlight under his bleached hair.

Hannah nodded.

Well, we might be going there. For a little holiday.

Is Dad coming?

No.

One minute her mother was singing to Charlie as she changed his nappy, the next she was looking out of the window, her face blank and bleak. One minute she was dancing to pop in her slippers in the kitchen, the next crying as she loaded the washing machine, sticking her head in the drum to hide her tears.

One evening her mother dragged down their suitcases from the loft. They were musty-smelling, fuzzy with cobwebs. Hannah watched as her mother unzipped them on her bed. Then Charlie woke up and needed a feed, so she left them there. Hannah looked at them, open like hungry mouths.

### 19 August 1986

I rang the rig this evening. Told Bobby I'm leaving. I can't do this any more. I've had enough. I can't face another winter in this place, in this damp awful croft, this croft meant for him and another woman.

I want to go home and stay somewhere warm and take my pills and be looked after for a change.

I told him, I'm going to Crowholt and I'm taking the children with me.

He begged, pleaded with me to stay. He'd been drinking, I could tell. I know it sounds awful but I was glad he was crying. I wanted him to suffer. The arrogance of it, of thinking he could pull the wool over my eyes, all these years.

No, I said. I'm leaving.

I didn't say it was forever. But I didn't tell him it wasn't.

Let him think that. Let him be frightened.

He deserves it.

### 20 August 1986

Bobby Bobby Bobby Bobby no no no no no no no no NO NO

Jane slams the diary shut. Shoves it away from her, hugs her knees to her chest. Squeezes her eyes tight.

The twentieth of August.

It was her first day back at school. Bright sunshine, a new

sky-blue pencil case, a new peg for her coat and bag. A new teacher, Miss Barnes, pretty and young in a polka-dot skirt.

'Now, class,' she said. 'We're going to write about what we did over the holidays. I want five sentences. You can illustrate them afterwards. Take a piece of paper and pass it on.'

Hannah sharpened her pencil, thought for a minute, then began to write: 'This summer I helped look after my baby brother Charlie. I went to the beach with Dad and looked at the little fish. We went to a wedding and there was a big cake.'

Hannah stopped. She pulled a strand of hair into her mouth and sucked on it, leaching its faint shampoo taste. Scratched at the sunburn on her shin.

She started to draw pictures instead, taking her time so she wouldn't have to go back to the writing, think about the cake, the kiss, her mother's pale face, her father's absence. She drew in the border, suns with long rays, ice creams, daisies. She was so absorbed in drawing that she didn't notice Mrs Reynolds, the headmistress, until she was standing next to her desk.

Hannah looked up at her. Mrs Reynolds had a pointed face and a mole on her upper lip, and Hannah was scared of her stern mouth.

But Mrs Reynolds didn't look stern today. She looked sad.

'Hannah,' she said, her voice low. 'I need you to pack up your things, and get your bag from your peg. I'm going to take you home.'

Hannah zipped up her pencil case, stood up with a scrape of the chair. The others in the class, seven of them, were looking at her, glancing up from their pages as she unhooked her satchel and cardigan from the peg by the door. Then she followed Mrs Reynolds to the staffroom, which smelt of coffee and potted plants, and Mrs Reynolds picked up her handbag. From it she drew a tin of mint imperials, and offered one to Hannah. Hannah sucked on it, the ice-cold taste. She had one years later as a teenager – a friend of her nan's had a dish of them on her sideboard. She'd had to spit it out. It had tasted of sucked hair, of sunburnt shins, of grief.

Mrs Reynolds ushered Hannah out of the school. The sun was warm, and there was a breeze which ruffled the grass. They walked out of the school gate and down the road.

It was strange, to be walking, alone with the headmistress, on a summer's day.

The soles of her sandals slapped against the pavement. She reached out and plucked grasses as she walked, stripping the seeds from them with her thumbnail. Neither of them spoke, save for the moment when they reached the sign for the Keen of Hamar, and Mrs Reynolds pointed and said, 'This way?' Hannah nodded, squinting in the sunlight, and they walked down the track, over the cattle grid, past Maggie's house.

As they came nearer to the croft, Hannah could see two cars: a blue Morris Traveller with a wooden frame – that was the doctor's car, Hannah knew – and a white car with a stripe down the side and lights on top. Police.

Hannah slowed. The police? What had she done? Her mind started to race. She'd been five minutes late for school the other day, dawdling on the beach looking for sea glass; was that it?

But then Mrs Reynolds turned to look at her. She held out a hand.

'Come on,' she said. And then, as if she'd read Hannah's mind, said, 'You're not in trouble. Don't worry.'

Hannah took her hand. It was warm, slightly sweaty. It gripped hers tightly.

As they walked up the driveway to the croft, Hannah could hear a strange noise. It sounded like a cow, lowing somewhere in the distance.

The croft door opened. Hannah looked up, expecting her mother, but in the doorway was a policeman, in a white short-sleeved shirt, black tie, black cap with a chequerboard stripe. He glanced at Hannah, nodded at Mrs Reynolds, said, 'Thanks for bringing her at such short notice, Marjolein; much appreciated.'

'It was the least I could do.'

'Would you mind sticking around for a minute? We might need you.'

'Of course.'

And then the policeman took off his cap, and looked at Hannah, his face unsmiling. Hannah shifted closer to Mrs Reynolds, who laid a hand gently, briefly, on her head.

'Hello,' he said. 'You're Hannah, aren't you?'

She nodded.

'Hello, Hannah. I'm PC Henderson. I'm a policeman. Shall we go inside?'

She nodded again.

They stepped into the porch. Mrs Reynolds wiped her feet on the welcome mat. The mooing sound, Hannah realised, was coming from inside the croft. The police officer motioned for them to go into the living room.

Her mother was there. On the sofa, next to the doctor – Dr Voss, Hannah saw him sometimes for check-ups on her heart – who was holding her hand. Her head was lolling back, and her eyes were closed, as if she was asleep. But then Hannah saw the tension in her jaw, the furrow between her eyebrows, as if she was in pain.

Her head rolled forward, and she looked at Hannah. 'Oh,' she said, and her mouth opened into a rectangle, like a postbox, and she let out a groan, that mooing sound, and a few sobs. Then her head lolled back again, and she shut her mouth slowly, and apart from a few hitching gulps in her throat, she was quiet.

'Your mother's sedated,' said Dr Voss to Hannah, in his gentlest voice. 'That means she's had some medicine to make her sleepy. But she'll be perfectly fine, don't you worry.'

Hannah looked at her mother. She wished she was back at school, with the rest of the class, colouring in her ice creams and sunrays. She glanced up at the headmistress, and Mrs Reynolds looked back at her, and Hannah was unnerved to see there were tears in her eyes.

'Hannah,' said PC Henderson, squatting down to look at her. 'I'm afraid I have to tell you something very sad.' He paused. 'Your father is dead.'

She stood there, while a silence grew in the room. She looked from one face to the other. They were all looking back at her, waiting for her to do something, expecting something, except for her mother, who was looking up at the ceiling and gulping.

Hannah didn't say anything.

'Do you understand what that means?' said PC Henderson.

Hannah nodded.

Then Dr Voss said, 'Hannah, why don't you go and get your pyjamas and a toothbrush. You'll be staying with Maggie tonight. Let your mammy get some rest.'

The rest of the day was a blur. She remembers eating dinner with Maggie and Charlie, cheese omelette and chips with tinned peaches for pudding, and after she'd brushed her teeth and got her pyjamas on, Maggie gave her some medicine. 'Phenergan,' she said. 'It'll help you sleep, sweetheart.'

Hannah can't remember much after that, except for waking in the night, howling, and Maggie being there, stroking her hair, and singing her back to sleep.

*23 August 1986*

I saw him today. His body. At the hospital in Lerwick. Maggie came with me.

PC Henderson met us at the ferry terminal. As we walked down the street, I thought, all these people, walking past, lives carrying on as normal. How can they? How can they be living their lives, going about their business, when Bobby is dead? I felt like a pebble in a stream. Life rushing around me while I stood still.

We got to the hospital. I'd last been there giving birth to Charlie. Strange thought. But we turned in the opposite direction to the maternity unit. Down a corridor, down some stairs, through some doors, to a waiting room.

It was just a normal room, like at the dentist's, with a water cooler and a potted spider plant and a stack of magazines. Such a normal room, and yet somewhere, just down the corridor, was my dead husband.

Thank God for the Valium, it was the only thing holding me together. That little bit of distance. Like I was watching everything on TV. It wasn't really happening.

Maggie and I sat and waited. I was shaking all over, like I had a chill, but I didn't feel cold. PC Henderson spoke to the nurse and then he came back and said, Sylvia. I have to tell you now, Bobby won't look as you remember him. He's had major injuries. He's covered by a sheet. The nurse has left his hand out, for you to hold, if you'd like. When you're ready, she'll show you his face. If you'd like to see the rest of his body you can, but it might be upsetting. I'm just saying this to prepare you.

Maggie squeezed my hand and I let go. Left her sitting in the waiting room. Followed PC Henderson down a corridor, through a pair of double doors, into a clean white room. The morgue. And there was a body, on a trolley, covered by a sheet. A hand dangling. A man's hand. It was grey.

A nurse there, standing with her hands behind her back.

Let me know when you feel ready, she said. And I thought, I'm dreaming, this is a dream, any moment I'll wake up, this can't be real. And I nodded, and the nurse folded the sheet down, neatly, quickly, uncovering his face.

I didn't think it was Bobby, at first. I didn't recognise him. I felt relieved, for a split second – they've got the wrong man, I thought. Bobby's still alive.

But it was him. His face was black and blue, and his head was – wasn't right, it was a strange shape, on one side. And his hair, his beautiful curly hair, was slicked straight back. Comb marks in it. But it was him.

His mouth was open, slack, and one of his eyelids was open too, just a touch. And his eyes, his beautiful blue eyes, I could see they were sort of milky white.

I just felt numb. Totally numb.

I took his hand. It was ice cold. And I said yes, it's Bobby. And I didn't cry. Not until I got back into the waiting room, and Maggie reached out to hug me, did I cry. Not really a cry. More like a scream, a scream I thought would never end.

The neighbours are keeping me afloat. Each night someone brings me dinner. A fish pie. A beef stew. Maggie cleans and irons for me. Does the washing-up and sweeps the floor and pegs out the laundry. Hannah is back at school. She wants to go.

All I have to do is take care of Charlie.

My Charlie. He doesn't know anything's wrong. He's still happy. Babbling away with his bright blue eyes. Bobby's eyes.

Bobby's boss from the rig came round today. A big man. He smelt like Bobby. Of salt and engine oil, but his hands were wrong, too skinny and pale. I miss Bobby's hands like hell. I can't stop thinking of how his dead hand felt in mine. Ice cold and heavy.

Bobby's boss talked. He told me what he knew. That Bobby had been drinking with some of the crew one evening, had been quiet and withdrawn, then disappeared. One engineer saw him heading up to the top platform. When they realised he was missing, they raised the alarm. Didn't take long to find him. Floating, face down in the water. Long dead.

Then he handed me a brown paper envelope full of cash. The lads on the rig had a whip-round, he said. It's not much but it might help.

My condolences, he said, and patted me on the shoulder, and left. And I stood there, clutching this envelope, feeling like I'd been tricked, somehow.

Doctor Voss called round today. He'd had Bobby's post-mortem report.

It said he didn't drown. He was dead before he hit the water. They think he might have fallen from a high platform and hit pipes on the way down.

His blood alcohol content was 0.18 per cent. I asked Doctor Voss if that was a lot. He said yes. At that level your behaviour changes. You might vomit, hallucinate. Black out.

My darling Bobby. My beautiful Bobby. What did you do? What have I done?

The funeral is tomorrow. Maggie's organised it. I'm dreading it.

Jane doesn't remember the funeral, because she wasn't allowed to go. She didn't even know it was happening. The mother of a boy she knew from school arrived one morning, brisk and cheerful, and took Hannah and her son on a day trip to Lerwick. They went to Woolworths for pick-and-mix, and then to the cinema to see *Return to Oz*, and then to the park, even though it was wet and freezing. When Hannah got home, her hands numb and the seat of her trousers damp from the swings, the photographs of her dad had been taken down from the windowsills, his boots had gone from the hallway, his coat from the hanger. He'd vanished.

Her mother was sitting in a black trouser suit in front of the television, her eyes vacant and glassy. She'd taken some pills, Hannah could tell. More pills than normal. She reminded Hannah of a deep-sea fish, swimming languidly below the surface of everything, down where the sunlight didn't reach.

Hannah lay in bed that night and thought about death. It confused her. That Easter, Miss Nisbet at Sunday school had told the story of Jesus' resurrection, holding up a big picture book with brightly coloured illustrations – palm leaves, three crosses on a hill, women in headscarves.

'And Mary stayed in the garden, crying,' said Miss Nisbet. 'And she saw a man who she thought was a gardener, but it was actually Jesus. He had a new, special body, and Mary didn't recognise him.' She turned the page. 'Jesus said to Mary, "Why are you crying?" and Mary said, "I'm sad because Jesus' body has been taken away. Have you taken him? Show me where you've put him." And then the gardener said Mary's name, and suddenly she realised who he really was.'

A couple of pages later, Jesus did the same trick again, disguising himself for a walk with two disciples. They didn't recognise him until he sat down for dinner and broke some bread with them.

This troubled Hannah. How could Jesus camouflage himself like that? What if her dad could do that too? What if he'd risen, and was wandering around looking like a dustman, or a fisherman, or the school janitor, and she didn't recognise him? That week, she searched the faces of the men she saw, listened to their voices, imagining them turning to her and saying her name, just like Jesus had done, and transforming, suddenly, into her dad.

It didn't seem possible that he was gone forever. That wasn't how stories ended. There was always a happy ending. Some magic trick that made things right. She made bargains with the universe. If she wished hard enough, really wished it, then he'd come back. She practised her magic at night, lying in bed with her face screwed up, her body clenched, her fists balled, wishing as hard as she could. That didn't work. She set herself tasks – touching every fence post on the road to town. Reciting the alphabet backwards. Counting all the stones in the crumbling garden wall. If she could do it right, if she could pass these tests, then maybe he'd come back. She tried her best, touching each stone, the lichen crumbly under her finger-tips, the fence posts knocking her hand as she walked, the letters whispered under her breath – but she kept losing count, or worrying she'd missed one, and then the magic was tainted, and she'd have to set a new task, or start again.

Maybe, Hannah thought, if she was good, really good, and ate all her vegetables, he'd come back. She swallowed the broad beans and boiled carrots that her mother dished onto her plate, grimacing.

Nothing worked.

'Are you going to die too?' Hannah asked her mother one morning. Sylvia was sitting at the dining table, smoking and looking out of the window as Charlie cooed in his playpen. Sylvia blinked at her daughter, an underwater blink.

'Well, one day I will,' she said. 'Everybody dies. But it won't be for a long time yet.'

'How do you know?'

'I'm not old. People die when they're old and worn out.'

'But Dad wasn't old.'

My mother's face dropped. 'That's different.'

'How?'

'I don't really want to talk about it,' she said.


One week later, Hannah watched the croft receding into the distance from the back of Maggie's car, Charlie's warm weight on her lap, the other back seat taken up with suitcases. Her mother sat in the front, her dark hair whipping in the wind from the rolled-down window, and Maggie drove. They took a ferry to the mainland, and Maggie took them to Lerwick, and then Hannah sat with Maggie and Charlie on some vinyl-covered chairs in the port while her mother pored over some timetables and bought some tickets, and then stretched her face into a smile and said, I think we're all sorted. Thanks, Maggie, for everything. The two women embraced, and then Maggie turned to Hannah.

Jane remembers the hug. Maggie's smell: Pears soap, woodsmoke, dog. She buried her face in Maggie's shoulder, breathed it in. Maggie embraced her fiercely, tightly. Looked at her as they broke apart, her face troubled.

Take care, sweetheart, she said.

Then she kissed Charlie on his cheek, and squeezed his fat hand, and stroked his flossy hair. And then she was gone.

They sat and waited. Sylvia smoked cigarette after cigarette, jiggling her leg. Charlie napped. Hannah's stomach growled. It was three in the afternoon and they hadn't had any lunch.

'Here,' said her mother, rummaging in the basket of the pushchair, pulling out a box of Farley's Rusks. Hannah sucked on one, felt it dissolve to sweet pap in her mouth.

The next couple of days were a blur. Jane can only remember snapshots: eating a packet of salt and vinegar crisps at the bar on the ferry while her mother drank a glass of brandy, her hand trembling. A visit to a bank in Aberdeen which had an escalator inside, which Hannah rode up and down, over and over, while her mother talked to the cashier. Charlie whining with exhaustion in a bed and breakfast next to a railway line where the trains whooshed past, the clack-clack, clack-clack of the tracks jerking him from sleep. And then their own journey on the train, at night, watching the ghostly reflection of her face in the window, the lights of towns sliding past. She remembers her mother ordering two cartons of orange juice from the woman pushing the trolley, giving one to Hannah, washing down three pills with hers.

And then, finally, waking on the train to a sunny day, her mother yawning, black creases below her eyes, her hair dishevelled. She stared out of the window.

'This is us,' she said.

Hannah stepped off the train, blinking in the sunshine. The conductor helped lift Charlie's pram down, hauled their luggage onto the platform. A sign on the wall read 'Crowholt Parkway'. Only two other people got off. There were cows grazing on the other side of the railway tracks. Hannah covered her nose.

'It smells,' she said.

'Muck-spreading,' said her mother vacantly. She pulled a pair of sunglasses from her pocket and put them on.

Her mother called someone from the phone box in the station. Then they sat on a bench in the thick air. Hannah breathed through her mouth. It was hot. Her mother gave her a fifty-pence piece, told her to get a chocolate bar from the vending machine at the other end of the platform. Hannah had never used one before. She watched the metal spring spin, drop the bar of Dairy Milk into the tray. It was melted. She sucked the sugary goo from the wrapper.

A taxi came. Hannah sat in the back, her mother in the passenger seat, holding Charlie on her lap. Hannah looked at the back of her head. Her hair up in a crocodile clip, the skin of her neck pale.

Out of the window the landscape was cramped and fussy, a patchwork of multicoloured fields, huge trees blocking out the sky. It all seemed too much, too crowded. As they wound through the narrow lanes with their high hedge walls, she gripped the edge of the car's seat, expecting another car to careen around the corner and smash into them.

Eventually they passed a sign saying 'Welcome to CROWHOLT. Please drive carefully.' They drove down a high street, passing a burned-out launderette, some teenagers smoking on a bench, a bookies, a hairdresser, a Gateway supermarket, and then they turned onto an estate of pebble-dashed houses. Some children were bouncing a football in the road, and the driver beeped his horn at them. They fell back and peered at the taxi as it drove past. Hannah turned her face away, looked down at her lap.

They parked up next to a grass verge with two tall conifers growing on it, and her mother paid the driver, and they stepped out of the car. An old lady in a blue cotton dress, her hair dyed the flat black of a fur coat, rushed forward to meet them. She hugged Sylvia tightly and said, 'Oh my sweetheart, oh my love, you're nothin' but skin and bones,' and then she cupped Charlie's face in her hands and said, 'Charlie, you cutie, oh you're gorgeous, I could just eat you up,' and then she turned to Hannah, let out an exclamation, bent down, hugged her tightly, pressing her to her sunburnt chest. She took Hannah's hands in hers and looked at her, said, 'Oh, bless you. She is the spit of him, isn't she, the absolute spit of him.'

She ushered them inside a house. Every surface was covered in knick-knacks: little vases of fake flowers, ceramic figurines of women in flouncy dresses, doilies on the tabletops, antimacassars on the chairs, net curtains at the windows. Even the spaces beneath the furniture were taken up: a life-size ceramic dog sat underneath the coffee table; a real Alsatian was asleep below the sideboard. Even the walls and ceiling were textured – the walls with peach-coloured woodchip that made Hannah think of tinned tuna, the ceiling with dimpled Artex. The brown carpet was moss-like, spongey, with a meandering pattern cut into the pile. There was a fireplace with plastic coals, and a massive TV, the picture clear and bright.

'George bought that telly,' Hannah's nan said, bringing them cups of tea and a Tupperware tub of chocolate digestives. 'A video player, too. Got them on hire purchase. Costs him a bloody fortune but he can afford it now, he's a manager at a music shop in Exeter.' She sat down on the sofa with a sigh. 'He's got into all that rock music. Goodness me, you won't believe it when you see him. Bleach blond hair, down to his shoulders. Christ knows what your father would have thought. If he'd survived the heart attack, the sight of George's hair would have finished him off.'

They watched television in silence for a bit, the screen reflected in Sylvia's dark glasses, Charlie's wide blue eyes. Hannah ate a chocolate biscuit, and was reaching for another, when her nan smiled at her and said, 'Here, love – did you know that you were born in this room? Right there, on the floor,' and she pointed to the patch of carpet in front of the fireplace. 'What a day that was. Sweltering heat, I remember. Like today. We'd left your mother; we'd gone out for the day, shopping with your Auntie Dot. Your mum said she had a stomach ache – we didn't think nothing of it, she wasn't due for weeks – and when we got back there was an ambulance outside. God, I had the fright of my life. And we rushed in, and there was Sylvia, sitting on the carpet looking like a bomb had dropped, holding you—'

'Don't,' said her mother softly.

'Eh?'

'Don't, Mum. I don't want to think about it.'

Doreen looked at her daughter, then shrugged.

'Fair enough,' she said. There was a silence. 'Anyway,' she said. 'This'll butter no parsnips. Let's get you all settled and unpacked.' She got to her feet, stiffly. Said, 'Hand us a suitcase, love, there's a good girl.'

They hauled their luggage up the stairs, Sylvia carrying Charlie. The landing was stacked with tins of baked beans and rolls of toilet paper.

'It's getting silly, now,' said Doreen. 'But I've nowhere else to put them. The pantry's full. George nags me – you don't have to buy fifty of everything, you know, Mother, he says. But it saves me a fortune. Hannah, love – I do apologise, you're sharing your room with some of our groceries.'

Her nan pushed open a door. There was no bed, just a chest of drawers, a wardrobe, and a window with a sagging curtain. One side of the room was piled high with more tins and cans – salmon in brine, chopped tomatoes, corned beef. A naked lightbulb hung from the ceiling.

'I know it's a bit bare at the moment,' said Nan. 'But we'll get it cleared out, do it up nice.'

'Where's the bed?' said Sylvia.

'We got rid of the single bed when George moved out. Sold it to the Normans – you remember the Normans down the road? But we've still got the airbed. George can blow it up later. Don't worry, it's very comfy,' she said to Hannah. 'And we'll get you a proper bed as soon as we can.'

That night, Hannah lay on the air mattress, staring up at the ceiling. The bed was topped with a heavy layer of brushed nylon sheets, woollen blankets, a counterpane, cold and heavy as a coffin lid, so unlike the soft quilts they'd had in Unst.

She listened to the noises – the occasional car driving up the road outside, whooshing on the tarmac, its headlights sweeping across the ceiling. She heard a couple of drunks arguing as they walked down the road, the clink of a glass bottle dropped, rolling. She heard the central heating click on, the boiler fire up, the pipes knocking. She heard Charlie wail in his sleep, her mother shush him. At one point Rex barked downstairs, although it sounded like he was dreaming, the bark high and weak.

Hannah chewed the skin around her nails until it hurt and the taste of pennies filled her mouth. The strange images of the past twenty-four hours jumbled together in her head – the escalator in the bank, the cows at the train station, the pale reflection of her face in the train window.

*Go to sleep*, she thought. *Go to sleep, and maybe when you wake up you'll be back in Unst, and Dad will be making toast downstairs, and it will all have been a dream.*

She woke in the morning to find the airbed half deflated, her hips and shoulder blades digging into the floor.

*10 September 1986*

I'm here in my childhood bedroom. It's just the same as before I left. I woke up this morning and thought I'd gone back in time. The calendar on the wall still turned to 1978. My poster of Donny Osmond. My golliwog on the shelf. And then I saw my hand. My hand with its wedding ring on. And it all came flooding back, like a weight on my chest. Crushing me.

What I wouldn't give to scrub it all out.

Mum's taking care of Hannah and Charlie. And me. Says to me I need to rest. Just to rest and she'll do everything else. She's moved Charlie's crib into her room. Does all the night feeds. Says I need my sleep. But I can't sleep. I lie awake staring at the ceiling.

I should have listened to Mum in the first place. I should never have left here. I was a foolish, naïve girl. Play-acting at being a wife, a mother.

And look what happened. Look what I did.

I was in the kitchen yesterday. Getting a glass of water. Looked at the spot next to the refrigerator where I sat, all those years ago, talking to Bobby on the phone when he first went back to Unst. Where he whispered down the line to me. Where I felt myself open like a flower blooming at the sound of his voice. His beautiful voice. Gone now, forever. His mouth, gone. His tongue, gone. All just burnt up to ash, scattered from the cliff.

I'm already beginning to forget what he sounded like. I try to imagine his voice but the harder I try, the more it slips away from me. Like trying to hold on to water.

It all started with that mill. The fire. Every time I look out of the bedroom window, it's there. The black shell of it. Fenced off with plywood but the stack still stands. Why haven't they torn it down? I asked Mum the other day. She just shrugged.

I want to go there and tear it down myself. Rip it apart. I keep the curtains closed so I won't have to look at it. I remember George and me watching the flames, greedily. A couple of stupid kids. Not knowing what it would lead to. Martin's death. Now Bobby's. Ashes to ashes.

My body feels like it's made of lead. So heavy. Can't get out of bed. I'm running out of pills, I need to go to the doctor's, get some more, but I just can't face leaving the house.

The life jacket is deflating. I can almost hear the hiss as the air escapes.

Hannah comes in sometimes. Brings me cups of tea. Food. I wish she wouldn't. I hate her seeing me like this.

Jane remembers. The drawn curtains, the silent room, the sour smell of over-breathed air. She'd creep in, quiet as she could, trying not to disturb the hump beneath the duvet. Setting down the tray of food, the cup of tea, taking the dirty plates, the half-drunk mugs with their scum of cold milk.

A nervous breakdown. That was the phrase she heard her nan use, a couple of days after they arrived. She'd been in the hallway, tying her shoelaces as slowly as she could, eavesdropping.

'She's having a nervous breakdown.' She paused. 'I don't know, Esther. I don't know. She's always been . . . a bit fragile, you know? But never like this. The first day she got here she took herself off to bed, and that's where she's been ever since. Nearly a week, now.' Another pause. 'Oh, I don't mind that. Oh, no. Don't begrudge them at all. They're lovely. The girl, she's no trouble. Ever so quiet, though; very serious little thing. Absolute double of her father, God rest his soul. Meant to be starting at the school soon, I'm going into Exeter to get the uniform tomorrow. And the baby's beautiful, little Charlie. I was thinking of entering him in that contest, I saw it in the *Gazette* . . .'

Days passed. Her mother stayed in bed, silence leaking from beneath her bedroom door.

Hannah took her job as big sister seriously. Helped get Charlie's sleepsuits on when her nan's arthritic fingers struggled with the poppers. Distracted him during nappy changes, dangling a rattle above his head. Fed him, cradling his warm weight in the crook of her elbow, watching him grow sleepy on the bottle. Kissed his peach-like head, his little nose. Marvelled at the smallness of him.

At night she'd hear his little hitching wails break the silence, like a cat meowing. And she'd listen to the creaking of bed springs and floorboards as their nan got up to feed him. Once, twice, three times. She heard her humming lullabies.

Sometimes her and her nan took Charlie out in the pram for walks up the road. Oh, said the old ladies who peeked into the pram. Look at him. Those eyes, those lashes. He'll be a heartbreaker. They touched his chubby cheeks with their dry-leaf hands like a charm. As if some of his youth might rub off on them.

She sat with him in the garden, the dappled shade of the tree, showed him things. A ladybird, a crab apple, an ox-eye daisy. Played the kazoo with a blade of grass as he watched, wide-eyed.

She made him laugh for the first time by saying ouch when he scratched her with his nails, paper-thin and sharp as razorblades. 'Ouch!' she said, and he chuckled in her lap, his eyes crinkling into half-moons. She said it again and again. 'Ouch! Ouch!' Giggles burbling up from him, pure and unselfconscious.

'Nan!' she said. 'Nan! I made him laugh!'

'Oh, well done, darling,' said her nan. 'Oh, he thinks you're the bee's knees, that boy. Idolises his big sister.'

Hannah whispered to him: I'll keep you safe. I'll protect you. Dad's gone and Mum's not right, but I'll look after you. I'll never leave you.

One afternoon she was sitting with her nan and Charlie, watching television, when a chiming tune struck up outside.

'Ice cream van,' said her nan, brightly. 'I think I've got some change – yes,' she said, rummaging in her pocket. 'Here you are.' She pressed a fifty-pence piece into Hannah's palm.

Hannah stepped outside, into the heat. The van was parked just down the street, and some children were racing out of houses, clamouring around it. Hannah hung back.

Someone tapped her on the shoulder. A girl with long ginger hair held back in a pink Alice band, her face screwed up against the sunlight. She shaded her eyes with a hand and looked at Hannah.

'Who are you?' she said.

'Hannah.'

'What?'

'Hannah.'

'I'm April,' she said. 'And this is Shelley. She's my sister.'

Standing next to April was a smaller version of April, her hair in bunches, who squinted at Hannah as well.

'Where do you live?' said April.

Hannah pointed at her nan's house, across the road.

'Where are you from?'

'Unst.'

'What?'

'Unst. It's an island. In Shetland.'

April and her sister turned to each other and giggled. Hannah didn't know whether to join in or not.

'Your voice is funny,' said Shelley.

Hannah prickled. 'No it's not.'

'No it's not,' April said, imitating, and they pealed with laughter again. 'Say summin' else.'

'Like what?'

'I dunno. Say – I live in that house over there.'

'I live in that house over there.'

The girls shrieked with laughter.

'Hoose!' Shelley said. 'Dat hoose over dere!'

'Yes, love?' said the man in the ice cream van. Hannah turned to him, feeling flustered. She leaned in and lowered her voice and said: 'A ninety-nine please. With a flake.'

Behind her, she could hear more laughter. Her face was hot. The ice cream man handed her the cone. She'd pictured herself sitting on the kerb with it, loose-limbed and lazy, like the other kids, but instead she took it back into the house and ate it there, although she didn't really fancy it any more. She looked at the living-room carpet where she'd been born and felt miserable. She gave Charlie a scoop of ice cream on her finger, his face brightening at the taste. She wondered if he'd have an accent like her. If he'd grow up and think she sounded silly. If he wouldn't want her as a big sister, with her stupid voice.

Hannah practised, whispering to herself at night. There. Then. That. Concentrating on putting her tongue between her teeth. Making the yawning vowels. House. Not hoose. The. Not da. You. Not du.

By the time she came back to Shetland, she'd lost the accent. That poetic lilt, the Scandinavian consonants, light and rhythmic like the flap of seabirds' wings. Her speech was rounded, low down, coming from the back of her mouth.

A soothmoother.

Jane, in her caravan, drinks a mug of tea with one hand, idly strokes Nell's ears with another. Her hands are chapped from cleaning. Maggie is coming home from hospital any day now, and Jane wanted to get rid of any traces of her stay in the house. She vacuumed, washed Laura's sheets, cleaned the oven, scrubbed the bathroom. She'd felt a sinking feeling as she'd locked the door behind her. It had been a mistake, staying so long there. She'd been getting too accustomed to bricks and mortar. The warmth, the fireplace, the soft bed. Now her caravan seems squalid, cramped, depressing. Its lightness doesn't seem comforting any more. It seems flimsy.

Jane looks, through the caravan window, at the croft. A seagull perched on its roof. As Jane watches, it stretches its neck and calls to the sky.

She thinks of the peeling wallpaper. The wallpaper she watched her dad put up, laying the strips on the ironing board, brushing them with paste. The jars in the cupboards, the Marmite. He was the only one who ate it, thick-spread on doorstop slices of toast. The algae-ridden bathroom – she remembers him singing in it, crooning in the bath where the echo flattered his voice.

The seagull on the croft roof takes off, propelling itself on white wings. She watches it go.

She should have taken care of the place, she thinks. Shouldn't have let it rot away. She looks at the boarded-up windows, like shut eyes, and her mind wanders again to fixing up the place. How long would it take? To strip it out, renovate it? She wouldn't know where to begin. All that damp, swelling and bubbling in the walls. Probably thick with spores, mildew – no good for a baby, she thinks, before she can stop herself.

Nell suddenly pricks her ears up. A low growl in her throat. She barks, once, twice, and Jane hears footsteps approaching. There's a knock at her door.

'Who is it?' she calls.

'It's me.' A woman's voice.

'Pat?'

'Yeah.'

Jane gets up, opens the door. Pat is standing there, woollen cap on her buzzed head, the tip of her nose pink with cold.

'You're all right,' says Pat. 'I'm not here to have a go. I'm here to apologise.'

'What?'

'I heard the news.'

Jane stares at her. 'What news?' she says.

'About your mother. The search, the . . .' She gestures to her hand. 'It was in the *Shetland Times.*'

Jane feels dizzy. 'Oh,' she says. 'Right.'

Pat looks at her. 'Why didn't you tell me, Jane? If I'd known that was all going on, I wouldn't have been such an arsehole to you these past few weeks. No wonder you were all over the place. After all these years, Jesus.'

Jane looks at the doorframe, fiddles with the door latch.

'Well,' says Pat. 'Like I said, I'm sorry. And I take back what I said, about – you know,' she says, waving a hand in the air. 'Being fired.'

Jane looks at her. 'Really?'

'Are you fit to work?' says Pat, frowning. 'If you're not, I don't want you coming in. I want you to take some leave.'

'I'm fine,' says Jane. 'I'm fine. I've got a doctor's appointment on Wednesday, but I can come in tomorrow.'

'You sure?' says Pat.

'Sure. Yes. I'm sure. I – I just want things to get back to normal. It'll help take my mind off things.'

Back to normal. Before this all happened. She's let herself get carried away. Fantasies of having a baby, living in the croft . . . stupid. Stupid, she thinks, as she grabs a tin of Nell's dog food from the cupboard, looks at it. The metal tin of her caravan, the metal tin of the factory, her sealed-off life. Vacuum packed, she thinks, as she grabs the can opener, pierces the lid.

As she scoops the meat into Nell's metal dish, her mobile phone buzzes on the countertop.

'What now,' she mutters, and picks it up. An unknown number. Area code: Crowholt.

She looks at it, her mouth going dry. She thinks about letting it ring out. But just before it goes to voicemail, she presses the answer button, lifts it to her ear.

'Hello?'

'Jane Douglas?' A woman's voice.

'Yes.'

'It's DI Sumner from the Devon and Cornwall Police. I just wanted to update you on the progress of the investigation. Is this a good time?'

Jane watches Nell eating her food, the bowl scraping on the plywood floor of the caravan.

'Sure,' she says, sinking down on her bed.

'The access and preparatory work were completed yesterday. We've cordoned off the area, got patrols set up. We're going to switch the pumps on tomorrow. If all goes to plan, we reckon it should take around three weeks to drain it clear.'

Three weeks. Jane swallows, her throat clicking. Listens to DI Sumner, talking about timescales, forensics, investigations. Media interest, she says. Be prepared. Reporters, journalists.

'This is only the beginning, of course,' says DI Sumner. 'The real work starts once the water's gone, and the excavators move in. All the material that gets removed will have to be checked by an anthropologist. Then the debris will be taken away. We'll have a team of specialist officers carrying out a fingertip search.'

Jane feels a wave of nausea roll through her body at the thought of fingertips digging into muck, searching for her mother's bones. She has a sudden urge to say, you know what, DI Sumner – switch the pumps off. Don't bother. Leave her down there, rotting in her pit. Let her stay there forever.

But of course she doesn't. She says okay, and thank you, and yes, I understand.

'And remember, Jane – if you feel you need any emotional support, there are services—'

'I'm fine,' says Jane. 'Thank you. Bye.' And then she hangs up, feeling cold all over.

She rolls a cigarette, her hands shaky. Lights it, inhales.

Looks at the diary on her bed. It feels as though she's dredging the body up herself, reading her mother's words. Threading a thin ink line into the past, the string of sentences trailing down, down, into the water. At the end, a hook in a monstrous mouth.

She stares at it. Then, on impulse, she stubs her cigarette out, grabs her lighter, sparks the flame. A steady hiss, a bright tongue. She picks up the diary. Brings the flame to the book's corner, watches it curl around the paper. It resists, at first, the pages dense and damp, but then the flame takes hold, brightening, stretching up the length of the pages, charring, blackening—

Then, with a sick lurch, she remembers Charlie's hospital bracelet, the lock of his golden hair, sandwiched inside. 'No!' she says, and drops the lighter, beats at the diary with her hand, smothers the flame, the heat searing her skin. She grunts. The corner of the diary is scorched, the edges glowing orange.

Jane flicks through the book, frantic. His hair, there, tips frizzled by the heat. The bracelet warped a little at the end, the plastic puckered. She clutches the book to her. The last of him, the only traces of him, and she nearly destroyed them.

'I'm sorry,' she says to the book. 'I'm sorry, I'm sorry.'

Jane throws the ball for Nell, hurling it along the windswept beach, watching the dog skitter across the ash-coloured sand. The horizon is smudged with distant rain.

She remembers coming here with her dad, as a girl. Trying to catch small brown fish in the shallows, searching for mermaid glass along the sea strand, hunting for razor clams on a low spring tide, watching them heave from their silty burrows. The air, the wind, the sea. Her dad. The happiest, she thinks, she's ever been.

She remembers being told, growing up, that her father died in an accident. He slipped and fell. Just like that, he slipped and fell, and then he was gone forever. After he died, she became earthbound, terrified of heights. She couldn't climb trees, or the ladders in the school gymnasium. Even the big slide in the playground made her sweat. She felt like a turtle crawling in the dirt, flattening herself to the floor. To slip, and fall. An accident. It could happen, she assumed, at any moment. That was the nature of accidents.

She can't remember exactly when things changed. When her father's death was ruled a suicide instead. Not a slip and fall, but a deliberate step into the void. There must have been an investigation, a coroner's report, but it was all kept from her. She saw it in the newspaper reports that came after her mother's disappearance, stated as fact: 'Some have speculated that her husband's suicide may have prompted Sylvia Douglas's nervous breakdown.'

It seemed to make sense. Blind drunk, reeling from the phone call from his wife telling him she was leaving him, he made his way to the highest part of the rig and did something stupid, reckless, tragic.

But Jane, picking up the sandy ball Nell has dropped at her feet, hurling it again down the shore, thinks: *I don't believe it.* He always seemed so solid, so reliable, so *there.* Compared to her mother, with her Valium fog and her deep-sea eyes and the sadness that seemed to shiver under her skin – he was as reliable as the tides. He liked a drink, yes, but he never got morose on it. Her mother had said it herself: *he just has this sort of confidence to him, that everything is manageable, that the world has a place for him, that everything will work out in the end.*

It could have been he went to take some air, clear his head, and slipped. A genuine accident. Or maybe he was killed. A drunken brawl, a whack over the head, a conspiracy of silence. Or a rusty grating, a dangerous hole in the platform. Negligence, a company cover-up. Who knows?

Not that it matters now, Jane thinks, looking at the pewter-grey sea. It was ruled a suicide. And that meant her mother was left destitute. Bobby's life insurance wouldn't pay out. The brown envelope full of cash was all her mother was left with. That and the croft.

Nell drops the ball at Jane's feet again, bright-eyed, panting. And as Jane bends to scoop it up, she feels something. A strange sensation, like popping corn, just below her belly button.

She stops, ball in her hand. Looks down at herself. Her stomach, bulging slightly against her cagoule.

Pop. Pop pop pop. Like a muscle spasm. Then a tiny, smooth, sliding sensation. A fish brushing against the sides of its bowl.

'No,' she says. 'No.'

She stands, breathless, her whole attention focused on her belly.

Nell barks, once, her tail wagging. Jane tosses her the ball, absent-mindedly. Puts a hand on the slithery surface of her cagoule. One small flutter, then stillness.

Jane stands there for a moment, heart beating. Then takes her hand away from her belly, jams it in her pocket.

'No,' she says to her stomach. 'No. I'm sorry. No.'


*15 September 1986*

Today I tried to get up and go to the doctor's. I need my pills. I got out of bed and went to the bathroom. Got dressed. Brushed my hair. I went to put some makeup on in the bathroom mirror but my face looked all wrong. Like a mask. I didn't like looking at it. It didn't look right. I couldn't face going outside looking like that, so I went back to bed.

Mum brought Charlie up for a cuddle and I held him with my face turned away. My dark glasses on. Thought I would frighten him if he saw me looking so strange.

*16 September 1986*

I need my pills. I have to get them or I think I'll die. But my body feels like it's made of lead. I can barely move.

*17 September 1986*

I'm going. Today. I'm going downstairs. And then I'm going to get my pills.

Jane remembers.

It was during breakfast – poached eggs on toast. Charlie was in his highchair, shoving fistfuls of mashed banana in his mouth. When their mother appeared in the kitchen doorway, wearing a baggy woollen dress which hung loosely from her bony shoulders, and a pair of big black sunglasses, her nan jumped and cried out, her knife clattering onto her plate, then got up, holding her arms out. 'Sylvia, sweetheart!' she said. 'Oh – come here. Come and have some breakfast.' She pulled out a chair, guided her daughter onto it. 'Here, love – have the rest of mine, I've had enough.' She slid over her plate of half-eaten eggs. 'I'll pop some more on for you – or if you don't fancy eggs, we've got cereal – or toast and jam, or porridge, if you'd like. Kettle's just boiled, do you want tea or coffee?'

Jane remembers staring at her mother, seeing herself reflected in the dark glasses.

Her mother shook her head. 'No. I just need to go to the doctor's.' Her voice was hoarse, low. 'I need my tablets.'

'Right,' said their nan. 'Of course, sweetheart. But eat something first. And have a cup of tea. Look, you're shaking. You must be hungry.' She filled the kettle, turned to Hannah, and said, 'Say good morning to your mum, sweetheart.'

'Morning,' Hannah muttered.

'Speak up, my love, she can barely hear you,' said Nan.

'It's okay,' said her mother. She swallowed and Hannah saw her Adam's apple bob in her stringy neck. 'It's okay, she doesn't have to.'

'Well,' said Nan. 'Come on, darling. Eat up before it gets cold.'

Sylvia ate slowly, in little bites, and sipped her tea.

'Why don't you take Charlie with you to the doctor's? In the pram? He needs some fresh air,' Nan said.

Hannah watched her mother put Charlie in the pram. Wedge his sunhat on his head. She didn't want her mum to take him. Felt nervous about it. She peered through the net curtains, watched her mother pushing the pram up the street, until they were out of sight. But it was only a minute before they were back.

### 18 September 1986

I made it to the end of the street.

I just couldn't go any further. My palm was sweating, gripping Charlie's pram. I stood there. Watching the cars and people going past. Willing myself to go on. To get the pills. But I just couldn't face it. What if one of the pram wheels fell off and Charlie spilled into the road, into the path of a lorry? What if we got to the doctor's and someone with a deadly disease coughed on him, and he got sick and died? What if there was an escaped lunatic on the high street, a crazy person, and they attacked us? I looked at Charlie, in the pram, his soft skin, his fragile egg-like head, his breakable bones. It was too dangerous, too dangerous. I turned and came back. Gave Charlie back to Mum. Went back to bed. Safer, for everyone.

I'm going to wake up soon. I will. It's all a dream, isn't it? It's all a dream. Ever since I went into labour with Hannah, everything has felt unreal. Maybe I lost so much blood giving birth that I'm in a coma in a hospital somewhere, and this is all just a big hallucination.

Wake up, wake up, wake up.

But if I wake up then there's no Charlie. Oh, my Charlie, my beautiful Charlie. Maybe that's why he is such a dream baby. Because he is a dream. A figment of my imagination.

Everything seems wrong. Off. Now that I've thought I might be in a dream I can't get rid of the feeling. I notice things everywhere. Signs that things aren't real. Colours are too bright, sounds too loud. I've been trying to retrace my steps. To think. When did the dream start?

I was wrong. It wasn't at the birth. It was the quarry. Swimming, with Sally and Judith. That was when things changed. When I dipped my feet in the water and felt that fear. I felt ill. Dizzy. What if I'd slipped into the water? Became unconscious? Drowned? What if this is all a hallucination? I remember reading once, that when you're drowning you have visions. Lack of oxygen to the brain.

If only I could get back. Back to where it all went wrong, and start again. A rebirth. A baptism. Water cleansing my body, my soul. I mus—

The charred edge of the paper eats into her mother's words. The diary trembles in Jane's hands. She doesn't want to turn the page, doesn't want to read on. She can feel it coming, the abomination, pressed between the pages ahead like some awful insect, waiting blackly there for her. She wants to shut her eyes, turn away. But she has to read. She has to bear witness.

She lifts the blackened edge of the page, turns it. Her mother's writing has begun to waver, the words lurching over the paper.

Could it be that the pills were hiding the truth? Numbing me – stopping me from seeing? Maybe Mum was in on it, recommending the pills, she was there to keep me in the dream, but why? I wish I knew what to do. What will make me get back to real life – there has to be something, something I'm missing, I keep feeling like I'm near an answer but it slips away.

Today I heard music, coming through the window. The most beautiful heavenly music – I drew the curtains, saw the mill there, the scorched tower stark in the bright sunlight – I realised the music was coming from there, like the pipe of a great church organ. I listened to it for hours, the most joyous music. Hannah couldn't hear it. That means something. If only I could hear it, it must be real. Because Hannah's not real and she couldn't hear it. It was just for me. I have to listen closely. I'm sure I'll find the answer.

Jane, her blood like ice water, remembers. She brought her mother up a mug of tea. She'd expected the dark room, the lump under the duvet, but instead, the room was flooded with sunlight, her mother kneeling up on the bed, her back to the door, looking out of the open window.

'Mum?' said Hannah.

Sylvia turned and smiled, a tearful smile. She patted the bed.

'Come here, sweetheart,' Sylvia said.

Hannah climbed up next to her. Her mother embraced her. Jane remembers her bony body beneath its polyester nightgown. She could smell the stale sweat, the grease in her mother's hair.

'Do you hear that?' Sylvia said.

Hannah listened. All she could hear was some birdsong, a distant lawnmower, her mother's breathing.

'Hear what?'

Her mother looked down at her. Hannah noticed her chewed lips, her bloodshot eyes. 'You don't hear that beautiful music?' Sylvia said.

Hannah blinked. Shook her head.

Sylvia laughed. 'Well,' she said. 'Never mind, never mind.' She held Hannah close, stroked her hair.

'Everything will be all right, Hannah,' she said. 'It will. I know it.'


*19 September 1986*

Music – and voices, now, words, but I can't make them out. They're English – at least, they sound English – but I just can't quite grasp them. They're having a conversation, about me, I think. I need to listen carefully, tune in to the frequency, just like a radio station.

I heard it! Last night. A voice coming from the stack, in the darkness. A voice so close I could hear it in my head. I concentrated hard, and listened, and then it was like static clearing, and I could understand. It wasn't frightening. It sounded calm. Like an old friend. Pay attention, it said, and it started to tell me things, lots of things.

Heat but no sunlight today. A muggy heat. A storm coming maybe. George wanted to take me for a walk. I didn't want to go. I wanted to listen to the mill. It was making music again, that divine music, not like any music I've ever heard before. But I went. Put my sunglasses on and my hat and we walked. I wasn't afraid this time, of going outside. It doesn't matter now. Nothing bad will happen to me, the mill told me. I have nothing to be afraid of.

George was talking to me. Reminiscing. Saying, do you remember when we were kids? Bringing out Mum's baking trays and sliding down that hill in the mud? And remember that man who lived at number sixteen, with the cat that sat on his shoulder? And the Jarrett brothers, do you remember them, standing in the middle of the roundabout, mooning cars? I could have laughed. It was so obvious what he was trying to do. Trying to convince me he is the real George. I saw straight through him but I played along, said yes, George, I remember. Those were the days.

We walked out of the estate. Down the high street. Everything seemed so threatening. People looking at me. I said to George, see — they're all staring at me because they know. And he said nobody's staring. You're imagining things.

I know, I said. I am imagining things, you're right, George. Imagining everything. He said what do you mean by that? And I said nothing, nothing.

We went to the park up the road. Same one we went to as children. Nobody in there but a cloud of midges scribbling in the air. We sat on the swings. I was sweaty from walking.

George said, Sylvia, I'm worried about you.

I said, you know what you should be worried about. Nuclear war.

What?

Nuclear war, I said. Mum should whitewash the house, it helps deflect the radiation. And the windows, too. And she should build a shelter under the stairs.

Okay, he said.

She needs drinking water. And enough food for fourteen days. I read it in a book.

Well, I don't think that'll be a problem, he said. She's got enough tinned tuna for fourteen months, I bet.

Then he asked me if I was taking my pills. I said no, I don't need them any more. They're not good for me. And he said he wanted me to see a doctor. I needed to get better. I can't just stay in bed all day. Hannah and Charlie need me.

Well I sat on the swing and scuffed the ground with my toes and smiled. And I said, do you remember watching the mill burn down? You and me, at the window.

Of course, he said.

Why is it still up there? Why did they leave it standing?

He shrugged.

I know why. I know why. My mind left it there. It's a way back, for me. A hole in the fabric between dreams and reality. A puncture. A gap, a rip. Like the pipes Victorians put in coffins, leading to the surface, in case they were buried alive. Fire − fire is the opposite of water, see. That's why it stayed, when I drowned. It all makes sense.

But I didn't say that to George. I didn't say a thing. If he knew − if they locked me up in hospital − I'd never get back. I'd be stuck here in the dream forever.


The mill was saying frightening things today. Whispering them under the grey sky. It told me exactly what I had to do, and I sat and wept and wept until I thought my heart would break. Mum came upstairs and said Sylvia, Sylvia what's wrong? What's this all about? And I said bring me Charlie, I want Charlie, and she brought me to him and I held him and kissed him, and said I love you, I love you, I'm sorry. Just because he's not real doesn't mean I don't love him. He feels so real, his hair, his skin, the scent of him, but it's all a trick, an illusion, I know. The mill started talking more loudly, right inside my head, so loud it was almost painful, saying you must not waver, you must complete the task, you must not falter, you must do as I say, and I was shaking my head saying stop, please, just let me have some time, and Charlie started to cry and Mum said now Sylvia, you're scaring him. You're scaring me. I'm scared, I said. I'm scared I'm scared I'm scared

A doctor came. A woman doctor. Mum brought her up to my room. The doctor said now, Sylvia, your family are a bit worried about you. Say you've been hearing voices, been having some strange thoughts, is that true? She asked me questions, questions. I couldn't hear what the mill was saying. And she said I'm prescribing you some medication. This is Haldol. Eight drops a day, she said to my mum, mixed into a drink. She should start feeling much better soon.

She left. Mum brought me a cup of tea. Come on, Sylvia, she said. Drink up. Before it gets cold. You've got to take your medicine. She wanted to watch me drink it. I wouldn't. She wrung her hands. When she left, I tipped the tea out of the window. Watched it splatter on the patio. I looked at the mill. It whispered to me. It said, Sylvia, you have to act fast. They won't let you get away with it. They'll put you in a straitjacket, inject you, put an ice pick in your eye, chop your brain up. They'll lock you away – you won't ever get back, you'll be stuck here forever.

Today it rained. Heavy, battering, rain, drops like ball bearings, hammering on the window, the roof. I wanted to go out in it and rip my clothes off and let it pour over me, but I didn't. I mustn't, they mustn't think I'm mad; if they do they'll send me to an institution, inject me with drugs, fry my brain with electrodes, and I can't go. I need to complete the task. The rain is a sign. Water from heaven. A sign that it's time. A baptism, a cleansing, get back to where it all started. Close the loop – make it whole again. Start again. Rebirth – the water of the womb – I will be protected – I need not fear – oh God but I'm scared – I

don't want to do it, I don't want to, I don't, forgive me, Hannah,
Charlie, I love you I love you I love you

Jane turns the page, her hand trembling.

Blank.

She flicks through, her breath shallow. Nothing. No more
writing. The end of the diary. But wait – here is a page torn out,
roughly. Jane runs her finger along the short, jagged edge. She
stares. On the sheet behind it is an impression of words, as if the
page on top was written on, ripped out. Jane touches it. Feeling
the indentations. The ghost letters.

Suddenly she realises, with a sick lurch, what she's looking at.
Her hand flinches back, as if burned.

The note her mother left at the foot of the stairs, before she
disappeared. The note the tabloids reprinted. Three lines. Eleven
words, scrawled in a jagged hand.

Jane knows the words. She knows them off by heart; they've
sat at the back of her mind for twenty years, a riddle she can't
solve, a dense, malignant puzzle. She doesn't need to read them.
But she wants to. She's angry, suddenly, at the diary ending this
way, with a missing page, a vanishing act. A dirty trick, a cheat.
It's not fair.

She looks at the indentations in the paper, the grooves where
the pen nib has pressed. Then she grabs a pencil from the drawer.
Presses the diary onto the bed. Begins to scribble, slantwise, across
the page, burying the white under a layer of graphite. A grave
rubbing, she did them in primary school, squatting in the grass of
the churchyard, sheet of paper taped to a headstone, purple crayon
revealing the etched letters.

And here they are. The epitaph emerges, white, from its grey
pall:

I'M SORRY

## THIS IS THE ONLY WAY
## MUM, DON'T GO UPSTAIRS

Jane stares at the page, shaking. Imagines her mother gripping the pen, scoring the words deeply into the paper, ripping it out, placing it on the bottom step of the silent house, while upstairs . . .

Jane slams the diary shut. Shoves it in the drawer. Sits on her bed, tries to breathe. She can feel it: the taste of water in her mouth, a pressure in her lungs, a burning in her nose, a roaring in her ears, and she feels herself dissolving, and the memories flooding back, a tidal wave, rushing, roaring, battering . . .

She is lying on her stomach in front of the TV, with a chocolate spread sandwich, a glass of milk. It's raining outside and the air smells electric.

Her nan is in the doorway, pulling her raincoat on. 'I'm just popping to the shops,' she says. 'We need some milk and bread. I've just put Charlie down for his nap. Your mum's running herself a bath.' She zips her coat up, unhooks her umbrella from the hat stand, smiles brightly. 'Just as well. She hasn't had a decent scrub in weeks. She must be feeling better. You'll be all right? I won't be long.'

Hannah nods, glued to the TV.

'All right, love,' says her nan. 'See you in a bit.'

She shuts the front door behind her.

Hannah watches the film, *The NeverEnding Story*. Her Uncle George taped it for her off the telly last week. She's vaguely aware of the thrum of the boiler stopping as her mother turns the hot tap off, and then a few minutes later, a small cry from Charlie. Dreaming, she guesses.

On screen, in a steaming swamp, the boy jumps off his white horse and begins to lead it through the water.

Hannah stares at the screen, chocolate spread sandwich forgotten in her hand. She is so engrossed in the film that she doesn't hear her mother calling her name, at first. But when she does, she scrambles for the remote, pauses the video.

'Hannah,' calls her mother, from upstairs. 'Come up here, please.' Her mother's voice sounds strange, flat.

Hannah gets slowly to her feet, looking at the screen, the boy and the horse frozen in the swamp, the picture juddering. She shoves the rest of the sandwich in her mouth, and heads to the bottom of the stairs. Looks up them.

'What?' she shouts, through a mouthful of bread.

'Quickly.'

She swallows the sandwich. Climbs the stairs. Looks down the landing.

'Mum?'

'In here,' says her mother. 'The bathroom.'

Hannah steps forward, past the tins and rolls of toilet paper. The carpet is damp underfoot. She lifts her leg, looks at her wet sock.

Jane, in the caravan, squeezes her eyes shut tight, shakes her head. 'No,' she says, 'no, no.' She can feel waves of panic lapping at her, a crushing feeling in her chest. She stands up, stumbles blindly towards the door, shoves out of the caravan into the freezing night air. Nell bounds after her, trotting out into the darkness, her white tail waving.

Jane leans against her caravan, her breath ragged. She stares wildly up at the stars, sharp and remote. Then she fumbles in her pocket, gets her phone out, taps a few keys.

'Jane.' Mike's voice on the end of the line is thick with sleep. 'Everything all right?'

Jane sniffs, swallows. 'No,' she says. 'No. It's not.'

'What's happened? Are you hurt?'

'No. No, I'm okay, I'm okay, it's just . . .'

Jane, suddenly, wants him more than anything. Wants him

holding her with his solid bulk, his safe embrace, her belly between them, with the baby inside − their baby. If she saw him, she'd tell him. She wouldn't be able not to. Now that she's felt it − now that it feels real . . .

'I just . . . wanted to hear your voice. I − they're switching the pumps on at the quarry tomorrow, and . . . my head's all over the place. That's all.' Her teeth chatter in the frosty air. 'I just wanted you. To hear you.'

'Are you sure? I'll come over, Jane . . .'

She shakes her head.

'No. It's okay. Can you just . . . talk to me? About anything. I just want to hear your voice.'

The sun rises over the sound, glistening on the water. Jane watches it from her caravan step, clutching a coffee, her sore eyes squinting at the light. She slept, eventually, after Mike read her *Yachting Monthly* magazine down the phone, but her sleep was shallow, shot through with strange dreams, and her body feels drained, brittle, a blown eggshell. She can hear a skylark making noise, its high, trilling song carrying on the soft breeze.

She finishes her coffee. Feeds Nell. Then, yawning, nauseous, she gets into the car and drives, following the grey ribbon of road as it winds towards the cannery. There is a thick blanket of cloud, now, and a brittle chill in the air which threatens snow. Jane, as she drives, tries not to think of the quarry. Have they switched the pumps on? Has the water started to be sucked up, sprayed out, the level dropping? She tries not to think of her tender breasts, her stomach pushing against her fleece, the appointment tomorrow at the hospital. She tries not to think of the diary, back at the caravan, the white letters. She tries not to think. Pushes the horror of it all to the back of her mind.

Over the cattle grid. Into the car park. Out of the car. She looks at the blue mermaid on the side of the building. A woman in the water. Jane turns her face away, shoves her hands in her pockets, heads in through the doors.

As soon as she enters the changing room, the smell of fish and blood and ice hits her. She swallows. Nods and smiles at the women greeting her, who tell her they've missed her, that Pat was a nutter, that she was in big trouble with the management for firing Jane like that, asking how she was, is there anything they can do, how's Maggie, how's the croft, Dawn's been talking—

And then Dawn appears. 'Jane,' she says. 'Have you found a solicitor yet? We need to get things moving with the sale of the croft; Pete wants to get started as soon as he can.'

'Dawn, can we talk later? I . . .'

'Ladies,' says a voice. 'Come on. Chop chop.' Jane looks up and sees Pat, clipboard in hand. Jane pulls on her rubber overalls, her boots, her gloves and hairnet, as the changing room empties.

'Right,' says Pat. 'Jane. Welcome back. How're you feeling?'

'Okay,' says Jane.

'Good. Now then. Heading. Sound okay?'

Jane sighs with relief. Heading she can do. If she'd been asked to strip roe, or use the suction hose, or go anywhere near the bath of ice water . . .

'Aye,' she says. 'Heading I can do.'

Pat nods. 'Good,' she says. 'And Jane – I'm sorry again. Really.'

Jane fiddles with her hairnet. 'Thanks,' she says. Then she heads out onto the factory floor. Takes a deep breath, tries to quell the bile rising in her throat.

Jane grips each salmon, shoves it beneath the blade, feeling the shock as the flesh splits, sliding the headless fish across to her right. The roar and rumble of the factory assaults her, scrapes against her skin. The violence of the place, the machines cutting and cracking and slicing. Her exhausted body feels sick with it. But she grits her teeth. Keeps going.

She imagines the pipes leading down into the flooded quarry. Sucking out all that rank, stagnant water. Spurting it onto the fields nearby. The water that has preserved her mother for all these years, pickling her like a foetal pig in a specimen jar. She thinks of her belly, the water in there, the pale translucent thing forming.

Spots swarm her vision. She feels like she's going to throw up. She steps back, braces her hands on her knees, lowers her head, breathes.

'Are you okay?' shouts Anthony, next to her.

Jane straightens up, nods.

She looks at the fish in front of her. She grabs a salmon, heads it, passes it on. Grabs a salmon, heads it, passes it on. Looks at their faces, mouths open as if appalled, wrenched gasping from the ocean, the clean salt sea, the moving tidal water, the water her father fell into, his broken body floating on the waves. She sees his blank bloodied face, looking down into the depths, sees a bathtub, its clear glassy surface – she shakes her head. Stop it. Stop it, stop it. Stay calm. Breathe, focus. Stop thinking of water, stop it. She grabs the salmon, pushes it towards the guillotine—

Only it isn't a salmon.

It is her mother's plastic arm.

Jane stares. Feeling ice cold all over with horror. She sucks in air and screams.

The arm pops out of Jane's slippery hands, slides off the belt onto the floor. There is a yell, someone hits the emergency stop button, the conveyor belt halts, suddenly. There's an intake of breath, a flurry, people shouting, saying it's Jane! Jane, what happened, are you okay?

Jane is breathing hard, her body ringing with terror, staring at the plastic arm on the floor. She blinks. It's not an arm. It's a salmon, just a salmon, a regular salmon, same as the hundreds of others.

Someone is yelling something about an ambulance. An ambulance? So there was an arm? What, thinks Jane, wait—

'Oh my God,' says someone.

'First aid kit!'

'Call nine nine nine! Now!'

Anthony has his hand clamped to his mouth, his face pale.

And then Jane notices the blood on her shoes. Dripping, splattering onto the ground. Quite a lot of blood. She feels woozy. She raises her hand. The hand that was holding the arm. Her first two fingers are missing. In their place are bloody stumps.

Water.

Water.

Jane hears a voice saying the word. Realises it's hers. Her mouth is dry. Something poking at her lips; a straw. She sucks at it. Feels water flood her mouth, drinks huge gulps. She blinks.

Mike. He's there. He's looking at her, his kind brown eyes, his rusty hair.

'Hello,' he says.

'You,' says Jane.

'Aye. Me.'

'Hello,' she says.

He kisses her forehead gently.

Jane looks around her. She's in a hospital, she realises. Blue corrugated curtains, bright strip lights, the beeping of machines. She looks down at herself, at the cannula poking out of the back of her hand. Her other hand is hidden in a lump of bandages.

'Oh,' she says, but she's not startled. She feels calm, clean, detached.

'Does it hurt?' says Mike.

Jane shakes her head.

'The painkillers must be working. They've given you some pretty strong stuff.'

'Did they . . .' She swallows, her throat clicking. 'Did they put my fingers back on?'

Mike nods. 'They sewed them back on. You've got pins in there. Wee metal plates.'

'Oh,' says Jane. She stares at the bandaged lump on the end of her arm. 'So my hand . . . it's going to be all right?'

'Well – they hope so. Thing is, your fingers got frostbite. From being packed in the ice. So they might not take the blood properly,' Mike says, wincing. 'If they don't, they might have to – well, unstitch them, cut the rotten bits off, sew them on again. You might be in here for a few days.'

Jane remembers. Hazily. She remembers watching Pat scrabbling in the bloody ice and fish guts on the factory floor, retching as she packed the severed fingers into a Tupperware box from the canteen. It's suddenly funny, the image, and Jane laughs, weakly.

'Well, I'm glad you're seeing the funny side of it,' Mike says, raising his eyebrows. Then he takes her hand, the unbandaged one, gently. Jane leans back on the pillow, looks up at the ceiling. Then she sits up.

'Nell,' she says. 'Nell – I'm meant to be looking after her—'

'She's fine,' says Mike. 'She's fine. Maggie's home.'

'Maggie's home?'

'Aye. She was discharged today. Just before you came in. You passed each other like ships in the night. I saw her when I went round to get your things.' He lifts up a holdall. 'Grabbed your toothbrush. Pants. Stuff like that. Maggie had a key to the caravan. Hope that's all right.'

'Thanks,' says Jane. She shifts in the bed. A bolt of pain shoots through her hand and she winces.

'Easy,' says Mike.

Jane lowers herself gently down, biting her lip as her hand throbs. She looks at it again, the bandaged lump.

'So,' says Mike, softly. 'What happened?'

Jane remembers. Remembers the arm. How solid it was, how real. The feeling of it in her hand, the cool smooth plastic. How clearly she saw each fingernail, the nicotine stain between the first two fingers, the scratch on the wrist, the nail polish. Cherries in the Snow. She swallows.

'I thought,' she says. 'I thought I saw—'

'Knock knock,' calls a voice. They turn to look as a nurse appears around the curtain, smiling brightly, pushing a trolley of medicines. 'How are you doing? Let me just check your notes . . .'

She looks at a clipboard.

'Jane Douglas. How are you feeling, Jane?'

'I want a smoke,' Jane says.

'No, no, no,' laughs the nurse, flipping the paper. 'Not good for healing. We want all the oxygen to the skin you can get.' Then she clicks her ballpoint pen, says, 'Shouldn't be smoking anyway, in your condition. When's baby due?'

Jane freezes.

'What?' says Mike.

The nurse looks up from the chart. Sees Jane's face. Mike's.

'Oh,' she says. 'Okay. Well.' She clears her throat. 'Any headaches, blurred vision, nausea?'

Jane shakes her head, feeling her face burning, Mike looking at her.

'On a scale of one to ten, ten being the worst, what number would you rate your pain?'

'Um,' says Jane. 'One.'

'Good. Now – let's take your blood pressure.'

The nurse puts the clipboard back at the bottom of the bed. Hums a meandering tune as she puts a cuff round Jane's arm, a clip on her finger. The machine whirrs, the cuff inflates. Jane glances at Mike, who is staring into the middle distance.

The cuff deflates with a hiss.

'Right,' says the nurse. 'Pulse a bit high. Blood pressure a bit low. Keep drinking water. Peerie sips. Try to eat even if you don't feel like it – the food trolley will be round shortly. And take these,' the nurse says, handing Jane two tablets in a paper cup. Then she draws the curtains around the bed, mouths 'Sorry' to Jane. Jane hears her shoes squeaking away on the linoleum.

They are alone. Jane looks at Mike, his face disbelieving.

'Pregnant?' he says. 'You're pregnant?'

Jane remembers telling the surgeons. In the operating theatre. Is there a chance you could be pregnant? they asked, and she nodded. Said yes, actually, I am. But I've got an abortion booked, tomorrow. So it doesn't matter. The surgeon and nurse looked at each other. One of them said well, you won't be making that appointment. As you're pregnant, we'll use a lighter anaesthetic . . .

Jane looks at Mike. She nods.

He stares at her. Points at himself. 'Mine?'

'Of course, yours.'

Mike leans back in his chair, his eyes wide. Looks at her. Then laughs. 'This is – this is nuts,' he says. 'You're – Jane, we're going to have a baby? But what – when – how long – oh my God,' he says. He leans forward. Takes her unbandaged hand again, gently. 'Jane. Why didn't you tell me?'

'Because,' says Jane. 'Because it wouldn't make any difference. I'm not having the baby.'

A pause. 'You're not?'

'I'm booked in for an abortion,' she says. 'Tomorrow.'

A silence. Then he says, 'Oh.'

Jane turns her face away. Mike's hand in hers feels limp.

'Why?' he says.

'You know why.'

'But what if it all went fine? What if you were fine?'

'I won't be fine.'

'You might be.'

'I won't be.'

'But—'

'Mike,' she says. 'Please. Stop.'

They're silent for a moment. Jane looks at her hand, in its white lump of bandages, like a fungus growing, some pale mushroom erupting from her wrist. She looks at it, and before she knows what's happening, she's crying, abruptly, pathetically, eyes and nose streaming, chest hitching with sobs. Mike tries to hold her, but for once his weight, his solidity, feels crushing rather than comforting, and she twists away from him, gasping as a hot surge of agony slams through her hand.

'Shh,' Mike says. 'It's okay, you're okay.'

'I'm not okay!' cries Jane. 'I'm not! I'm losing it. My mind is . . . it's just dissolving, like − just like hers did, at the end. My grip on reality . . .' She wipes her tears away, takes a few shuddering breaths. 'Today, on the slime line, I reached out, took a salmon − only it wasn't a salmon. It was my mother's prosthesis. Her hand. As clear as day, as clear as you are now.' She feels panic surging through her. 'I'm losing my mind, Mike,' she says. 'I'm going mad.'

'You're stressed,' says Mike, leaning forward in his chair. 'That's all. It's just stress. The investigation, the search, Maggie's fall, losing your job, selling the croft . . . a pregnancy,' he says, incredulous. 'It's too much for anyone to handle. You're not losing your mind. You're exhausted. You just need to rest.'

'How could I look after a baby, Mike, when I'm hallucinating my dead mother's prosthetic hand? When I'm seeing water in dry bathtubs? Next thing I'll be hearing voices, telling me to − to . . .'

She puts a hand to her face. Feels the panic flooding her, a tide of cold shimmering water rising around her chest. She shuts her eyes, tries to breathe, breathe. Her heartbeat thuds in her ears.

She looks at her hand, the white lump of it, thinks of her mother's hand, in the factory, in the quarry . . . she can feel a burning in her throat, her nose, hear the roar of water in her ears − breathe, she thinks, breathe, breathe, but she can't, her throat closing—

'Jane,' Mike says, 'Jane, it's okay.'

*'It's okay, Hannah,' says her mother.*

*Hannah hesitates. She holds on to the doorframe. A drop of water falls from the tap into the full tub, sends ripples over the surface.*

*Her mother is sitting on the edge of the tub. She's out of her dressing gown, for once, wearing a summer dress, a pattern of yellow flowers that hangs from her bony shoulders. The dress is wet, dark and clinging to her front. Her plastic arm is off, sitting on the bathroom windowsill. And her face is odd. Pale, her eyes wide.*

*'Come on, Hannah. Come and get undressed.' Her mother's voice is low, soft. Hannah can see the pulse in her neck, fluttering against the skin like a trapped insect. Her whole body seems to tremble slightly, as if with an electric current.*

*'But it's not bath time,' says Hannah.*

*'That doesn't matter,' says her mother. 'That doesn't matter. I need you to get in the bath.' Her jaw ticks. Her hand clenches in her lap, the knuckles pressing whitely against the skin.*

*Hannah doesn't move. She looks again at the tub. The shining water. She sees a blond hair dimpling the surface. One of Charlie's—*

Jane squeezes her eyes tight shut, shakes her head. 'No,' she says, 'no, no.' She struggles upwards, kicks the sheets off, rips the cannula from her hand. Mike tries to stop her, but she shoves past him, stumbles out of the ward, trying to ignore the pain in her hand, sharp and clear as cut glass, Mike calling her name. She runs, fast, bare feet slapping on the polished linoleum, her breathing coming hard.

'No,' she says, and she clenches her fist, hits the side of her head. 'No, no.' But the images come, like a flock of vicious birds. 'No, no—'

*'No,' says Hannah. 'No. I don't want to.'*

*'You get in,' says her mother. 'Get in here. Now.'*

*Hannah looks at her mother, with her eyes too wide, too white, in her taut face, her clenched fist, her gritted jaw, and some primordial part of Hannah's brain sends a ping of adrenaline shooting down her limbs, sounds an alarm, a warning: run.*

*Hannah lets go of the doorframe. Backs away, on weak legs. Her mother stands up, fury contorting her face, her mouth turned down.*

*'You come back!' she shouts, and her voice breaks, as Hannah stumbles backwards, bumping into her nan's bedroom door. 'You get in here!' Hannah turns, grabs the door handle.*

*'Don't go in there,' says her mother, 'DON'T GO IN THERE!' And Hannah darts into the bedroom, slamming the door—*

Jane, blinded by panic, turns one corner, another, stumbles into an empty lift. She hammers the ground-floor button. The doors glide shut as Mike rounds the corner. As the lift descends she sees herself in the reflective wall, pale, wild, as mad as her mother, and she turns away, covering her face, trying to stop the images coming—

*She is only in the bedroom for a second before her mother comes bursting through the door, but in that second time seems to stop.*

*She sees Charlie. He is lying in his crib. For an instant, stupidly, Hannah thinks someone has put a blue lightbulb in the room. Because he is the wrong colour . . .*

The lift doors open. Jane stumbles out, past a nurses' station, down a corridor, ignoring the raised voices behind her. She breaks into a sprint, shoving through the double doors—

*Charlie is blue. Why is he blue? His eyes are open, and there is a bloody foam around his open mouth, and his blond hair is dark, wet, plastered to his scalp, a muslin cloth draped over his naked body, and at that moment she realises, and her body goes limp with horror, and her mother bursts into the room, bellowing like a beast—*

There are shouts behind her, Mike's voice the loudest, but she doesn't look back. She tears across the car park, down the hill, over the road, stumbling towards the sea, scrambling over the low wall, over the spiky grass, onto the rocks at the shore, the stones slippery underfoot. She wades into the ocean, cold water foaming at her ankles, her shins. She pushes forward, forward, wanting to give herself up to the waves. The water has been calling her, ever since that day – all of them, her father, her mother, Charlie, all given up to the water, and she tried to escape it but it's no good, it's in her blood. She forces her legs forward, pushing into the waves, the gasping shock of it, up to her navel, up to her ribcage—

*Her mother hauls her, screaming, into the bathroom, gripping her hair, Hannah thrashing, her feet skidding on the tiles, and her mother drags her to the tub, shoves her head under – Hannah writhes, surfaces, gulps air, is pushed under again. Breaks the surface, chokes out Mum, Mummy, under again, roaring in her ears, gulps of burning water, shooting down her nose, her throat, flooding her, like fire, and she's going to die – staring at the avocado-coloured plastic, the bubbles escaping from her lungs, her mother's iron strength pressing on her skull, in her hair, her scalp burning – and she's dissolving, disintegrating, blackness like a gaping mouth—*

There are shouts behind her but it is too late. The water is up to her neck now. Her useless hand flails as a wave knocks her off her feet, and she is sucked beneath the surface, the water claiming her at last.

*She wakes in a puddle of water, vomit. A light shining in her eyes. Something strapped over her mouth, her nose. Strangers in dark green uniforms, lifting her onto a stretcher. Hannah glides down the stairs, out of the front door. Blue lights swing over the houses.*

*A hospital. A ventilator. Beeping instruments. A night, a day, a night, a day. Kind nurses. Bad food. Dried-out jacket potatoes and pots of watery jelly. Her nan comes, and her Uncle George, both ashen and wet-eyed. A policeman is with them, and he tells her that her mother is missing and her brother is dead. She feels numb, unreal. That night, Hannah dreams her mother is hiding beneath her hospital bed. She can hear her breathing.*

A psychiatric nurse comes. Jane expects to be strapped into a straitjacket, or at least injected with something. But it's not like that. The nurse just talks to her. Asks her questions. Jane answers, abruptly. No. She doesn't want to kill herself. Yes, she's been having hallucinations. Yes, there is a family history of mental illness.

'Could you tell me a little more about that?' asks the nurse, gently, and Jane laughs, bleakly, flops her head back on the pillow. She has never felt so exhausted.

She swallows.

'I'm scared I'll kill my baby,' she says.

The nurse looks at Jane. 'Why would you kill your baby?' she asks.

Jane shrugs. 'It feels like destiny.'

The nurse listens. 'Go on,' she says.

And Jane looks at the nurse, with her neat silver bob and kind brown eyes, this total stranger with her carefully neutral face, and feels insulted, almost. Why should I tell you? she wants to say. What gives you the right to know? And she takes a deep breath to say those things, but instead, Jane starts to talk. And she finds herself telling everything. Like puncturing an abscess, the pus draining out, it won't stop once she's started. Her mother's arm. Mike. The pregnancy, the factory; Maggie and Dawn and Pat, the diaries, Charlie, her father, her nan. The pills.

The drownings.

The police helicopter, hovering over Crowholt, its beam slicing down through the night. The lines of yellow-jacketed officers combing the fields. The frogmen, slipping into the flooded quarry. The black and white pages flapping in the wind, her face replicated, duplicated, stapled to telegraph poles, Blu-Tacked in shop windows. The flowers and teddies, piling up against the garden fence, a drift of them against the fence, going slimy with the rain. The funeral. A winter's day. The tiny white coffin, lowered into the frosty earth.

When she is finished, she is trembling all over, but feels cleaner, clearer somehow.

In her stomach, there is a swish, a nudge. Jane feels like a plastic bag at a fairground, a goldfish swimming inside her. She puts a hand on her belly. The nurse pours her a beaker of water from the jug by her bed. Jane drinks it greedily.

'Postpartum psychosis,' says the nurse. 'In my opinion, anyway. That's what your mother had.'

Jane looks at the nurse. It seems unreal, being able to label the horror that neatly. To pin it down, like sticking a pin through a great black insect.

'Postpartum psychosis,' she mutters. Then: 'Will I have it, too?'

'There is a higher risk if there's a family history,' says the nurse, gently. 'Nobody can guarantee you won't become unwell. But things have changed since your mother gave birth. We have more knowledge now. Better treatments. We can monitor you, look out for warning signs that things are going downhill. We can plan and prepare. Forewarned,' she says, 'is forearmed.'

Forearmed. Jane thinks of her mother's plastic limb, floating in the lake.

Jane sleeps. When she wakes, her fingers ache, a low, throbbing ache. The nurses unwrap the bandages, inspect her fingers, suck air through their teeth.

A doctor comes and tells her that her fingers are too frostbitten to save. They'll need to amputate. She is wheeled off to theatre again. She wakes with two neat stumps, the ends of the bone trimmed, smoothed, covered neatly with flaps of skin, black stitches across the top, like a row of wiry kisses.

Pat comes from work, with a huge card, a teddy on the front with a sticking plaster on its ear. An enormous fruit basket, cellophane wrapped. Bananas, grapes, nectarines, satsumas, a passion fruit, a pineapple.

'Bribery,' Pat says drily, 'from management. 'So you don't sue the pants off them. They should have put guards on those blades years ago.'

A nurse unwraps the basket for her. Jane peels, with difficulty, a satsuma. Tears a segment off with her teeth. Then another, and another.

She looks at the last satsuma segment, glistening in her hand. She remembers her mother, pregnant with Charlie, tearing into her brown bags of oranges, a wadded tea towel under her chin to catch the drips.

A few more days, and she stands blinking in the spring sunshine outside the hospital. She grips a plastic bag. Inside it is a box of tablets ('Valium?' Jane had asked, her mouth prickling at the memory of the bitter yellow pills. 'No,' said the doctor. 'Sertraline.'), a wad of leaflets – 'You and Your Pregnancy', 'Severe Mental Illness After Childbirth', 'Postpartum Psychosis', 'Life After a Hand or Finger Amputation' – a bottle of folic acid pills, and a Post-it note on which is scribbled three telephone numbers, and the words 'talking therapy / hand therapy / midwives'.

She stands there, gripping the bag, feeling the sunshine on her skin, the cautious warmth of it.

'Ready?' says Mike.

Jane looks at him, nods.

May. The island teems with life. Wildflowers speckle the grass, walls of pale yellow primroses, marsh marigolds like gold coins floating on the bogs, the delicate pink lollipops of sea pink. The spring migrants have arrived, birds falling onto the island in their hundreds, the shearwaters, terns, ospreys, swallows, settling onto the velvety grass, the stony beaches, the jagged cliffs. In nests and hollows, muddy burrows and grassy ledges, eggs are laid – smooth, round, pointed, conical; speckled, pale as porcelain, the delicate blue of sea glass. Lambs and calves are born, slithering out of their bloody darkness, the farmers out in the night with torches and gel, arms aching, straw in their hair. The dark hours begin to disappear, the days stretching and expanding, and Jane expands with them. She keeps thinking she can't get any bigger, but she does, puffing up like rising dough. She feels vast, superhuman. It is so strange, this feeling of her body announcing itself; even in her shapeless fleeces and baggy T-shirts her belly bulges. With its popped-out navel it reminds her of a service bell, the kind you see on hotel reception desks, and demands attention in just the same way.

Other people greet her, smile at her as she passes, smile at her stomach. Round is a friendly shape. Her body feels friendly. Soft, pliant. No more boniness, no more hard edges. The undersides of her breasts rest against her ribcage, her beach ball stomach touches her thighs when she sits, her jaw and neck meet now in the shadow of double chin. Her flesh greets itself.

In Mike's bedroom is a full-length mirror, and one evening, in the soft dusk light, Jane draws the curtains, takes off her clothes, looks at herself. She runs her hand, with its two stumps, over the full moon of her stomach, over the dark line that starts at her sternum and runs down into the mass of pubic hair, splitting around her belly button like a river around an island. She runs her hands down her thighs. They are massive, dense, huge buttresses, trunks of oak trees. Veins marble the skin of her breasts, taut with blood. On a poster at the midwives' office she read that when you're pregnant you get half as much blood again. She seems compelled to keep topping herself up with water, pints and pints of it, gulping them down. She wants ice, too. Makes trays of it in the freezer, three of them on constant rotation so that she always has some. She cracks the cubes into bowls, spoons them into her mouth, crunching them, the creaking and cracking filling her skull. She wonders if the baby can hear it. Wonders if it feels the chill slipping down into her belly. She hopes the cold doesn't bother it.

Jane eats. She still craves tart things, sour things, bitter things, things which catch in the throat and make her eyes water. She eats slices of lemon like crisps. Dips a teaspoon into a jar of horseradish, sucks it clean.

'Nobody will be kissing you,' says Maggie, smiling.

That's not true. Mike is all over her, and she responds in kind, feeling round, rich, voluptuous. She doesn't tell Maggie this.

Maggie, bedbound while her hip heals, is crocheting feverishly. Booties, hats, a cardigan, a teddy bear. Yarn balls turning in a teapot, unspooling from the spout. Everything is yellow, or white, because Jane doesn't know the sex of the baby. At the scan, she asked them not to tell her. Still, she studies the photographs they gave her, taking them from their white slipcover, looking at the ghostly outline of her passenger, pale in its cavernous darkness, its ribs fine as fish bones, its necklace of a spine, its head, round and inscrutable. She paid five pounds for a printout of the photographs, and on the ferry back looked at them over and over. Put them in her wallet. Took them back out. Touched them, touched her belly.

'Why didn't you want to know the sex?' asks Maggie.

Jane shrugs. 'Just thought it'd be nice to have a surprise,' she says. But really, she's thinking of her mother, lying on the couch as Esther swung the wedding ring over her stomach. Best not to know. Best not to have any expectations at all. Except for low ones. That way, any surprise will be a good one.

In the caravan's medicine cabinet, alongside the first aid kit, sanitary towels, and paracetamol, is the box of sertraline. She takes it dutifully. She has the number of the Samaritans and the Shetland Mental Health Team stuck on a Post-it note to the telephone. She has researched, on the internet, all the symptoms to look out for. Irritability. Difficulty sleeping, appetite changes. Feeling suspicious or fearful. Thoughts of harming yourself or your baby.

Thoughts that your baby is the second coming of Jesus. Thoughts that a burned-out paper mill is talking to you. Thoughts that you need to hold your baby underwater until it is dead.

Jane holds her mug of tea, looks out of her caravan doorway at the croft. It is encased in scaffolding and blue tarpaulin, the sound of hammering and drilling reaching her on the wind. Breeze blocks, buckets of plaster, planks of wood litter the field.

Mike, sitting on the bed next to her, hands her a paint chart, says, 'What do you think for the nursery? Sea Urchin? Willow Tree?'

She looks at the colours, a range of pale greens that remind her of the lichen that grows on the stone walls of Maggie's garden. 'I like Willow Tree,' she says.

Mike nods. Marks a cross on the chart.

Jane looks at the workmen. 'Do you think they'll be finished in time? Before the baby comes?'

'Aye, I reckon. Just about. Just make sure to keep your legs crossed.'

Two weeks later, she is loading up a paint roller with Willow Tree. She starts to roll it on the sloping wall, then steps back, looks at it.

'What do you think?' she asks Mike. 'Not too dark, is it?'

Mike looks up from where he's assembling a flat-pack crib. 'Looks fine to me,' he says. 'It'll dry paler, too, don't forget. And that window faces south, so it'll get light all day.'

'We should get one of those blackout blinds,' says Jane. 'To help the baby sleep. Judy was talking about them. I remember trying to sleep in here, during the Simmer Dim, with the midnight sun coming in . . .' She looks around her, at the smooth walls, the plastic sheeting on the floor, the new space-age heater, a slim white square, like something from a sci-fi movie. The radio is playing, the sunlight streaming through the new skylights. The room smells of plaster, of sawdust, of fresh paint. 'I can't believe it's the same room,' says Jane. 'I can't believe it's the same house.'

Mike looks at her. 'Still glad you decided not to sell, then? No regrets you spent your savings on this place, and not a villa in the Costa del Sol?'

She smiles. Shakes her head. 'No regrets. Dawn's still seething that I didn't sell up though. Didn't even sign my leaving card from work.'

Mike rolls his eyes. Looks at the crib, the diagram. 'Ah shite,' he says. 'Left the Allen key downstairs.' he gets to his feet. 'Want a cuppa?'

'Can I have a glass of water?'

'Pint?'

'Yes please.'

'Ice?'

'Aye.'

He grins. Kisses her. She watches him go. Then she loads up the roller again, lifts it, touches it to the wall – and feels a sudden pop. Like a taut string has snapped, somewhere deep inside her. And then, a gush of warm liquid, flooding down her thighs, down into her socks. She watches, helpless, as it pours from her, running over her shoes, pooling on the plastic sheeting.

She stands there, the roller in her hand, the radio playing. The smell rising from the fluid is sweet, fleshy, clean, like mown hay, like warm skin.

'Mike?' she says. 'Mike!'


The helicopter lifts into the air. The air thrums around her, the sound of the whirring blades drowning out the voices of the paramedics. The sun angles through the windows, moves around the cabin as they change direction. She feels her belly tightening, contracting, her bowels knotting, the weight of the baby pressing against her spine. She sucks in air, breathes it out. Mike holds her hand, tight.

Twenty minutes later, she is being wheeled into a room, helped onto a bed. A band is strapped around her belly, a dial is turned, and the room is filled with the sound of galloping horses.

'A lovely strong heartbeat,' says the midwife.

She puts Jane's legs up, slots her ankles into two stirrups. She snaps on a glove, lubricates her hand, says, 'This may be a peerie bit uncomfortable, my love,' and pushes her fingers inside. Jane squeezes her eyes shut, grits her teeth. Mike looks on, pale.

'Oh my goodness,' says the midwife.

'What?' says Mike.

'You got here just in time. Another half an hour, that baby would have been born one thousand feet up in the air. You're nine centimetres dilated.'

Mike laughs, squeezes Jane's shoulder. Another contraction tumbles over her and she's away for a moment, lost in the darkness of her body.

It's so hot. Mike brings water, Lucozade, biscuits, but Jane doesn't touch them. All she wants is air, breath, in and out like waves on the shore.

Half an hour passes. An hour. Two hours. Three. The midwives change shifts.

Darkness falls. Jane looks at the moon, a razor-sharp sliver between the venetian blinds. Her body heaves downwards, like it's trying to purge itself of something, the contractions pulling and sucking at her body like waves, rushing and roaring through her. She gets on all fours, clinging to the bed like it's a life raft. She grunts, moans, the sound coming from somewhere below her chest, somewhere deep in her guts, some place unchanged since cavewoman days. She sucks gas and air, the mouthpiece whirring, the taste of it slightly metallic. Her head floats, dissolves, briefly. She doesn't like the feeling. Lets the mouthpiece clatter to the floor.

Her legs are shaking, uncontrollably, with exhaustion, with adrenaline. Mike rubs her back, says, 'You're doing so well, so well sweetheart, keep going, keep going,' as Jane gasps.

Another hour passes. The midwife frowns at the printout, the little needle tracing a line from the machine.

'Looks like baby's getting a wee bit tired,' she says. 'The heart rate's getting low.' Another contraction. Jane watches, blearily, the red numbers on the monitor, dropping, dropping. Again, and again, it dips, erratic, like a butterfly with a torn wing.

Five minutes later, Jane is wheeled into a bright white room. Mike is sitting by her, a blue hairnet on his head, like the ones she wears at the factory. A blue screen cuts Jane in half. Anaesthetic cuts her in half again. The baby is in limbo. Stuck between worlds.

*Don't die*, Jane thinks. Tears run down the sides of her face, pool in her ears. *Don't die. Please, don't die.*

'Okay,' says the surgeon. 'Here we go.'

Mike grips Jane's hand, looks her in the eyes. She looks at him. Tries to ignore what is happening below the screen. She can feel something, like they are trying to stuff her into jeans two sizes too small. She is jostled, jiggled. She dry heaves, retching, coughing. She thinks of the salmon on the slime line being gutted, squeezes her eyes shut, tight.

The baby is dead, she's sure of it.

All this, for nothing. Nothing.

The beeping of monitors, the clinking of metal instruments on trays. But from the surgeon, the nurse, the midwife, silence. Awful silence.

And then one of the doctors says, 'Here you are,' and Mike says, 'Oh. Oh Jane, oh look!'

Jane opens her eyes. She looks.

Suspended in the air in the doctor's blue gloves, the theatre lights blinding white around it, like a halo, is a baby. Moving, alive. Oh God, Jane thinks. You're beautiful. Huge. And beautiful.

'It's a bonnie wee lad,' says the surgeon.

'A boy,' says Mike, laughing, in tears. 'Our boy.' He kisses Jane's head.

The baby is dried, handed to Mike, wrapped in a blanket, a little white hat on his head, and Mike lowers him, showing him to Jane.

She looks at him, his inky, blinking eyes, and he looks back at her, his small face.

'Look at him,' says a nurse. 'No tears at all. He's an old soul. Been here before.'

Jane shakes her head. 'No,' she whispers to the baby. 'No. You're brand new.'

Jane pushes the buggy across the sand. Mike walks beside her. It's the middle of September. Sunny, but a chill breeze. Autumn just beginning. There is nobody else on the shoreline except a man further along the beach, throwing sticks into the surf for a black lab.

Jane stops.

'Right,' she says. 'Let's get this over and done with. You okay to wait here with him?'

Mike nods. 'Are you sure you'll be okay on your own?'

'Yeah,' says Jane, squinting at the ocean. 'Shouldn't take long. At least there's no wind.'

She reaches into the hammock underneath the buggy, lifts out a clear plastic bag, knotted at the top, full of cigarette-grey ash. Five pounds of it. She thought there'd just be a couple of eggcups full, like in films. And the ash isn't ground up as fine as she thought it would be. She'd expected flour, or icing sugar, but it's more like cat litter. There are some visible shards of bone. She grimaces. Then, as if to cleanse herself, she looks at their son. Robbie. He's asleep, his pouchy cheeks slack, his mouth slightly open.

She kisses her son's head. Kisses Mike. Cradles the bag of ashes in her arms, and steps into the surf.

It's a shallow beach, the sand sloping gently, and she has to walk out quite far, saltwater foaming up her wellington boots. She feels that tug, like an invisible rope between herself and her son, and can't help but turn and look back. Robbie in his pushchair, Mike holding the handles. He is watching her. She wonders how he feels seeing her walk into the sea again. She raises a hand to signal that all is well. He raises one back.

She turns to face the ocean.

Jane wasn't sure about putting her mother back into water after so many years in that stagnant quarry. But this is different: saltwater, flowing currents; she'll be moving again. Free. There was a photograph of her here, on this beach, as a little girl. Standing on the sand. Long before she had her prosthesis, long before the mill burned down, long before everything went wrong. In the photograph, she was grinning, in a T-shirt and shorts, feeling the sun on her skin, the sand between her toes. Written on the back of the photograph, in her nan's hand, was 'Minehead. August '66'.

They'd found her at the bottom. Stuck in the silt, the soft sediment. She'd been well preserved by the cold, airless water, down in the depths where no light could reach. The pockets of her summer dress full of rocks. Why her arm had appeared, they don't know. Perhaps there had been a shift in the water, a movement. Maybe some of the limestone rock face had crumbled into the lake, and the disturbance had let the arm break free, loosed it like an arrow, shooting towards the surface.

Jane had gone down to Crowholt. Collected the ashes, the arm. Had visited the cemetery where Charlie was buried. His heart-shaped headstone, engraved with the words: *Charles Robert Douglas. Our dreams are buried here.*

She'd left flowers. In the florist, the woman had tried to sell her a white arrangement. Calla lilies, white roses, baby's breath. Jane had recoiled from them. Hated their bloodlessness, their funeral parlour neatness. Instead she'd gone for a huge bunch of sunflowers, their thick fleshy stems fat and vital, their blooms like smiling faces. Ten of them. The brightest things in the whole cemetery.

No flowers for her mother. Just the kelp and seaweed.

Jane untwists the knot in the plastic bag, using her left hand

– the right is still healing; she has to massage the amputated finger stumps every day, do painful exercises. She opens the pouch, holds it at arm's length, and pours the contents into the water. Some of the ashes pool on the surface, some blow and stick to Jane's hands. She shakes the bag out. A grey scum floats around her boots. She steps back, swishes her feet around, dips one hand in, then the other, sluices the ash off.

The grey slick moves, shifts, starts to sink. Jane watches it getting broken up by the waves, slowly disappearing. She doesn't know how to feel. And then she hears a noise, from the shore. Robbie, his cat-like cries. She turns to look. Mike is pushing the stroller back and forth, back and forth, but he needs his mum, he needs Jane. She turns and splashes back through the surf to him; Sylvia, the ash, forgotten, the empty plastic bag crumpled in one wet hand. She runs up the sand to him, his little face, scrunched and wailing. She unclips his buggy straps, lifts him up, clutches him close, buries her face in his soft neck, feels the fine floss of his hair against her cheek.

She sways from side to side, shushes. His cries soften, quieten.

'All done?' asks Mike.

'Aye.'

'You okay?' he says.

'Yeah,' says Jane. 'Yeah. I am.'

Jane and Mike sit on the sea wall as the sun climbs, the day warms. Jane feeds her son, his hand on the white swell of her breast, his fingers splayed like starfish on a rock. He is four months old. He is seventy centimetres long, weighs sixteen pounds, and Jane loves him. She loves him so much that she feels like she might burst with it, sometimes. She never knew she had such capacity for love.

She strokes his hair, the colour of peaches, just beginning to thatch across his scalp. She runs her little finger lightly over the fontanelle, the soft spot in his skull beneath which she can just feel his heartbeat ticking, and feels the familiar shiver of anxiety, low in her chest, which rises whenever she thinks of his fragility – his thin skin, his birdlike bones, his eggshell head. After his birth, her brain went into overdrive, ruminating on all the ways he could be hurt, maimed, killed. She was hypervigilant, her mind a radar, scanning for threats. For weeks she had a recurring nightmare of working in the cannery, emptying a crate of salmon and finding his body packed in the ice. But the nightmares soon went away, her mind purging its fears like her body shed the remnants of pregnancy – the lochia which soaked pad after pad, the hair which clogged the shower drain, the night sweats in which all the ice water she'd drunk seemed to seep from her pores. She is taking her tablets, and going to therapy, and she will not work in the cannery again. Her caravan sits abandoned in the long grass. She has taken the wheels off it, but can't bring herself to scrap it just yet.

The croft is clean and bright and warm. In the porch they are growing geraniums, their petals glowing red against the glass. And buried in the garden, wrapped in silk, is her mother's arm. Pointing towards the sea, its outstretched palm turned upwards, as if asking for forgiveness.